THE SPIRIT OF SUNFLOWERS

THE SPIRIT OF SUNFLOWERS

KRISTINE K. MCCRAW

Kristine K McCraw

Contents

First Printing, 2021

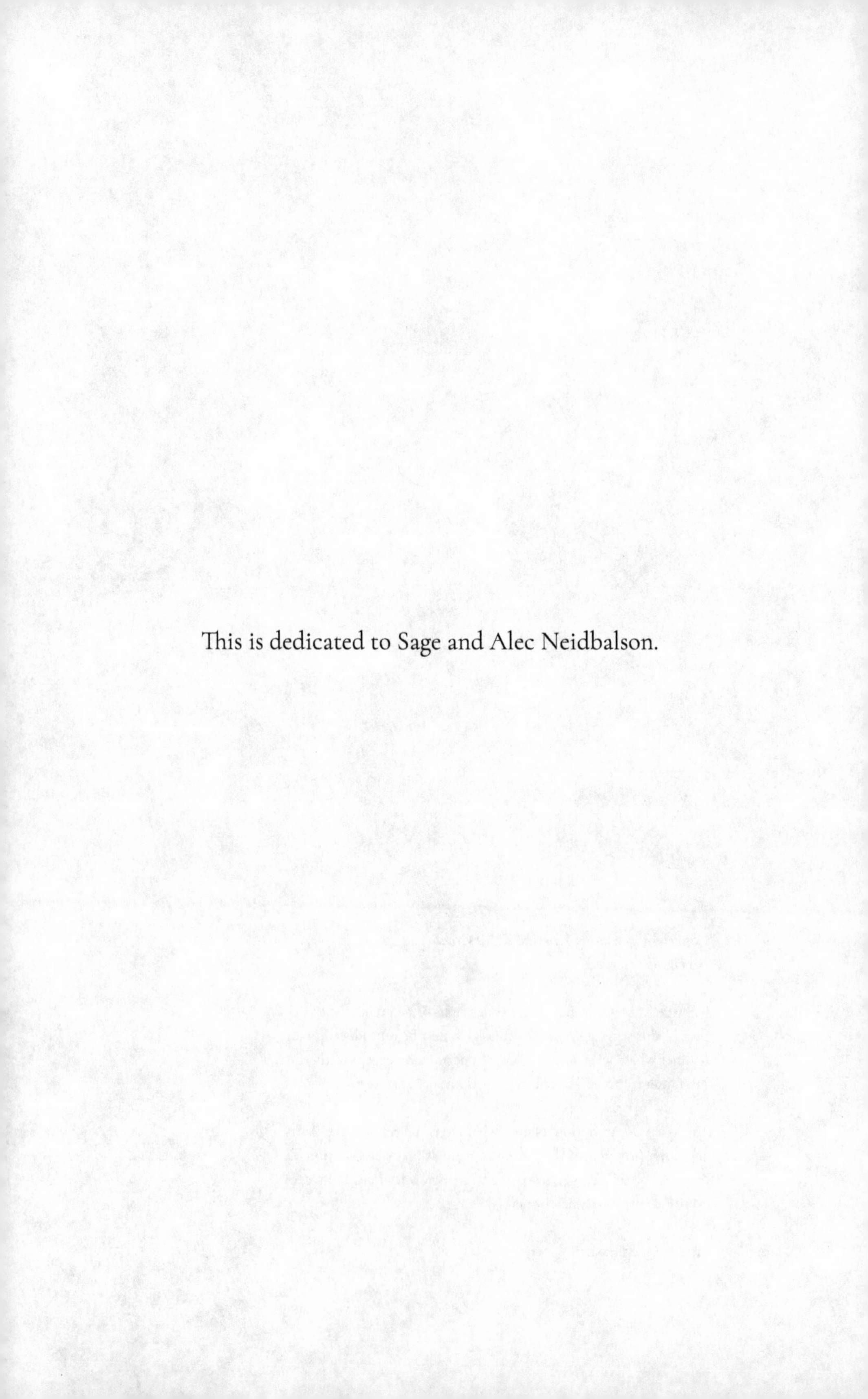

This is dedicated to Sage and Alec Neidbalson.

I

Chapter 1

The Keepsake Box

Willow stepped out of her car and walked over the cracks in the driveway, avoiding the chance that her heel would sink into one of the crevices, and then paused when she reached the stoop of her mother's house. A flash of the door from the house on Old Rock Road permeated her thoughts, and when she came back to reality, she noticed the grain and the stained wood on this door—dry and brittle from aging. This worn door was comforting, she realized, for she knew her mother would be there on the other side waiting for her arrival. It had a six-pane window at the top that was too high for a person of her mother's height to see outside, but right after Willow rang the bell, she noticed her eye peering through the peek and then the sound of the locks turning, click, click, click.

One. Two. Three. Willow said to herself as she bobbed her head in time with each unhinging lock.

It was always the same; nothing had changed since they left Sol Valley and moved to Pequot, a small-knit community with salty air and a gentle breeze that blew from the sea. Barbara took the same precautions for everyone, including expected guests and her own daughter. She grabbed Willow's hand pulling her inside the house, then with haste, pushed the door shut followed by the snapping of the locks.

"Thank you for coming right from work." She hugged her daughter, then Willow followed Barbara, her mother, a middle-aged woman with rounded hips and bouncy brown hair, through the entry hall to a living area where Barbara motioned for her to sit.

Willow plopped at the far end of the sectional sofa and sank into the cushion while sliding off her black leather three-inch heeled pumps. Any higher than three inches and Willow wouldn't be able to make it through the day without feeling as though someone took a bat to her ankles. Willow breathed out the stress of a hard day with a deep sigh.

"You've certainly stirred my curiosity. I suspect this is good news by your urgency and enthusiasm." She relaxed into the white puffed cushion of the couch.

"I bought a house," Barbara told Willow without hesitation.

"You bought a house? You never told me you were looking for a house. Where?"

Barbara drew in a deep breath letting out an audible sigh before she was able to return the answer. "This house!"

"You're buying this house?" Willow questioned as her eyes trailed around the main room noticing a crack that zigzagged from the crown molding to the tip of the door frame.

At one time the place served as a carriage house. It was built in the early 1900s for high society guests to store their carriages while they vacationed at the historically famous Pequot Colony resort, a one-time grand estate bestowed with ornate trimmings, and lustrous gardens. By the early twentieth century, it was turned into a museum to tell the history of the lighthouse, located where the mouth of the James River meets the Atlantic Ocean: a place where Willow and her mother had enjoyed an afternoon picnic or a leisurely walk when Willow still lived here.

The first time Willow noticed its stately appearance, she thought of Edwin Mann, the one rich person living in the valley when she was a child. At one time, the museum had given off the same luster as Edwin Mann's mansion on the hill. Willow had never lived in such fancy places, but "*The Carriage House*" sounded fancy when she read the name on the envelope of the rent check in her mother's print. It wasn't until after they moved in, Willow realized it was a fixer-upper, only the owners had no intentions of fixing it. Ten years had passed since they first rented this house.

"Yes. Yes. The owners let it go into foreclosure and left town. I bought it dirt cheap from the bank. I couldn't pass it up."

"Wait a minute. This old carriage house is falling apart. I mean it still has its charm but why not look for something more modern and in less need of repairs? You might be getting yourself into a money pit," Willow said. She changed her tone when she noticed her mother's brow lines scrunch. "I'm shocked and happy for you!"

"I'm shocked too," Barbara replied. "It was a spur-of-the-moment decision. I managed to get a loan that would cover the expenses. Well, I hope they cover it. I'm aware that old houses have hidden costs when it comes to renovating but I am determined to get this house in mint condition."

"I'm happy for you mother. I think it's a wonderful idea." Willow wasn't sure if she really meant that; nonetheless, she would be there to support Barbara.

"Thank you, Willow. That means a lot to me."

Her mother drifted for a moment as if she was envisioning the possibilities of a renovation. Then, Willow recollected the farm, a place where she spent a summer as a nine-year-old, the summer her mother disappeared. Her mother had worked hard to get to this point of success in her life. After the day they were reunited at the police station, Barbara promised she would make a good life for them and she kept that promise.

"Why didn't you tell me this before today?" Willow asked.

"Oh Willow, honey. I wasn't quite sure about it. I wanted the house, but I'm scared. What if I can't handle the responsibility? What if the project flops? You know, we've lived many places, but I've never actually owned a home."

"Mamma," Willow called out to focus her mother's attention. "Get a hold of yourself. Have you forgotten the squalor you brought us out of over the years? Every obstacle since we left the valley many years ago seemed like a mountain, but we made it over every single one."

"Oh Willow. You always give me unwavering credit. You are my inspiration."

"Mamma, you were the strong one. You had to be. I was still a child. I say take it. Take it. Take on the challenge!" Willow's voice grew emphatically louder.

"You always call me mamma when you're passionate about something." Barbara smiled at her daughter.

"When we moved here, I finally had a yard, a decent bedroom, and a neighborhood with people who would wave when you passed them. I'm happy for you."

"I couldn't fathom anyone else living here but us. I mean me or one of us." Barbara paused to consider another idea. "Willow, why don't you move back in with me? We could do this project together and you would be able to save money instead of paying your high monthly rent. It's not right on the water like your condo but only six blocks from the beach."

"Mother, you know how I pride myself on being independent. Moving back in here is not an option, but I will help you; you won't be in this alone."

"Fine, then. I can do this. I know I can."

"And I'll be here to support you," Willow replied. *I just can't live on this property again.*

In the evening, Willow celebrated with her mother, having dinner at a waterfront restaurant near the lighthouse. Willow picked at her salad heaped with arugula leaves and vinaigrette dressing as she and Barbara conversed. After they finished their meal, they listened as the pianist played a classic rendition of Chopin. Willow and Barbara sat in silence until the end of the song, before leaving. Barbara tipped the musician as she followed her daughter out of the restaurant and then fetched her keys from the bottom of her Vera Bradley purse. As they drove home, they discussed the renovations with Barbara giving details about the company she elicited to complete the job. She was passionate about fixing the house and Willow noted as she patiently listened while her mother described her ideas. Barbara wound around the bend and veered left at the yield sign. A glimpse of the lighthouse and water beyond its tall stature could be captured at this angle.

"Mom, you are ready for this."

"There's much I need to learn," Barbara replied nervously as Willow stared out the window watching the shoreline dwarf in the distance as her mother drove toward her condo.

"One step at a time," Willow comforted her.

Barbara had the radio set on the station that played 70's hits and she sang along as she dropped Willow off at her place, a contemporary complex that sat next to the water. Willow's condo had a balcony that faced the estuary of the river. She looked forward to relaxing there with a glass of wine to end the evening. It was an exquisite summer night for stargazing, something she enjoyed ever since she searched for Leo the Lion at the farmhouse all those years ago. Willow stepped out on the balcony and watched the pink horizon slip away. The sky was clear as if it had been sharply focused with a high-powered camera lens. Tonight, she would be able to see an abundance of celestial objects with her telescope.

#

Barbara had a meeting with the architect and asked her daughter to join in the consultation as a second pair of eyes and ears. Willow arrived 30 minutes earlier, noticing the house was prim to impress like she was proving her capability of seeing this renovation through to its finality. The bell rang and Willow dashed to answer it. When she opened the door, Willow caught a glimpse of the architect's black Lincoln Town Car parked next to the curb and a full view of a woman standing in the doorway. She was slender with long pencil-thin legs. She wore a light pink suit jacket that extended below her waist with the same colored matching skirt. The white blouse underneath was flimsy, and the collar had wide pointed tips that stuck out over the top of the jacket. Blond hair draped over her shoulders and fell at the tip of her pearl necklace.

"Good evening! I'm Willow, Barbara's daughter. Come in. My mother is in the kitchen."

She entered the house and introduced herself in a formal business-like manner. "I'm Marybeth Dawson from Keller Designs."

Willow held the door open for Marybeth who was encumbered with a camera case slung over her shoulder and a bag of files. She walked slowly gazing around at the walls and ceiling of the dwelling as she moved toward the kitchen area. Her attention was immediately drawn to the house's structure. She hadn't wasted a moment and her keen observant manner seemed unforced. Barbara greeted her and directed the woman to a chair at the kitchen table. After Marybeth sat, she reached into her bag and pulled out a file. The file had Barbara's first and last name on the tab, Barbara Jones. Willow recalled the day she was told her last name wouldn't be Hitchens any longer. After they left Sol Valley, her mother, with the help of the detective, had their last name changed. Every effort Barbara had made to wipe out her life in Sol Valley gave her a smidgeon more of security.

Marybeth opened the folder and glanced over the manuscript before she spoke. "The house was originally built as a carriage house in 1902 and was converted into living quarters in the 20s. Then in the 50s, a small addition was made to the west side of the house to create more living space as well as adding a second floor. The front room was once where the stables were located. The living room is where the carriages were stored. Interesting!" She glanced around as she unpacked the house's history and listed changes. "And upstairs, there are two bedrooms?"

"Yes, that is correct. Two very small and claustrophobic bedrooms," Barbara answered. "Would you like to have a look?"

"Eventually, I'll make my way up there, but I'll need to take some pictures here first. Do you mind if I just walk around the bottom floor? I'll need to do a full assessment of each floor and the outside as well."

In a judicious manner, Marybeth perused among the bottom floor snapping pictures and taking notes on a yellow legal pad. She did the same thorough examination of the outside before asking Barbara to take her upstairs. The split staircase was an enclosed, dim space with narrow steps that felt unsteady as the three of them lurched up each one. The rooms of the second floor were tiny, and the sloped walls of the gabled roof made it feel as closed in as the stairwell. Marybeth took the same precision with the upstairs. After she finished taking photos and making notes, they reconvened at the kitchen table.

"Before I draw up a plan, I would like to get a feel for your main priorities of this renovation," Marybeth inquired.

"Priorities?" Her mother asked with a concerned tone. Willow noticed her mother seemed daunted by the question. "I haven't thought much about it."

"Let me explain. You have hired me to draw up plans, which is a meticulous process. While I am going to make sure the job is done well with the highest of standards in mind, you are the one paying for the materials and ultimately the person who will be living here. So, what do you hope to get out of the renovation? Do you want to preserve the original style of the house or are you more interested in comforts? Do you want every quirk fixed to perfection or are you ok with imperfections? Personally, I think the imperfections are what give the house its charm and uniqueness but that is up to you."

"Oh, I see what you're getting at, Marybeth. I'm sorry; I just haven't thought that much about it."

"Can my mother have a little time to think about it?" Willow asked.

"Of course; this is a consultation. Take your time and think about it."

"No," Barbara jumped in. "I would like to preserve its history as much as I can but make it more comfortable. I agree with you, Marybeth. The quirks give the house its charm."

"Well, that can be done. You will be pleased you decided that."

"Are you sure mother?" Willow asked.

"Yes, I'm sure," Barbara replied.

"All right then. I will start the planning. It's important you are available throughout the process because I will be asking you a lot of questions over the next few weeks."

"I'm committed to this. I work at the woman's shelter in town during the day. I can be reached there and at home in the evenings."

"Thank you," Willow said to the architect. She saw a release of worry lift from her mother's expression.

Marybeth gathered up her items and handed Barbara a business card with her contact information. After the consultation, Willow spent more time with her mother conversing over a bowl of chocolate ice cream before leaving. On the drive home, Willow thought about how her mother always managed to make any shabby rental they ever lived in a comfortable home but now she was finally able to have a place to call her own. It was quite a leap from Old Rock Road, but the memory of that house was still etched in Willow's mind as if it had been yesterday when she lived there.

Inside her condo, Willow rushed to her closet and shifted around boxes stored snugly under a row of hung clothing, until she found the mahogany keepsake box. It was a gift from her mother for her sweet sixteen. Inside the box had been a necklace holding her birthstone. She opened it with her mother's loving eyes gazing down at her. Now Willow peered at the flowery relief with her name finely carved in a flowing cursive font, under the design. When her mother told her it was a keepsake box, Willow had known exactly what treasures she would store inside. She gazed at the vessel and ran her fingers over the top feeling the bumps and curves before she gingerly lifted the lid. Inside was the carnelian stone, the pink crystal, and the gift she received from Bonnie on their last day together, a dried sunflower. These little trinkets at one time, in her mind, held powers. As she fumbled with the relics, she vividly remembered receiving each one. Her fingers delicately held the flower ever so careful not to unhinge the petals from the voluptuous centerpiece. Willow didn't believe the superstitions anymore, but they held memories.

#

Lying flat in my bed, I had heard them fighting once again as I had clutched my bear tighter. The oak floorboards had muffled their shouting, but I could tell, mamma was crying and begging daddy to stop, to please leave her alone. Tears dripped from my eyes and gathered in the pockets on the side of my nose. The noise trailed from the main room, where daddy always sat in his tattered pea-green armchair after coming home from working in the rock quarry to the kitchen, where Mamma worked. Today, she had just finished boiling the jars to get them ready for canning strawberry jam. I counted twenty before I left for school and when I came home, the jars were neatly placed on the shelf above the harvest gold oven. I heard the legs of the kitchen table skid and a chair thumped as it fell to the floor.

"Floyd, stop," Mamma shouted. "Stop this!" I pushed tightly with the tips of my fingers against the outer part of my ear hoping to block out the uproar, but it didn't stop the sound of shattering glass — Mamma's jars. The kitchen door slammed with one sharp thud shaking the side of the house, the same side where my pillow leaned against the wall. My head felt the vibration and my heart felt Mamma's sobs. I peered outside. Below my bedroom window in the dark cool night, Mamma leaned with her forehead against the screen door, crying for Daddy to let her back in the house. The porch lamp threw its beams on Mamma, making her visible. Beyond the scope of the lit stoop and driveway, was a wall of darkness, where the forest began. I waited and watched for what seemed like an eternity listening to the bush crickets' chirp. She eventually sat on the concrete step with her head resting in her cupped hands, her long straight toffee hair hanging from the crown of her head and over her shoulders. I wanted to go and be with her, but I was to stay in my room in line with Daddy's order. I finally went back to bed and drifted asleep soon to be woken by the sound of the Gremlin rolling over the sticks in the yard and backing up through the gravel driveway. I could hear stones spitting from under the tires. The headlights briefly shot through my window with a twisting light beam across my bedroom walls before it was dark again. The house was quiet. I knew Mamma was gone.

2

Chapter 2

The Letter

The yellow bus with the name Sol Valley Public Schools painted on its sides, stopped at the end of Old Rock Road. There was nothing around for miles in this part of the valley. Once the bus pulled out of the elementary school and past the little town consisting of a mechanic's garage, a general style store called Powel's Market, a mom and pop home cooked restaurant named Lucille's, a gas station with a rusty swinging sign that read Shell Gasoline and Motor Oil and a few other stores that sold hardware and farming supplies, the rest was fields and farms.

Willow hurried down the steps and onto the hard surface of the road. She glanced back when she heard the bus driver say bye and the doors flapped shut. The bus hissed and pulled away motoring down the highway, leaving puffs of exhaust behind it. It would amble to the end of highway 49 where it met the steep hillside. Willow heard the wheels muffle in the distance as she ran toward her house. This was the first burst of energy she had all day for she spent half the evening awake in bed wondering when her mamma would return, and the lack of sleep dragged her through school. She pushed her legs anxious to see Mamma at home waiting with a glass of milk and cookies for the afternoon snack. While she wasn't there this morning to get her ready for school, Mamma had all day to find her way back to the house and make everything normal again.

Willow came to the stoop and paused listening for sounds of dishes in the kitchen but there was nothing except air rattling the newly grown spring leaves of the oak tree. Willow felt her heartbeat faster as she placed her foot on the first step. Heaviness weighted her legs and she felt as if she was lifting tree limbs as she moved up the stoop. The door was locked. As if she wasn't already tired enough from being awake half the night, she would have to wait for Daddy to return home from work to get inside. She sat on the ground drawing lines in the dirt with a stick clasped in her fingers like she was holding a pencil.

Homework would be hard today without Mamma here to help. Willow struggled to learn as well as the other kids and wasn't sure if she would get through it alone, that, and the exhaustion. This morning, Mrs. Twine scolded her for not turning in her spelling homework which was collected right after the pledge, but then she must have caught on those things at home weren't right because when the math homework was taken up, she slipped by Willow without asking for it. Willow wanted to please her teacher and she always tried her best at school but today she couldn't muster up the same motivation.

Mrs. Twine would patiently work extra with her, giving her further explanation to the math problems and quizzing Willow with multiplication flashcards, but today, she let Willow be. Willow usually soaked up this attention from Mrs. Twine, who seemed to be her only friend in fourth grade. Tammy used to be her best friend until she began to gravitate toward the click of girls who didn't play tag anymore or climb on the monkey bars. They found it more fun to giggle and talk about boys where they gathered behind the basketball hoop.

Willow peered down at the stain on her polyester blouse. Mamma had always made sure Willow had a clean dress to wear. Willow especially loved her red dress with black and white plaid stripes that she wore over top of a white, puffy-shouldered shirt and frilly cuffs. On cool days, she wore it with stockings but on warmer days, she wore it with her white knee socks and always with the shiny, black Mary Janes. She loved these shoes because they had quarter-inch heels, and it made her feel as if she were a grown-up. Mamma always pressed her clothes before she dressed for school. But this morning, Willow found herself scrubbing off dirt marks when she picked an outfit from her dirty laundry pile. She would have to learn how to work the washing machine if mamma didn't come home.

Mamma always called it fickle, after she had to toggle the knob between settings for the cycle to start. *This fickle thang*, mamma would complain.

Daddy rambled down the driveway and pulled beside the house where he parked his matted, firehouse red Chevy pickup, the square headlights faced the oak tree that stood ten feet from the stoop where she sat waiting. Finally, he was home. Willow watched as he wound the handle to roll up the window before turning off the engine. He stepped out of the car, his navy work clothes dusty from a day's work of digging into the mountains and shifting rocks. He wore tan, steel-toed boots and carried his hard hat and goggles, his dark brown sideburns and mustache dirty and damp from sweat.

"Willow," he said in a flat voice as he passed her on the stoop where she was waiting. He made no eye contact, nor showed any expression. "Let's get in the house."

She noticed a brown paper bag dangling below his folded hand. He had stopped at Lucille's for dinner. Willow followed behind her father and into the kitchen where he dropped the bag on the table. He ordered her to get plates and bring his dinner to him in the living room. Her mood, forlorn, left her with little energy yet she managed to follow her father's command. She served Daddy his food where he sat in his chair staring at the television. He mumbled thank you but after that, he only spoke again to tell Willow to go to bed. Willow had the urge to ask him about Mamma, but she did not dare approach him this evening. Daddy was more cranky than usual, and his appearance was extra stern.

#

A week went by and still no Mamma and no explanation as to her whereabouts. The food was dwindling. There was nothing but a few shriveled apples and a bag of brown carrots in the fridge, peanut butter, stale bread in the bread box, and the cans of soup mamma stocked up for the winter sitting in the pantry closet. With only a dozen cans left, Willow found the courage to ask her father to take her to Powel's where she could persuade him to buy the kind of food mamma would use to make dinner. She was tired of the peanut butter sandwich and soup. He obliged to her request and they shopped at Powel's. When they got to the checkout, Floyd was impatient with the clerk and began complaining about how the place was run. He held a scowled face the whole time he was griping. Willow shrunk with embarrassment as she noticed the unfavorable reactions of the people nearby. After she got in the car, Willow slumped below the window so no one would see her.

At home, Willow slid the TV dinners in the oven. She had learned how to work it over the past week out of a matter of survival. As usual, she served Floyd dinner in the chair as he kept himself glued to the television. She ate in the kitchen next to Mamma's empty chair. Daddy finished eating and brought his empty dish and utensils to the kitchen, leaving them on the counter for Willow to wash. When she finished her meal, she quickly cleaned the dishes, wiped the table, and then escaped to her room where her thoughts drifted to her mother's absence. Daddy had told her Mamma left because she didn't want to be a mother anymore. This news stung Willow. Mamma would never leave her, she thought, but she hadn't come back either. She wouldn't be able to call the house because their phone service was discontinued after Christmas when Floyd was laid off from his job during the slow winter months. They hadn't been able to save enough money to continue paying the bill, and Mamma complained that Daddy had spent too much at the lodge, a place where Floyd went to meet up with his father, a place where women weren't invited.

Willow changed into her pajamas and then slipped into bed pulling the musty-smelling covers up to her chest. It had been a while since her sheets were washed. In fact, the last time was the day before Mamma prepared the jars; she had washed a load of laundry and hung the sheets on the line. Willow remembered how fresh her sheets smelled, like clean air. She decided. Tomorrow would be the day she would teach herself to wash clothes, only she wondered if she would be able to reach the line to clip the laundry with the wooden clothespins.

#

Willow, standing at the end of the driveway, saw the bus coming east on Route 49, also called Marshland Highway. She took off running, loping down the dusty road and kicking dirt clouds behind her heels. By the time she reached the end of Old Rock Road, she was winded. The bus driver waited impatiently.

"Hurry up, Willow," he yelled.

Willow pushed her legs a little quicker. She hated to keep the bus waiting again. Her feet hurt already, and the day hadn't even begun. Only two more weeks and she wouldn't have to catch the bus for the rest of the summer, yet she worried about being home alone. Who would be there to take care of her while daddy went to work, she agonized? Mamma always looked forward to having her home for the break.

Mrs. Twine told her good morning when she walked into the classroom. Her smile warmed Willow. Since Mamma left, it was the only warmth she got.

"Willow dear," Mrs. Twine addressed her. "Can you come to my desk please?"

Willow did as she was asked. She stood next to Mrs. Twine who turned to face the young hapless child. The troubled expression on the teacher's face made Willow think again why Mrs. Twine had asked to see her. The flashcards weren't in her hand this time.

"Willow, honey," she said softly. "You need to go to the principal's office."

Willow dithered. She never had to go to the principal's office before. She had watched other children being commanded to meet with Mr. Spencer and their nervous faces revealed that such an occasion was never good. Mrs. Twine placed her dainty hand on Willow and gripped her shoulder bone lightly as if she was anchoring Willow.

"You're not in trouble, sweetie. Don't worry," Mrs. Twine assured her.

The principal's office was a cool, damp, square room. The walls were painted blocks of concrete, stark white. The only picture on the wall was a photo of the school taken when it first opened in 1958. Mr. Spencer motioned for Willow to sit in the chair directly in front of his desk. The stiff material of the seat made the back of her thighs itch. She nervously tapped her foot against the chair leg, feeling the coolness of the metal brush her shins. He leaned and peered at a piece of paper with words typed on them, then glanced at Willow with a sympathetic expression. Whatever it was, it seemed official.

"Uh umm, Wilhelmina, it's nice to see you but I'm sorry for the reason you are here."

No one called her by her full name unless the person didn't know her and was reading her name from a list. "Why am I here?" Willow squeaked nervously.

"I have been trying to get a hold of your parents, but I just can't get in touch with them. It seems your phone is no longer in service."

Mr. Spencer shifted forward waiting for an answer from Willow who remained silent in the chair. Then, he rephrased his statement into a question.

"Wilhelmina, how can I get in touch with your parents?"

"My mamma is gone and my dad," Willow paused to catch herself before she started crying. "My dad, he's at home. I mean he is working at the quarry during the day, but he usually gets home around five."

"I've called his place of work, but he hasn't returned any of my phone calls, and I've sent a letter to your house, but I did not get a response, so I'm going to have to ask you to give him this letter."

Mr. Spencer, who now seemed indignant at his inability to render the situation, handed Willow a white envelope with the line '*To the Par-*

ents of Wilhelmina Hitchens' typed in the front center. She dragged her hands from underneath her legs and reached out, reluctantly grasping the envelope. Her thumb and pointer finger pinched the corner and she brought it to her lap.

"Wilhelmina, I'm sorry to have to tell you this, but it's for the best." He stopped anticipating a reply from Willow who was by this time, sullen. Mr. Spencer revealed to Willow how Mrs. Twine always spoke fondly about her and that he knew she worked hard in school, but it wasn't enough to let her go to fifth grade. "This letter states that we are going to have to hold you back in fourth grade next year. I need your dad to sign this notice, and please bring it back tomorrow."

Willow's face flushed with embarrassment, and her eyes filled with water. She tried to hide her sadness from Mr. Spencer by tipping her head down toward her legs. A tear slid out and dripped on her thigh.

"I'm sorry, Wilhelmina. It will be a relief for you. Maybe next year won't be so hard and you will know more about fourth grade than any of the other kids."

"All right, Mr. Spencer."

Willow couldn't argue the decision for Mr. Spencer was right; this year had been exceptionally hard. She didn't care as much about staying back in fourth grade as she did about what the other kids would say. It seemed to her like she was the only one in her class that had ever been held back. Her school had only one fourth grade class. In fact, each grade had only one class. "*Everyone would know*," she balked.

She left his office and thought about running out the front doors of the school to escape the embarrassment, but home was too far away and what if Daddy had the house locked, then she'd have to wait on the stoop all day.

Mrs. Kelp, the school secretary, saw Willow crying as she was traipsing from Mr. Spencer's office, with heavy steps and welded wet eyes. She directed her to sit in the chair beside her desk for a while, *till she could calm down*, Mrs. Kelp had said in a soft, sympathetic voice. Willow listened to the continuous click of the typewriter keys and it calmed her. When she felt ready, she told Mrs. Kelp she wanted to go back to class.

3

Chapter 3

Summer at Last

When Willow got home, the house wasn't locked, so she let herself inside. The dank smell overwhelmed her as she passed through the doorway. She would have to start cleaning like Mamma did. Springtime was when Mamma dove into a deep cleaning frenzy, washing windows and walls, moving around furniture, and rearranging cabinets. She dropped the letter in the middle of the dusty, kitchen table. Mamma had painted it yellow last summer, a creamy rich yellow like the center disc of a daisy. She couldn't wait to see them bloom this year but wished Mamma was here to experience it with her. When they first flowered last summer, Willow remembered sitting on the stoop admiring the pretty petals with Mamma beside her. Thinking about this memory drained her energy again. The laundry would have to wait.

It was past six and Floyd hadn't come home yet so Willow searched in the pantry for dinner. She counted six cans. Mamma's winter stock was almost gone. She forewent making a peanut butter sandwich because the bread was moldy and stale. When she had pulled it from the bag, the edges crumbled. As she waited for Daddy, she ruminated about how she would approach him. She had to get him to sign the paper and ask him to go to Powel's Market for some fresh bread and milk. She made a list like Mamma did and decided that while she was at it, why not write him a note to sign the paper. That way she could avoid talking to him. Hopefully, he would be able to read it, she thought, for her spelling was sometimes indecipherable.

Floyd came home late after the spring sun had set, and he was especially distant. He smelled of liquor, liquor he drank at the lodge, and he was roweled up with energy, stumbling around the house, making random sneers about what angered him. He groused about Mamma.

"Your Mamma didn't love you anymore. She took up with someone else." His voice was harsh as he spoke those words. Willow ran up to her room and covered her head with the flowered sheets. *I have never known Mamma to love anyone but Daddy.*

Floyd was always making up things that weren't true like the night they came home from the dance at the lodge. The one and only time, Mamma was invited, Daddy was angry with her because she spoke to Joseph, the preacher at Church. Willow recalled the words her father spoke about Joseph. He called him a traitor because he let certain people join the church and then he put a stop to attending Sunday service. Willow remembered how heartbroken her mother was for she loved singing and the kind people. Willow wished she could be in church again with Mamma.

Why would she leave me?

The house quieted and she heard her dad collapse on the couch followed by loud rolling snores.

#

Willow had the letter in her hand Friday morning. She stealthily slipped it from her bag and dropped it on Mrs. Twine's desk when the other kids were unpacking their school bags and sharpening pencils. She hoped with the distractions, it would go unnoticed that she was turning in her failure. She sagged her head in shame avoiding eye contact with her teacher as she turned to go back to her desk.

"Thank you Willow," Mrs. Twine said. "Next year is a new year."

Willow would miss Mrs. Twine over the summer. Now that she had her letter signed and turned in, she contemplated staying home the rest of the year, hoping it would go unnoticed. There was only one more week left. That afternoon, she hugged Mrs. Twine before she got on the bus, something she usually never did. Willow had made up her mind; she wasn't coming back to school. She didn't need to be there for the annual end-of-the-year picnic. Mamma wouldn't be there this year anyway and the thought of all the other children lighting up in bright smiles when their parents arrived in the classroom just before lunchtime, pained Willow.

The bus dropped her off at Old Rock Road and she sprinted off before the doors slid to a close, her long legs scuttling down the country road to where her old house stood, blanketed with shade underneath the oak tree.

Summer at last!

#

Knowing she didn't have to go to school, Willow slept soundly. She woke to the sunshine filtering past the branches of the oak tree and through her bedroom window screen, creating a shower of light on her face. The chorus of the cicadas meant summer and how she relished those noisy creatures right now. She dragged herself downstairs and glanced in the direction of the orange marmalade shaded clock; its metal sunburst arms encased the face and sparkled in the morning light. It caught her eye when she stepped into the kitchen. She slept late this morning. Willow couldn't tell time precisely, but she knew it was somewhere around ten o'clock because that is where the little hand pointed. Daddy hadn't noticed that she didn't go to school. A feeling of relief brushed through her insides.

Willow stepped into the pantry and when she reached for the box of Rice Krispies, a mouse ran over the tip of her big toe. Startled, she jumped back and let out a bellow. Mamma would have swept that creature outside with a broom. By the time she grabbed the handle, the mouse had disappeared into the kitchen and under the harvest gold oven. She vigorously swiped the bristles behind the oven, eventually scaring it out of hiding, and managed to trap the mouse against the floor with the bottom of the broom. Then, with the broom head bearing down on the creature, she carefully slid it across the floor and out the door. She had seen Mamma do it many times.

All morning she occupied herself with television, watching reruns of old timey shows, the kind that you can't get in color, the same one's mamma grew up watching. Dennis the Menace was her favorite. Several hours later, when she had to get up too many times to adjust the antennas for a clear picture, she decided it was enough of lying on the couch and ventured outside. Without Mamma, outside was lonely and Willow almost wished she was in school.

She walked to the field behind her house where the uncut grass was shaggy and thick. She waded through tangling blades, pushing her legs with exertion until she made it to the dirt patch where Bartholomew's corn crop began. He had passed over the winter, but someone had moved into the house and took over the farm. Willow heard of a family living there, Bartholomew's son's family, but she hadn't been given the opportunity to meet them.

I wonder what they're like.

Curiosity got the better of her and she wandered on further, following the path between the line of trees and the edge of the field. Daddy never minded Bartholomew, but he always warned her to stay away from the odd lady on the other side of Marshland Road, across from Bartholomew's farmhouse. The lady lived in the woods nestled at the bottom of a hill where a rich man's mansion stood proudly as if it resided over the cottage. Floyd despised the rich man, Edwin Mann, except he liked that Mr. Mann was trying to get the lady off his property. 'We don't need her kind 'round here putting curses on this place', her Dad had said. She didn't know her, but she must be a witch, Willow gathered, and it was enough to spook her.

Willow stayed in the trees watching Bartholomew's property, waiting for something to happen and when nothing worth an ounce of excitement came about, she hesitantly edged closer to the house where she eventually found herself at the end of the tree line. She hopped out of the woods and onto the grass as if she was a rabbit and almost fell into the old wooden shanty that sat on the same property of the farmhouse. Willow hadn't known what this old structure had been used for but she did know that it had weathered to gray and spaces parted the clapboards, letting enough light in to see the barren floor. Behind it, her eye caught a glimpse of the field. It struck her as odd. Something was different about this year's corn crop. The usual elongated leaves jetting from a stalk about knee's height were, instead, round like the shape of a heart, and there were only about five to six leaves per plant, unlike corn.

It doesn't look like Bartholomew's corn.

On the other side of the farmhouse, where the barn was located, she could hear the motor of a tractor. She waited for movement from the farmhouse but nothing—it sat still, only a gentle breeze and chirping birds filled her ear.

Willow became distracted by a squirrel capering through the forest floor and along tree branches. Willow followed the squirrel, frolicking along with him as if she were a nymph in the woods, and before she realized it, she was close to her house. Her stomach growled, so she paused for lunch. Inside, Willow took out the package of Wonder bread from the metal bread box on the counter.

Fresh!

She spread the usual peanut butter and added grape jelly on both slices. Today, she would attempt to do the laundry. After lunch, she gathered her sheets and the sheets off Mamma and Daddy's bed. If Mamma came home, she would be pleased with clean sheets. Willow fussed with the knobs on the washing machine and became anxious when she couldn't get it to start.

"Mamma's right. This machine is fickle," she said out loud.

She had already filled it with the bedding and had poured a cupful of the white soap granules on top. Daddy would not be happy if he had to come home to a broken washing machine. *Why would you even start this?* She imagined him grumbling.

"I have to get this to work," she panicked.

Willow gave it one last toggle and to her relief, the machine started. She released a breath and the sound of the water gushing into the basin soothed her worry. She began to sweep the dirt off the kitchen floor and found some shards of glass sitting beneath the edge of the oven which reminded her of the night mamma left. She glanced up at the empty shelves.

The jars should be filled with strawberry jam.

Her mood turned somber, but she persisted with her task thinking of how Mamma would be grateful. After the cycle ended, Willow pulled at the wet material and slid it over the top of the rust-colored Kenmore washer. She dumped it in a plastic laundry basket and topped the heap with a handful of wooden clothespins. She tugged at the heavy load until she managed to drag the basket outside and without spilling a single piece. Standing in front of the clothesline, she stared at the feat in front of her pausing to think about how to get the sheets over the string. She could barely even touch the line let alone clip the pins.

Luckily the air was still, nothing gusty that would blow the sheets away. Her plan, which was carefully thought out beforehand, was to throw the sheets over the line then spread them out as much as she could. After several attempts, Willow got the first set of sheets hanging almost evenly and then went on to finish with the second set. That was the best Willow could manage, and she hoped the pillowcases wouldn't slip off or blow away. The wooden pins stayed at the bottom of the basket and she took off again through the woods.

The bus was coming from the east on Marshland Road when she arrived back at the farm where she waited again at the edge of the forest. There would only be three days left if she had stayed in school. Willow was searching for the squirrel when she heard the wheels of a car pull into the driveway next to the farmhouse. A forest green station wagon, with brown paneled sides, was parked next to the front porch on the same side where the porch swing hung. Two girls stepped out of the back seats from each side of the vehicle. The older girl looked to be about twelve and the other one was around her age.

Willow remembered they were the new students at Sol Valley Elementary. Two sisters who started school in March or April, Willow couldn't say exactly but she recalled it was around the time when she heard the tractor pulling the plow across Bartholomew's fields. They must be Bartholomew's granddaughters. Mamma had said when the weather got nicer she would take Willow to meet the new family. Willow was timid when she thought about meeting them. She was afraid they wouldn't like her, like Tammy, who stopped being her friend.

"Bonnie, get your school bag," the mother shouted.

The young girl was dressed in a brown, white and blue plaid dress with a rounded collar and a ruffled hem. She had on light blue knee socks and shiny shoes. Her reddish-brown short, bowl-cut styled hair lay flat on her forehead and was curled under at the ends. It was different from her sister's, who had long dark brown hair feathered at the tips around her face and she wore a hint of makeup. Bonnie retrieved her bag, dropped it on the porch then eagerly ran down the steps and into the grass, heading toward the sassafras tree.

"Wait a minute, young lady. You take that bag into the house and change out of your school clothes before you start climbing that tree you love so much."

Bonnie followed her mother's instructions as Willow watched inquisitively. She recognized the younger girl coming out of the third-grade classroom one day, but she never saw the older one before today. A few minutes later, the thin, energetic girl ran back outside, now wearing a pair of jean shorts, a white T-shirt with a rainbow on the front, and a pair of white tube socks double striped in red at the top. The pieces of hair near her temples flopped in the wind she created when she sprinted, making a beeline for the tree. She jumped for the lowest limb, pulled herself up into the tree, and straddled the branch; her gaze settled on the empty road. The heat of the day was at its peak and beads of sweat speckled Willow's hairline as she sat under the brush watching. The girl started pulling off twigs and breaking them, making crackling noises. She saw her pluck a leaf from its stem and push it in her mouth, chewing it like it was candy.

"She eats leaves?" Willow said out loud.

The girl turned in her direction, but thankfully Willow went unnoticed.

It was getting closer to the time Daddy would be home. *I had better get home on time. If Daddy catches me here spying, he'll give me a lickin'.* Just as she pulled herself from the itchy ground, she heard a voice call out.

"Who are you?"

Willow had turned back into the woods, but it was too late. The girl called out to her again.

"Hey, come back here. What are you doing?"

Willow swung around and saw the girl had flipped and flung herself out of the tree to the ground. Willow wished she could do such things. She was not as nimble as this girl seemed to be. They both began to walk toward each other. Willow was nervous, but the stranger was not shy at all.

"Who are you?" She asked Willow again.

"I'm Willow."

"Hi, I'm Bonnie. You want to climb my sassafras tree with me?"

Willow was unsure she should be here, but she felt comfortable in the presence of this girl.

"I guess. I can try," she mumbled bashfully with a quiver lacing her answer.

"Come here. I'll help you," Bonnie offered.

Willow ran behind Bonnie. Bonnie was back up in the tree in no time, while Willow struggled to hoist herself off the ground.

"Here," Bonnie said, extending her hand to Willow.

Willow clasped Bonnie's wrist and with a tug from her new friend, she was able to get her body up high enough to swing around and settle securely on the branch. The roughness of the bark scratched her legs. Bonnie pulled a three-lobed leaf that looked like a hand with two missing fingers and put it to her nose taking a whiff of its pungent scent.

"What does it smell like?" Willow asked her.

"It's sweet. Like lemon pie."

"I've never had lemon pie, but I've had lemon meringue pie," Willow stated.

"That's what I mean," Bonnie said eating the leaf.

"You can eat those?" Willow asked confused.

"Yeah, try one."

Willow pulled a leaf off the tree. This one only had two lobes. It looked like a mitten. She put it in her mouth and chewed it slowly deciphering whether she liked it or not.

"It's sweet," she said in a surprised tone, "but it doesn't taste like lemon meringue pie.

"I don't think so either," replied Bonnie agreeing with Willow.

Willow was relaxed in the presence of this girl, a refreshing change to being at her house.

"Do you go to Sol Valley Elementary?" Bonnie asked.

"Kind of well, not anymore!"

Bonnie looked confused but Willow was having such a good time she didn't want to explain her hopeless situation, so she just left out the other part—the part where she didn't go back to school. A burst of wind twisted the leaves and blew up Willow's bangs. She worried about the sheets for a moment.

"I go there but only three days left."

Willow pulled another leaf from the tree.

"This one looks like an egg."

"The leaves are different," Bonnie said. "But they taste the same."

Willow stayed in the tree a while longer enjoying being with Bonnie. Bonnie climbed a little higher in the tree, but Willow stayed on the first branch too timid to try. Off in the distance, she heard a truck turning at the intersection of Marshland Road and Old Rock Road.

Daddy.

She had better get home.

"Where are you going?" Bonnie asked when she saw Willow project her leg over the branch.

"I got to go home. I think I heard my daddy's truck."

Willow nervously slid from the tree scraping her arm on the trunk as she plunked to the grass. Pinhead dots of blood appeared on her arm, but she ignored them and ran quickly in the direction of the woods.

"Will you come back again?" Bonnie shouted at Willow's back.

She bellowed out a *yes* as she took off running.

#

Willow saw her dad waiting on the stoop glaring with that look he gives people when he's mad. It made her heart tight and she shivered with rattled nerves.

"Where you been?"

Willow feared telling him the truth about going to Bartholomew's farm, so she said she went for a walk. He scolded her for wandering off the property. He never let Mamma go too far either.

"Get the laundry off the line before you come in the house," he said sternly and then huffed as he went inside, slamming the door. The door bounced off the trim with a piercing bang as if it was talking back to Floyd's harshness.

Right away, Willow followed his order and quickly carried herself to the clothesline. The clothespins were no longer in the basket but, instead, were clipped to the sheets on the line.

Willow paused for a moment staring at the wooden clips sticking up against the pale blue sky. She wondered how they got from the basket to being clipped on the sheets. It couldn't have been her dad, she thought. Not once did Willow ever see him do housework, that was 'mamma's job' he always said, and since mamma had been gone, when her dad saw her struggling to clean, he never offered help. *Why would Daddy clip the laundry then ask her to take it down*, she asked herself, and obediently began her task.

4

Chapter 4

Sunflowers Instead

Another week would pass before Willow could draw the courage to return to the farm. Her dad threatened her with a drubbing when she arrived home that day to him sitting on the stoop. She was aware that her dad did not want her to wander off their property in fear of people knowing Barbara was gone and in a small-town, this kind of news would spread fast. Some people must have gotten wind of the situation because when they went into town for provisions one evening, Floyd was confronted with a question about Barbara which he answered with a quick and concise *'she left and didn't' tell us where she was off to'*, avoiding eye contact, and he added *'Willow and I are doin' fine'*, to ward off an inquiry of the plight he had put Willow in without her mom at home. But Willow, who reveled at the idea of having a friend nearby, a few evenings later, broke down and asked her dad if she could take a walk to Bartholomew's farm, giving him several plausible reasons to let her go, but he adamantly grunted, *'you stay 'round here Willow'*, talking out of the side of his mouth with his mustache twitching at the corner as he spoke.

"Yes, Dad," She acquiesced to his wish but secretly devised a plan.

She would wait until Bonnie was out of school and then, would sneak off in the morning and return long before Daddy got home.

#

So, after a long and insipid weekend being stuck in the house subjected to her father's unpredictable moods, Willow was finally home alone. It was Monday morning and she had woken up with a different feeling. By now she was accustomed to her mother being gone and looked forward to going to the farm. She watched television for a while and then checked the sunburst clock. It was sometime between ten and eleven. Willow poured herself a bowl of cereal, then put the empty bowl in the sink and hurried upstairs to change out of her pajamas. She scrubbed her teeth with vigor and quickly brushed the knots from her hair. She looked into the mirror to make sure she was presentable, something her mother always reminded her of before leaving the house, and she ran down the steps. Once she was outside and past the field, Willow meandered through the same path to the edge of Bonnie's yard, where the old shanty sat. Today was the first official day of summer vacation, and she hoped Bonnie would be home. Willow sat in the bush, watching the farmhouse, too timid to knock on the door. She would wait for Bonnie to come outside like last time. The waiting dragged on and Willow began to grow restless, so she inched to the lawn and fixated on finding a four-leaf clover until she heard a girl's voice squeaking behind the farmhouse.

Curiosity took hold and Willow found herself at the corner of the field, where she could see a bigger view of the land and the covered porch which abutted the back of the house. She couldn't quite make out the words she was hearing but knew it was the same high-pitched, enthusiastic voice of the girl she met in the sassafras tree. Finally, Willow, after keeping her eyes on the field, spotted Bonnie skipping between the rows of plants while a broad-shouldered man with slick, dark hair and sideburns was inspecting the leaves of the plants and taking samples of the soil. The older sister was sitting on a step of the back porch, clutching a hard-covered book, deeply engrossed in reading. Seconds later, the mother, using her back to push open a wooden-framed screen door, struggled to bring out a tray of refreshments. The older girl hurried to hold the door while the woman placed an avocado green, crinkle glass pitcher of tea and matching tumblers on the table before she tootled back in the house. The sister filled her glass and then resumed her reading on the steps with her drink comfortably beside her.

Willow gazed upon the scene, thinking of how it had been a while since anyone served her something to drink. She remembered how Mamma would bring out two glasses of lemonade to the stoop where they would sit together chitchatting and sipping homemade lemonade, which Mamma proudly made from real lemons. Soon, the man moseyed further down the field and the sister, who was still intently reading, seemed unaware of Willow's presence, so she took the opportunity to approach Bonnie.

"Bonnie, Bonnie," Willow called out in a low almost whisper voice, her hand cupped at her mouth.

Bonnie paused as if she thought she heard something but then continued her enjoyment in the field, unaware that her attention was being summoned. Willow called out again, more loudly and quickly this time.

"Bonnie!"

The spirited girl turned her whole body around and saw Willow. A smile lit up her face.

"Hi Willow. Come play with me in the sunflower field."

Sunflowers Willow realized as she said the word to herself. *Not corn. That's why the leaves look different.*

"What happened to the corn Mr. Bartholomew planted?"

"My dad decided to plant sunflowers since last year's corn crop didn't grow as well as before. It's something called *roshon*."

"Rotation," a voice smugly called out from behind Willow.

Willow turned to see Bonnie's sister descending the porch steps and saunter toward the field, leaving her book next to the glass. "Crops need to be rotated in order to produce more vegetables." She emphasized the word rotated. "Corn leaves an excess of nitrogen in the soil and sunflowers like nitrogen. Since last year's crop of corn did poorly, daddy planted sunflowers to improve the soil for next year's corn crop."

Willow was stunned at the explanation as she tried to grasp what the girl was saying. All she knew was how pretty flowers can be, and Mamma loved flowers.

"That's my sister Jenny. She thinks she knows everything."

"Bonnie," Jenny looked annoyed, "Mom said time for lunch."

"Well, tell her I'm not ready. My friend Willow just came over to play."

"Bonnie, you have to come in for lunch when mom tells you," Jenny said giving her sister a firm directive. "I'm sure your friend can eat with you."

Although Willow was nervous to be at a stranger's house for a meal, she was delighted at the thought of having lunch. She was hungry. Dinner last night was another bowl of soup, which wasn't enough bulk to stave off hunger for too long and this morning's bowl of cereal was measly. Bonnie darted past Willow and Jenny, then leaped the steps of the porch and stopped at the door.

"Mom," she yelled robustly through the screen. "Mom, can my friend eat lunch over?"

Bonnie's mother came outside to investigate her daughter's request and saw Willow, who nervously backed up a step, lowering her eyes to the grass. Willow felt shame. She wondered if Bonnie's mother knew about Floyd, knew about his unfriendly manner, knew that she didn't have a mother at home, knew that she struggled in school, and had to stay back in fourth grade.

"Sure, she can eat lunch with us. And who is your little friend, Bonnie?" The mother asked, her voice sounding melodic.

"This is Willow," Bonnie replied.

"Hi," Willow said meekly.

"Hi, Willow. I'm Mrs. Murphy."

Willow demurely smiled back at the kind woman.

"Welcome," Mrs. Murphy said showing her perfectly aligned teeth and soft smile. Her strawberry blond hair was pulled back into a ponytail at the nape of her neck and she wore a thick checkered headband which pulled her bangs from falling into her face.

"Thank you, Mrs. Murphy."

Mrs. Murphy motioned for the children to come inside with one hand while holding the screen door with the other. Willow noticed her long, slender fingers. Bonnie resembled her mother in every way except that Mrs. Murphy's hair was lighter.

"Mom, can we eat on the porch? Please, can you bring us the peanut butter and jelly outside, and we can make it ourselves?" Bonnie begged.

Mrs. Murphy thought for a moment. "Well, I guess that will be all right; come get the things, Bonnie."

Willow waited on the porch while Bonnie went into the kitchen to retrieve the food. In no time, she came bounding outside juggling a jar of peanut butter, jelly, two butter knives, a loaf of bread that dangled from her fingertips and swung like a pendulum with every step she took, and two paper plates. She set them on the cedar log table. The two girls sat across from one another spreading the peanut butter and jelly on the pieces of bread. Bonnie folded each piece into a triangle. Mamma never did it that way, Willow thought; she puts the bread together and cuts it into rectangles. Bonnie chewed as she gazed over the fields.

"My dad says the Sunflowers could grow taller than him. Some sunflowers grow 12 feet."

Willow turned her head to look at the field. The plants were about two feet now, with only four to six leaves jetting from around the stem. She couldn't imagine a flower growing to 12 feet. To Willow, that was as tall as her house. She thought about her mamma and wished she could have met Mrs. Murphy.

When Willow turned back around, Bonnie stuck her finger in a hole encircled by a knot in the wood.

"This house is old," She begins to tell Willow. "My dad said this house needs a lot of fixing. Since grandpa died, he's been patching up holes with this white stuff. Maybe I can patch this hole in the table."

"How are you going to do that?" Willow asked.

Bonnie looked at the jar of peanut butter and then looked at the hole. "This would work," she stated. "The stuff my dad has is white like the walls and this peanut butter is brown like the table."

Bonnie took the knife and scooped out a goop of peanut butter then stuffed it into the hole. Carefully, she took the tip of the knife and smoothed out the lump.

"There," she exclaimed looking quite pleased with herself.

"That looks perfect," Willow complimented her friend.

A cat walked up the steps and strutted over to Bonnie, rubbing the side of its body against her friend's ankles as it bobbed between her legs. Then it leaped onto the table.

"Is this your cat?" Willow asked.

"Yes, this is Oliver. He's a tabby cat," Bonnie said, petting the back of the cat's head.

"He's pretty." Willow reached over to join Bonnie in petting the cat. By now, the cat was purring loudly.

The cat, decorated with grey, black, and white markings, stepped over to the hole that was filled with peanut butter and started licking.

"Stop that Oliver," Bonnie reprimanded and pushed the cat to the ground. The cat then scurried off the porch, pattering its paws as if it were in trouble.

Bonnie and Willow started eating their peanut butter and jelly sandwiches, leaving the jars open and the bread bag untied. Bonnie was distracted looking at indentations on the table, rubbing her pointer finger in the tiny crevices she found in the wood. She started counting every imperfection, but when she reached fourteen, she stopped.

"There're a lot of dings in this table. Want to help me fill them in?" Bonnie asked Willow.

"Do you think it's OK?"

"My dad will be happy that I'm trying to help him. He's been so busy with work since we moved into Grandpa's place. Then when we're done, we can paint the table like my dad painted after he patched the holes in the walls. That way, you won't be able to see the peanut butter."

Bonnie handed Willow a knife. She scooped a glob of peanut butter, and Willow followed her lead. The two of them got busy spreading peanut butter in the indentations. When they were just about to finish, Mrs. Murphy walked out on the porch to see them engrossed in their task.

"Bonnie, what on earth are you and Willow doing?"

"I'm helping dad by fixing the holes in this old table."

"Bonnie," her mother emphasized her name, "those are not holes; they are natural imperfections in the wood. And the table is not old, Grandpa just made that table last summer, before he passed."

Bonnie started to cry. "Mom, I'm sorry, I didn't know. I thought..."

"Ok, Ok, well you need to wipe every bit of peanut butter off the table."

Willow felt frightened. She just met Bonnie's mother and already they were in trouble. Bonnie ran into the house and Mrs. Murphy followed behind her. Willow stayed on the porch feeling stupid. Oliver strutted back up to the porch and jumped on the table, licking at the peanut butter. When Bonnie came back outside, she shooed Oliver away again. The two girls went to work scrubbing the table with soapy water. Mrs. Murphy came out to inspect and when they finished, she wiped the table dry with a towel.

"I know you meant well, Bonnie, but you should never spread food on anything; do you understand me, child?"

"Yes, mom."

"Why don't you two run along and play, and Willow," Mrs. Murphy looked directly at her, "Don't do everything Bonnie tells you to do." Mrs. Murphy smiled warmly at Willow.

Willow felt a sense of relief. Mrs. Murphy made her feel as warm as her mamma and Mrs. Twine did. Daddy wouldn't have let her off the hook so easily. The two girls ran carelessly through the sunflower field, up and down every single row, brushing their calves against the heart-shaped leaves. Their ankles were brown from the dirt and their socks smelled like the manure Mr. Murphy spread in the field of flowers, which were just about ready to grow buds. Willow heard the growling of a truck popping over rocks along Old Rock Road, yet it was too early for Daddy to come home. Still, she panicked at the thought of being late, and besides, she had some cleaning to do.

"Bonnie, I have to go home before Daddy gets back, or he'll be mad."

"Why, Willow?"

"He just will."

"Oh. Can you come over tomorrow?"

"I can in the morning. Bye, Bonnie," Willow said, and she scurried off finding her way to the path between the field and the trees. Daddy couldn't know she'd been playing at Bonnie's house, and she would need to wash and dry her smelly socks. Willow hurried home.

#

The morning brought a strong summer sun, and as Willow got dressed for another day with Bonnie, it was rising to shine its glory over the valley. She had been playing with Bonnie for several weeks without her dad having a clue that she was leaving the house. Today was like no other and she ran to the farm and noticed a remarkable difference as she navigated the path. The sunflowers were taller, maybe the height of her, and tiny bumps of green topped the stems. The plants looked as if they were wearing crowns. Willow, who was now strong enough to climb the sassafras tree, hoisted herself up to have a bird's-eye view. She saw a field of green buds, each, a wreath of encased leaves, with its tips, perky and pointing toward the sun. She stared in awe at the magnificent scenery and felt the anticipation of what was yet to come when the buds would expand and open to a yellow flower.

Feeling a flutter of excitement—she had something to look forward to—as she did nearly every morning when she thought about going to the farm. Willow had become more comfortable with the Murphy family and today, after sliding out of the tree, she went up to the door and knocked. She heard footsteps in the house before Mrs. Murphy appeared behind the screen. An iron horse and buggy relief splayed across the mid-section of the metal door.

"Hi, Willow. Bonnie's in here watching television."

"Can she come out and play?" Willow asked eager to get back up in the sassafras tree.

"Sure, she'll have to get dressed first. Come on in," she told her.

Mrs. Murphy opened the front door and Willow readily stepped into the house. This was the first time she would come in through the front door, a sign that she was now comfortable with the Murphys. It was unlike Bonnie to still be inside at this time of the morning. When she walked to the living room, she heard *Come on Down* blaring from the television. Bonnie and Jenny were sprawled out on the couch watching a game show and still in their pajamas. Mrs. Murphy hurried back to the kitchen.

"Hi, Willow," Bonnie stated when she noticed her standing in the entryway to the living room. "Come in. We just got a new television last night."

That's why she hadn't come outside yet. Jenny's eyes were glued to a screen encased in a brown wooden box that held the television set. It had a column of round knobs on the right and was decorated with intricate latticework around the perimeter. Mrs. Murphy must have just dusted because it was shined up and a bottle of Pledge furniture polish was sitting on top. The contraption was much nicer than hers, a 20-inch black and white television on a metal stand, with wheels that annoyingly squeaked every time it needed adjustment. The Murphys' new television didn't have antennas like hers. There was a cable box that got reception for extra channels and a color picture. Willow sat on the couch next to Bonnie and watched the rest of the show.

After Bonnie changed, they headed outside through the kitchen. Mrs. Murphy was making chocolate chip cookies again. A big bowl of dough with a wooden spoon stuck in the mound sat on the counter, and the warm smell of sugar filled the kitchen. Bonnie attempted to stick her finger in the bowl when Mrs. Murphy caught her and slapped her finger away.

"Just one lick, please mom?" she begged.

"Ok, Bonnie you each can have a spoonful of dough." Mrs. Murphy scooped a tiny bit for each of them.

The two girls ate the dough and licked the spoons clean before dropping them in the sink and continued to the back porch. The screen whined as it swung to a close behind them. Mr. Murphy was fiddling with the irrigation system. He warned them to stay out of the field because he would be heavily watering the crops and the fields were going to be saturated. The sunflowers were at a crucial point, and with the high temperatures, they required an exuberant amount of water, he explained.

"Oh Shucks, all right Dad," Bonnie reluctantly complied with her father's instruction.

"Let's climb the tree again," Willow suggested.

Willow and Bonnie climbed the sassafras tree and settled on the lowest branch. Oliver was on the front porch observing. He seemed to be watching for birds, Willow noticed, and she pointed him out to Bonnie who then explained how he catches birds, moving her hands like cat paws, as she imitated his hunting maneuvers.

Willow noticed the house directly across the road, a stately structure that sat at the top of a hill; the grounds were bright with green grass and manicured shrubbery. The driveway, a long thin filament of pavement, curved upwards and led to the home of Edwin Mann. The large 1940s tutor-style house was a myriad of stone and stucco holding three front-facing gables that pointed tall and proud. Willow remembered Daddy saying Mr. Mann felt as if he owned the valley because he was richer than everyone else. High up in the tree, Bonnie pointed to the white cottage at the bottom of the hill, beside Mr. Mann's mansion. The structure was minuscule in comparison, and the abundance of plants that surrounded the place, made it look comfortably, tucked away.

"I know Mr. Mann lives at the top of the hill, but I wonder who lives at the bottom," Bonnie asked.

"I'm not sure of her name, but my dad told me to stay away from her. She cast spells on people," Willow cautioned.

"Is she a witch?"

"I don't know. I guess because witches are the only ones who cast spells."

"Not all witches are bad. Some witches are good," Bonnie told Willow.

"That's true. Maybe she's a good witch."

"Well, let's go find out for ourselves," Bonnie suggested.

Willow nervously agreed. Daddy was at work, so he wouldn't know. After all, he didn't know that she'd been going to Bonnie's for some time now. They climbed down from the tree and crossed Marshland Road *and* Willow's fears disintegrated with the novelty of the adventure. The girls walked along the edge of the road until the entrance of the white cottage appeared. A rusted metal mailbox sat on a rickety post that leaned slightly west. The numbers painted on the side were faded except for the two at the beginning of what was once a four-digit address. Willow and Bonnie stood quiet for a moment surveying the property. There was no carved-out driveway but, instead, a patch of dirt led to the house which was surrounded by thick forest. A creek babbled alongside the river birch trees several yards from the cottage and underneath one of the trees, was an unoccupied metal lawn chair, a waffled pattern of square cuts-outs on its seat and back. It was as rusty as the mailbox. The front porch was bare except for an old-fashioned water basin and a pitcher sitting on a wood table stand right next to the door. From a distance, the cottage looked cozy, nestled in the trees, and not sinister like one might think of for a witch's house.

"Let's go up to the house," Bonnie urged.

"Are you sure Bonnie? Are you sure we should just walk up to her house?"

"Yeah!" Bonnie answered and she couldn't wait a second longer. She confidently skipped toward the house; Willow followed right next to her.

When they reached the porch, they stopped to inspect the water pitcher and basin. There was a well pump off to the side of the house. The windows had cobwebs in the corners with tiny pieces of leaves caught in them. A Garden Orb Weaver spider constructed a web that stretched from the post at the corner of the porch to the side of the house. It sat in the middle as if it was satisfied with its creation and now patiently waiting for prey. They peaked in the windows and noticed the light that filled the house was dim and grey with dark corners. Natural light, shadowed by the trees, filtered in the windows, which was the only light in the house. In fact, there were no lamps or overhead lights, only an oil lamp on a table next to the couch. There was a kitchen in the back with a freestanding pantry cupboard, a small round oak table and matching chairs, a terracotta sink with a deep basin, and a hand pump like the one on the outside. Off to the right of the kitchen was a closed-door that must have led to another room.

"Look at that," Bonnie exclaimed, intrigued by what she saw.

"What is it?" Willow asked curiously.

"There's a black dress and a broom. She is a witch." Bonnie's voice grew louder and more intense.

Willow moved her head closer to the window and placing her hand over her brow, she peered inside, inspecting thoroughly. Sure enough, there was a black silk dress hanging from the ceiling on a hook in front of the fireplace and a broom leaned against the wall right next to the mantle which was lined with candles. She quickly jumped back, spooked at the sight of witchery paraphernalia.

"Bonnie, this is spooky. We should go back to your house."

But Bonnie, unafraid and curious, suggested, "Let's go around to the side of the house and peek in the window to see what is behind the door. Maybe the witch is in that room. I bet she's sleeping. Witches sleep during the day."

Willow couldn't believe how fearless Bonnie was; she didn't seem to have inhibitions about snooping around someone else's house. The two girls stepped off the porch and tiptoed stealthily to the side of the cottage to where the window of the room behind the mysterious door, was located. They saw a woman with long gray hair sleeping in a metal-framed bed. They heard springs squeak when she turned to face the opposite way.

"You kids get off my property," a shrill voice came from behind the house.

Willow and Bonnie, startled, looked up in the direction of the austere command. There stood Mr. Edwin Mann. He had gray hair and a bushy gray mustache below a fat nose. His red face and beady eyes were filled with ire. The woman, now awake, opened her eyes and saw Willow and Bonnie standing at her window. The girls, frightened at what they had stirred up, screamed, and ran from the scary man, their feet kicking up dust and gravel as they dashed to safety. When they made it to Marshland Road, they stopped to catch their breath.

"That was close," Willow said panting heavily.

"Did you see how mad Mr. Mann was? I thought his eyes were going to pop out of his head," Bonnie snickered.

"I thought he was going to bust his pants when his fat belly shook."

Willow and Bonnie laughed the whole way back to the sassafras tree. Oliver was waiting for them at the bottom of the trunk. They sat down, resting from their risky quest, and talked about what they found. Oliver settled in Willow's lap. His fur felt soft on her bare legs and when he started to purr, the vibrations relaxed her. A gentle breeze brushed by and cooled her off. They listened to the sound of a tractor off in the distance as they rested their heads against the bark of the tree. Willow felt content, as if the world stopped for a moment.

"My dad must be planting the corn today, I hear the tractor," Bonnie said.

"Where is he planting corn?"

"On the field behind the barn, the one closer to the mountainside.'"

Willow remembered the sound of the tractor the first day she met Bonnie. That must have been Mr. Murphy getting the field ready. Bartholomew had planted soybean in that field before. The cat's purrs grew louder, and his eyes were closed as he rested in Willow's lap.

"Oliver likes you, Willow."

"I like him too. I never had a pet. My grandparents on my mother's side had a dog but when my Papa died, my Grandma had to be put in a home, and the dog had to be given to a new owner. Daddy wouldn't let us keep him."

"Why not?" Bonnie asked.

"He said we couldn't afford another mouth to feed."

"That's too bad, Willow. You can pet Oliver anytime you want. That's if he's not prowling."

Willow wistfully thought about what she was missing. She wanted what Bonnie had, a family, a pet, Mamma. "Bonnie I'm going to head home."

"Already? Don't you want to stay for lunch like usual?"

Willow wished she could stay, but she had chores and besides, Mamma taught her to never overstay her welcome. The Murphys have been nothing but kind to Willow, but it was time to leave, to head back to where she belonged. "No, I really need to get home. I have chores."

"Come back. We have to find out more about the witch."

"I'm not so sure about that."

"Don't be scared, Willow. We can do it together."

"Yes, Bonnie, together," she repeated. "Bye Bonnie."

Willow felt Bonnie's eyes on her back as she walked past the old shanty, its dilapidated frame feeble from the years that had passed, and found the path beside the field. She turned around and gave a quick wave. Bonnie waved back.

Willow walked back to the house in a fog. Her mind seemed to drag her away from the world for a moment, and she felt a wave of melancholy sweep over her. It slowed her pace and she stared at the ground as she walked with slow heavy steps.

My dad is not as nice as her father.

She thought about Mr. Murphy and how he takes Willow, Bonnie, and Jenny for rides on the tractor and lets them pick beans from the garden. Sometimes they eat the beans right off the vine which taste bitter at first but then have a robust crunch, and a squirt of liquid when bitten. Bonnie finally made it to the stoop where she found a bowl of strawberries sitting on the corner of the square landing. Someone left her strawberries and her first inkling was that maybe her dad put them there for her to eat at lunch, but she quickly brushed off that notion. Floyd was never known to leave the quarry until the day was done. Willow then thought maybe it was Grandpa, but he doesn't bother much with his granddaughter, Willow noted.

Willow picked the strawberries from the colander and ate one after another until the colander was empty with its tiny evenly spaced holes now visible and dots of red showing the remnants of the sweet fruit. She quickly washed the bowl and hid it in the pantry so her Dad wouldn't think people were coming to the house. That would make him mad, she had thought. He had never liked unexpected visitors, especially if they had been for Mamma.

5

Chapter 5

The Cabin

Willow's one o'clock appointment was canceled, leaving her with an hour she didn't expect to have free, so she decided to give her mother a call. They had been talking at least once a day since the plans for the house were put into motion. Barbara asked for Willow's advice at every decision to the point that it was starting to become stressful. Willow hoped the afternoon phone call would ward off a long evening discussion after work; tonight, Willow planned for a quiet evening alone on her balcony with a glass of wine and maybe stargazing. She pushed the buttons to dial the Pequot Women's Shelter listening to two rings before her call was answered. Her mother's voice was a pleasant greeting for an unknown caller but sounded urgent when she realized it was Willow. Willow rolled her eyes. Not another issue with the plans, she thought. Marybeth was meticulous, but Willow wondered if it had to be this difficult to draw up a blueprint for a renovation.

"I'm afraid I have some news," Barbara blurted.

"News? Is there another problem with the plans?" Willow asked as she listened to her mother heave a heavy sigh. That could only mean bad news, Willow gasped. "Mom, what is it?"

"It's Floyd. He's reached out to me."

"What? How did he find you?"

"Willow, I received a letter from him. It came this morning to the shelter. I don't know how he found me after all these years."

Willow wanted to jump through the phone to console her mother, but she felt as helpless as she did when she was nine. "What does it say?"

"Basically, the letter expressed his sorrow and..." she paused sucking in another breath of air, this time, a deeper and more intense breath of air. "He asked to meet with us. He said he wants no harm and wants to apologize."

"Did he say where he is living?"

"He's still living in the valley. I'm not familiar with the return address that was on the envelope, but I know it's Sol Valley."

"Don't go. Let me go. I'll find out what he wants or if he has really changed." Willow quickly responded as if it was a reflex.

"Willow, don't. We can't just believe what he says is true, and it will drudge up the pain we spent so many years trying to get over. I don't trust his intentions."

Willow couldn't fathom what compelled her reaction because after she and her mother left Sol Valley, she vowed never to return. "I'm an adult now. I understand things differently."

"Willow, I guess I can't stop you. You are an adult now. But if you go, please be safe."

"Mom, I'll let you know what I decide." When she ended the call, her mother's anguish echoed in her head.

Willow spent what was left of the hour speculating the outcome of opening a chapter in her life that had been closed. She made a list of pros and cons and when she read over her thoughts, two reasons she scribbled in the pro column, *why* and *Bonnie*, nagged at her so ferociously that she immediately put in notice for time off. She hoped this would bring closure to the unanswered questions that were written in her story for twenty years. She indulged in thoughts of Bonnie, her best childhood friend, the one who saved her that summer, and Floyd, her father, the one who she hadn't heard from since before he went to jail.

When she went home that evening, she called hotels and booked a stay in Sol Valley. There goes my quiet evening she thought. Her decision warranted another call to her mother. Barbara picked up after the first ring, and without hesitation, Willow explained her plans to visit Floyd. Barbara grew quiet and let a moment pass before she warily voiced her concerns.

"When we left the police station that day, I vowed never to let Floyd ruin our lives. I was determined to make a good life for us, Willow. That's why I got a restraining order in place upon his release from jail, but I guess too much time has passed for that order to still be viable."

Willow understood her mother's concern, but it wasn't enough to change her mind. She had questions and she wanted answers. She contacted Floyd by telephone after her mind was set and the plans were made. Hearing his voice for the first time since she was nine, left her feeling insecure and unsure of who she was, as if the past twenty years never happened, like her life after reuniting with her mother never existed. She felt as if facing the past was the only way to overcome the piece of darkness that still lived inside her.

#

Sol Valley was further away in Willow's mind than it was in distance. The trip was about two hours without traffic and as close as it was, she had never ventured back since they moved to Pequot, the beachside of the valley. She pulled into The Holiday Inn which never existed in the seventies. The little town in the valley had grown. Lucille's was no longer in business but a chain restaurant, named Friendly's sat in its place. Another gas station with a minimart was added; there were now two grocery stores, several chain restaurants, and a strip mall of retail stores. She could have made it a day trip, but she needed a good night's sleep before facing her father. She was determined to shelter her mother by not telling her where she was staying, but Willow broke down and left the name of the hotel on her mother's answering machine late last night. Willow showered and dressed. It was a muggy morning and her shorts and tank top didn't seem to make the heat any more bearable.

Willow preferred that he meet her at a restaurant, but he had no transportation. She offered to pick him up and bring him back to Friendly's for a meal which she would pay for, but the reluctance in his voice convinced her to not probe further. He spoke insipidly and slowly as if talking to people was unusual. The low tone of his voice forced her to press the telephone receiver closer to her ear so she could hear the directions he recited. After hanging up the phone and rereading the directions she had written on the hotel note pad, she highlighted the route on the map realizing it would take her through her past: Old Rock Road, the farmhouse, Mr. Mann's Mansion, and Miss Kora's cottage. She conjured images in her mind. After passing the actual locations of these places, she would then make a right at the mountainside. Beyond that point was unfamiliar territory in her recollection, nothing but trees and dirt roads she surmised. A long, empty, gravel road was etched somewhere in the back of her mind that she associated with Grandpa's house, but she couldn't be sure. Grandpa was gone now; Floyd had let her know that during their initial phone conversation.

Willow was ready to leave by 11 AM and with the gas gauge tip pointing on the F, she set off on the journey into her past, nervously making supplications for a cordial visit with her father as she drove away from the hotel. After all, she had told her mother she wouldn't go to his house on the first visit and here she was doing the opposite. Her heart sped up when the street sign that read Old Rock Road caught her attention. Just ahead, the farmhouse was coming into view and by now, she could feel the pulse of blood at her temples and the sweat that glazed her palms. The sassafras tree still stood plump with greenery and taller than Willow imagined, but behind that, the old shanty was nonexistent, a piece of history gone, and a patch of grass took its place. The farm had changed from a small family-owned farm to more industrious and twice as big. The barn was extended, and several silos stood beside it. Trees had been cut to make room for more crops. Willow noticed the crop behind the house was corn and not sunflowers.

The station wagon wasn't parked in front. Instead, there were several heavy-duty trucks side by side on a paved lot, different from the one-car pebbled driveway of years ago. She glanced up the hill and noticed Mr. Mann's mansion, not as stately as the vision she had in her childhood memory. The hedges were no longer shaped into neatly trimmed constructions but were overgrown and bushy. The house was showing its years with its dull façade and worn trim. The entrance to Miss Kora's cottage was grown over with a lunker of bushes and there was no indication of a rusty mailbox leaning in an obscure direction. The scene passed and Willow would get another chance to have a view on the way back. Right now, she needed to focus on the directions. She followed the route and after turning right at the end of Marshland Highway, her stomach flipped with nerves to the point of nausea. Was she making the right decision, she asked herself? Nothing seemed familiar but somehow, she knew this part of the valley remained unchanged. Her intuition had been correct for beyond Marshland Highway was nothing but coiled mountainous roads and forests. Willow slowed down. The street signs were hard to see; the green backgrounds of the signs blended with the woods, which were lustrous with oaks. Floyd had said about four miles past the turn she would be making a right on Crumpler Road and then a left in about another mile. The road he lived on wasn't named but the number 1008 was assigned to it, and it was the only landmark, besides more trees. When Willow noticed the odometer read 3.7, she decelerated again and kept a vigilant watch for Crumpler Road, all the while becoming more anxious with a tumultuous stomach and clammy palms. What would she say to a man who didn't care for her and abused her mother? Why was she even coming? She thought deeply about her decisions before the trip and this visit would give her answers, she hoped, answer she wanted since she was abandoned. While her father never touched her physically, he neglected her needs and his actions caused her to live with angst. She grew up with an overly cautious mother, who was cautious to the point of obsession and overcome with worry much of the years after leaving.

Willow found the entrance to Crumpler Road and made the turn.

She pushed the odometer back to zero and watched for a mile to pass. At last, she came to the pole with the white, rectangular sign attached to the top and labeled 1008 in bold black letters. This was the road that would lead to her father. She drifted back in time for a moment to the night of the chaos, hearing the scream, the skidding chair, and the frightening sound of shattering glass as if it were happening right now. The road started out paved, but the smoothness of the asphalt gave way to dirt and gravel. Eventually, her sedan was bouncing over dips and bumps of the uneven earth and her tires hissed as it crunched over rocks. Then his shack appeared. It was a mere 20 by 20-foot cabin, Willow guessed, and stupendously humble. It had a pipe attached to the side and a stocked woodpile stacked against the house. There was a narrow front porch, just one step off the ground, with wood beams attaching the roof to the floor. The front door was accompanied by a window on both sides. It was livable but very much opposite from the place her mother was constructing. How dissimilar their lives had become, Willow said to herself. She turned off the ignition after pulling in front of the cabin. There was no driveway, just barren land covered with brown pine straw and pinecones. The place was shaded by trees with a subtle hint of sunshine streaming through branches, the beams scattered throughout the lot. It felt comfortably cooler underneath the shade she noticed as she stepped out of the car and shut the door, which creaked giving off a sonorous moan. She'd have to spray it again with W-D 40. Her dad heard the noise and came outside. He stood on the porch staring at Willow with sorrowful eyes. Calmness encumbered him like Willow had never known in her father. He said nothing.

"Floyd?" she questioned. His hair was grizzled, and his eyes were sunken. The years had aged him. He had wrinkled lines jetting from the corners of his eyes and creases at the base of his cheekbones. He looked wearied and his once tawny skin was washed over with a pallid yellow.

"Willow," he answered, "It's me, your dad." He stated as if to confirm, "Come in."

Willow was too scared to enter his house, yet she allowed herself to be alone in the woods with this man she hadn't seen in 20 years, her reasoning didn't make sense, yet she couldn't pull herself away. "I'll sit on the porch."

"That'll be al 'right," he replied.

Several aluminum-webbed, folding lawn chairs and a wooden bench sat on the front porch. It looked as if he may have had company over with all the available seating. Willow hesitantly inched to the porch, second-guessing her decision with each step, and sat in one of the aluminum chairs still unconvinced she should be there. The chair was ragged, and the edges of the material were frayed at the ends. The middle dipped when she let herself sink into the seat. She placed her elbows on the cool metal arms and tapped the fingers of her hands in a nervous beat as if to soothe herself.

"Would you like something to drink?" he asked.

"No thank you," she replied. "So, this is where you've been living?" she asked, trying to think of something to say.

"Yes. For the past 10 years."

"Where were you before then?" She asked as if she didn't know.

"Willow, you know right. You know I was in jail." He talked to her like she was still that young nine-year-old child with learning problems. That innocent, naïve being who didn't know that people could be bad.

"I know, Floyd."

"You don't call me daddy anymore. Heck, I know you're grown now. Look at you. Just look at you." He stared at her as if she was a figment of his imagination making the moment more surreal than it already felt. "You are a woman now. All grown up."

"Floyd, you were never really a dad to me. I'm grown up and successful because of my mother, Barbara."

Uncomfortable silence came next. Floyd, who was at a loss for words, stared out beyond the porch saying nothing. Willow knew this to be her father — those painful nonexistent exchanges of colloquy that ensued many evenings when Barbara was missing. Her father was never one for conversation. Waiting for him to respond, she could see in his eyes he was searching in his head, but he couldn't seem to find any words, so she spoke again.

"It was hard for a while. We had no money and Mamma had to take handouts. She always had to keep a watchful eye to protect us. She didn't know if you'd come after her like you threatened that night. Remember Floyd!" Willow spurned. Her voice grew deeper and her tone became harsh.

"I do remember. I'm sorry, Willow. I'm sorry. Your mother, she was a beautiful woman when I knew her. She deserves better than me."

"That's no excuse dad, Floyd." Willow corrected herself. He didn't deserve the title of Dad.

Silence. Floyd looked away again as if this was too hard to face, his countenance barren.

"My saving's grace that summer was meeting Bonnie and my outings to Bartholomew's farm. I met Miss Kora who told me stories about you. She warned me to stay clear of you but here I am. I came here for answers, Floyd."

"I know you did Wilhelmina."

"I don't go by that name anymore. Just call me Willow. Willow Jones, not Hitchens."

"Ok, Willow," he paused. "I'll try my best. What do you want to know?"

"Why? Why did you do that to my mother? What did you say to her that night?"

"Willow, she found out I did something wrong and she threatened to take it to the police."

"I know what you did. I found it in a newspaper clipping. Actually, Bonnie, my friend, did and read it aloud to me, not knowing what she was reading. You see, I couldn't read very well as a child, but you didn't know that either."

"I knew that Willow. I just couldn't help you. I can't read very well either so how could I have helped you? Your Mamma did a fine job of that."

Willow never knew her Dad couldn't read. "You couldn't? So, you know how frustrating it is or was?"

"Yes, I do. It stopped me from doing a lot of things. And my dad never let me forget it either. I still don't read well but I see you have overcome that disability."

"I did. It took time but I did, and I found ways to compensate for it." She knew the statistics from her studies; incarcerated males have a high percentage of the inability to read. "What mamma did was the right thing, and you shouldn't have laid a hand on her. You deserved to go to jail." Willow stopped herself. Although she was right, she didn't want her dad to become angry when she was alone out here in the middle of the forest.

"I did." He replied. "Can you excuse me for a moment?" Floyd went inside and came back out holding a glass and a pill that he flung in his mouth and swallowed after a gulp of water. "Are you sure you don't want some water? It's fresh and clean out here from the well."

"Sure, I'll try it."

Floyd went back inside and brought Willow a glass filled with ice cubes and water. Not realizing how thirsty she was, she chugged half the glass. The ice clinked when she took the glass away from her mouth and set it down on a plastic table beside her. "Refreshing. It's been a while since I had well water."

"Willow, I know what I did was wrong. I was an angry, angry man. I still have anger, but I've learned to cope. That's why I live out here. I'm better off alone. This is no excuse, but I know where it came from. I saw my father push my mother around almost every day of my life as a child. He beat her and he beat me." Floyd abruptly ceased his explanation and sat still while he gripped the arms of the chair as if he had to keep himself from falling. He took a deep breath before he spoke again showing how painful it was to speak of his father. His voice crackled. "My father was always full of hate. He took it out on people he didn't like; well hell, he took it out on my mother and me. But my mom, she isn't or wasn't like Barbara. I knew there was something special about your mom. I had to make her leave that night."

"What do you mean? You threatened her she was scared and left."

"Yes, but I wanted to end it after I..."

"After you what?"

"At some point, I realized what my life was and all it would be. I realized I was carrying on like my father and if your mother stayed, I would continue to be abusive like my father. My mother never had the guts to stand up to Robert, but your mother stood up to me that night and I got angry and hit her. And then it dawned on me. If she stayed, I'd only abuse her as my father abused my mother and me. So, I told her to get out, but I couldn't let you go. You were the only being in this world that didn't see my ugly faults. I just couldn't let you go at the time. Your mother wanted to come back in, but I knew I would hurt her again and again. She banged on the door for me to let her back in, but I wouldn't. She sat on the stoop and cried and when she wasn't aware, I opened the door and threw an envelope of money on the porch and told her I'd never hurt you and I made her leave."

"Dad, you threw her out like some old used-up dish rag that needed to be discarded, like garbage."

"I did Willow. I'm sorry."

They both sat in silence for a while listening to the sounds of nature. Birds whistled in trees nearby, which contrasted the somberness on the porch. An occasional pinecone dropped from a tree making a soft thud on the cushioned forest floor and unseen animals scampered in the brush. Willow, now pensive, was coming to realize why her father lived in this lonely cabin with no one around him. He needed his life quiet to survive the demons that haunted him. The seclusion is what made him able to cope. The once morose man was now ashamed and sad, something he must have felt all his life, being with a father who treated him with insolent disregard and a mother who let it happen. Willow realized, her father was abused too, except unlike his mother, her mother stopped the cycle. Right then, she appreciated her mother's strength more than ever. This strength brought them out of a suppressed life she would have lived if her mother didn't influence the change of circumstances. Floyd continued expressing sorrow. It seemed that maybe this was part of a redemption process he was seeking for his life, something he wanted to do to right his wrongs.

"Dad, I need to go now. I can come back tomorrow if you wish."

"I would very much like that. Thank you for coming."

She took one more look at the shell of a man sitting on the porch relieved that the initial meeting was over. The door squeaked again when she opened it to get back in the driver's seat. Backing out cautiously, Willow turned her head observing her surroundings carefully to avoid hitting trees or large roots. When she turned back for one more glance at Floyd, she realized her father's eyes had stayed on her as she pulled away. He lifted his hand and gave a wave; she returned the gesture. Ambivalence gnawed at her as she left the cabin. Willow had hoped this trip would close that part of her life forever. She wanted to wash her hands of this dim part of her past. She wanted to hate him, but she couldn't.

On the way back to the hotel, Willow passed by the farmhouse, it was busy with tractors and movement around the barn. She stretched her neck and traversed the fields with her eyes but noticed no one. The Murphys must have sold it, she speculated. That evening after a lonely dinner, she recoiled in her hotel bed to watch television. The light on the hotel phone was lit indicating she had a message. She spoke to a woman at the front desk who told her Barbara Jones called. It was her mother as she suspected, but she didn't have the gumption to talk with her yet. Willow had hoped she would have closure and could move on with her life, but she only had more questions. A movie of the day's events played in her head, the reel repeating over and over.

6

Chapter 6

Gunshot

I gripped the spindles of the staircase with both of my hands and peered over the edge of the steps. Mamma and Daddy didn't know I was awake. Daddy was pacing in the kitchen. I could see his body pass through the doorway, clutching his gun. He was arguing with Mamma.

Mamma pleaded with him, "Put your gun away, Floyd. They are not coming back here. You don't need your gun. Gina's husband is not coming back here."

"Barbara, did you hear what he said. Ray doesn't think you should be here with me."

"No Floyd, he just said you didn't need to speak to me like that and they thought it was best to leave. Ray thought maybe you were tired."

"No Barbara, he has it out for me. All I did was tell you to hurry up in the kitchen. He left to get his gun. I know he's coming back."

"Floyd, no he's not."

"Why were you talking with him and Gina outside? I was standing at the door, Barbara. I saw it."

"Floyd you called me a whore. I was making an excuse for you because I

was embarrassed. I was telling them you had a little too much to drink and you were tired."

"Well Barbara, I'll drink what I want. Ain't you or Ray or Gina gonna tell me what I can drink."

"Put the gun down Floyd. Give me that gun!"

Then I heard mamma scream a high-pitched cry. She was trying to talk, but her words were muffled and hollow as if Daddy was covering her mouth with his hand. Low pitched moans and pleas escaped her mouth in staggered cries that grew louder with each attempt to articulate a clear plea, but the words came out distorted. Then suddenly, the gun sounded a quick but powerful bang that ricocheted off the walls leaving an echo ringing through the house. I ran down the stairs to see Daddy standing over Mamma. Her lifeless body was strewn across the floor and her head cocked toward the kitchen cabinets. She was still while blood seeped from a black mark in the center of a patch of slicked, matted, fluid-drenched hair. The patch stuck to her scalp while the rest of her hair was frazzled from the struggle.

"Mamma," I yelled. "Mamma. Mamma." My screams grew louder and louder, and my mouth, agape, as tears fell in streams, streaking my cheeks. When I focused on Daddy, he was still clinging to the rifle, resting the end on his hip. I tried to run to Mamma, but Daddy stopped me when he put his arm out and swept me up keeping a tight hold around the middle of my tense body. I kicked and kicked with all the fight I had in me.

"Let me go. Let me go." I screamed to no avail. Daddy dragged me up the stairs as I reached for Mamma. My outstretched hands waited for her slender fingers to reach mine, but they remained untouched. My cries were unanswered. Mamma was dead.

#

Willow sat up swiftly, overwrought with fear. Her whole body was sweating. She kicked the covers, trying to cool off but the fright wouldn't pass, and heat clenched her body as if it held her. Willow's chest pounded to a rhythm as the blood coursed through her temples with the same beat. She gulped for air in-between heaves. She glanced at the phone and it reminded her that she never returned her mother's call. The clock said 3:20 AM.

7

Chapter 7

Into the Past

The hotel was fully awake with guests by eight in the morning. Willow could hear doors opening and closing, which was occasionally followed by children running in the hallways clamoring with laughter and exchanging conversation. Her head felt groggy as she tried to come to reality, recollecting the memory of her dream in pieces as if it was being played back to her. The nightmare haunted her thoughts, so she immediately decided that a phone call to her mother was past due. Barbara should be at work by now for Tuesday was her early day. Willow picked up the receiver and pushed 9 before dialing the number for the woman's shelter of Pequot. A different woman, who went by the name of Brandy, answered with a hello that sounded as if she worked at a busy pizza parlor. Her voice was nasally and extremely loud. She asked who was calling and added the word dear to the end of just about every line she said. Willow waited on the other end while she heard this woman shuffling papers as she talked.

"Willow, dear," she sounded as if her mouth was flush against the phone, "Here she is dear."

"Hello," Barbara said softly.

Finally, it was a relief to hear her voice.

"Hi, mother, it's me Willow."

"Yes, I know, sweetie. How's it going? I called you yesterday. Did you get the message?"

"Yes, mother. The front desk told me you called but I was just too tired to call back. I saw Floyd." Willow slipped in that last sentence, nervous to talk about her encounter with her mother.

Silence.

"He lives in a cabin. Alone."

More silence.

"Mom, are you there?" Willow asked.

"Yes, I'm here. I'm a little shaken up about you going to see him. How did he act? Was he hostile?"

She wouldn't tell her mom about the dream.

"No, he was very calm, actually subdued is more like it. Much different than what I remembered."

"Are you going back to see him? I'd rather not have you..."

"Mom, I'm 29, remember. I'm sorry mother, I know you're worried. I'll leave if I feel any sense of danger. When I was a child living with him while you were gone, I never felt like I was in physical danger. He was just rather distant and gloomy, and he embarrassed me when he got angry in public, but he never laid a hand on me. I know it was different for you mom and I'm sorry. You never deserved to go through what he put you through. I just have to put closure to this part of my life."

Willow paused for a moment waiting for a response on the other end, but Barbara remained silent, an uncomfortable silence that made her feel as if going to see Floyd was some sort of betrayal. She didn't want to hurt her mother yet felt compelled to find answers.

"We had a good conversation yesterday. I'll call you as soon as I get back today. Trust me, mom." Willow thought about her dream and felt a pang of worry like she heard in her mother's voice.

"I trust you, honey. It's Floyd I don't trust. But I know he's your father and I understand the need to find answers. Please be careful Willow. I wish you had a mobile phone."

"It wouldn't work where he lives anyway." Wrong information to tell her mother. If she knew how isolated his place was, she'd be even more disconcerted.

"Has the valley changed or is it still the same small town?" Barbara asked, changing the subject.

"No, it's bigger. There are places to shop for clothing and a few more restaurants. Lucille's is now called Friendly's and there is a Chinese take-out place here. It's big-time," Willow mocked.

"Wow, it sounds quite different like it finally moved on to the next decade," Barbara chortled. "Well, you can tell me all about it when you get back. It was nice to hear from you."

"Yes, mother. I'm sorry I didn't call you back last night but I'm glad we talked. I know you're busy at work and at home with the renovation. How's that going?" Hearing her mother's voice waned the anxiety she had been holding since she woke.

"I'll tell you about it tonight."

Willow could hear a woman's nasal voice. Brandy must be the new receptionist at the shelter her mother had mentioned.

"Brandy is asking me questions. I've got to go now. Don't forget to call and be careful. I love you."

"I love you, Mamma." Willow felt the brevity of those words as she spoke them. It carried her back to childhood when her mother was the loving constant in her life always making sure Willow had everything she needed and comforting her through every move and difficulty she experienced in school. Barbara worked two jobs much of the time, yet her weariness never held her back from being an attentive mother.

Willow showered and toweled herself dry, yet she still felt sticky. Another hot day. She draped a T-shirt over her head and pulled on a pair of overall shorts after making herself presentable with spiral-styled curls and a touch of rouge. She strolled over to Friendly's for a hot breakfast. After she paid her bill, it was time to drive to the cabin. Her father said eleven o'clock and remembering the length of time it took to drive the trip yesterday, she would make it to the cabin right about eleven. Her timing was impeccable she thought priding herself.

Willow passed Old Rock Road and slowed down when the farmhouse came into a clear view. She didn't notice any movement in the field but was able to steal a quick glance of the front porch before she passed the house and was quite sure she saw a woman who resembled Mrs. Murphy swaying on the porch swing. The scene passed too quickly to be sure, but it roused her curiosity enough to make a stop on the way back if she had the courage that is.

Willow pulled in the front of the cabin. Sticks crunched beneath her wheels as she maneuvered her vehicle to the same place where she parked yesterday. Floyd heard her arrive and came out from the cabin. Willow fixed her gaze upon his face as she walked toward the porch where he was standing, watching her as well. His mouth bowed in a partial smile and his eyes were more alert than she remembered from yesterday when they had their first physical connection since she was nine.

"Hello, Willow," he initiated.

"Hi Floyd," Willow replied. He didn't seem hindered today that she hadn't addressed him with dad.

"Would you like a drink of water? I'm sorry, that's all I have to offer you to drink. I have some deer jerky. There's a man in town who makes the best deer jerky you'll ever taste."

"Are you still fishing?"

"Every day. I gotta eat somehow."

"That's how you eat?" Willow asked. It just dawned on her that her father hadn't mentioned having a job. He didn't have a car to get himself anywhere. She remembered Miss Kora. Willow always wondered how she survived and now her dad is living the same way Miss Kora lived. Willow wondered if her dad knew anything about Miss Kora. She wondered if Joseph was still around. She had more questions than she realized.

"Dad, do you have a job?" Willow inquired.

"A job? It's hard for felons to get jobs. I work from time to time, but I can't get anything steady. Most jobs I land are for people who need extra workers temporarily and pay me under the table. That's why I live off fishing as much as I can. I've learned to make things from scratch, like bread. Miss Kora sends me herbs."

"Miss Kora? Miss Kora is still around?" Willow asked, her curiosity piqued.

"Yep, she's getting old, but she still grows her garden of herbs."

"It looks like her place is overgrown with bushes and no one lives there. Her mailbox is gone."

"Look a little closer," Floyd said.

"I'm shocked. How does she get to you, she never had a car and you don't have a car?"

"Joseph," he replied.

So, Joseph was still around, Willow thought, and he was continuing to spread his charity to the dejected folks of the community and Floyd was officially one of them. Joseph's sagacity helped Willow's father, a man whose judgment was always impaired, change into a man who can now live with some sort of semblance. While his life was nowhere near what one would consider fulfilling, he was no longer a threat. He survived.

"Do you see Joseph often?"

"Once a week, he comes out to visit and usually brings Miss Kora with him. That's when she delivers her herbs. She is quite the healer. Willow, she told me about you coming to her house." Floyd's eyes became watery with despondency. "I always forbid you to leave the house because I never wanted anyone to know about my hostility but I'm glad you did. The Murphys, Miss Kora, and Joseph kept you safe that summer. My actions were unforgivable, I know that, but I'm hoping one day you and your mother can find it in your heart to forgive me."

"That explains the chairs on your porch," Willow remarked.

"If the weather is nice, we sit on the porch. Joseph starts with a prayer and reads scripture. It's peaceful."

Willow was astounded at what she was hearing. After her dream, she was partially afraid it was a sign that she would come to the cabin and find her dad dead by his own gunshot. Until now, she couldn't shake off the feeling that the dream was indicative of some other meaning. But she had found quite the opposite. Her dad never talked this much in all her life and while he seemed sad, he also had a glint of hope in his voice.

"Dad, do the Murphys still live in the farmhouse?"

"I believe Jenny lives there with her husband and Mrs. Murphy. Mr. Murphy passed away. Jenny has children but I'm not sure how many."

"What about Bonnie? Do you know anything about Bonnie?" Willow asked with eager interest. Her desire to know about her friend kindled delightful childhood memories, some of the best childhood memories she had.

"I don't know, Willow. I don't know that much about the Murphys." Floyd changed the subject. "Would you like to come in and see my cabin? I've been doing some woodworking and I just finished making a cabinet."

Willow was curious and felt more comfortable today, so she accepted the invitation inside. It was a simple cabin with three rooms. The large room held a living room area with a couch, fireplace, and a kitchen. There were two rooms at the back end, a bedroom and a bathroom. Her eyes swam over the place and stopped at the kitchen area where she saw the cabinet.

"Come over here and see what I was telling you about."

Willow schlepped behind her dad to a meager six by six-foot kitchen with a sink, a two-burner stove, an oven range, and two cabinets. On the wall perpendicular to the kitchen cabinetry, was a wonderfully crafted cherry wood hutch ornately carved around the trim. It held an array of dishes. Willow was both surprised and impressed with her dad's talent.

"When did you start building with wood?" she asked.

"I took a class in jail and I built a desk for the warden's office."

"That's a beautiful piece," Willow complimented her father.

"Thank you, Willow."

Floyd offered Willow water and then directed her to the porch where they continued their conversation. His communication was now more than a skein of words mumbled in surly tones like she remembered as a child. He described the grim experiences in jail as well as the opportunities he encountered to improve skills and heal from trauma. He learned ways of coping. His father, Robert Hutchins, had only contacted him once and when Floyd was released, he learned Robert had died. Floyd never did get a chance to confront him nor say his goodbyes but with his dad gone, he now seemed unfettered by the grip his father once had on him.

Several hours passed before Willow ended the visit with her father when they both seemed as if there was nothing more to reveal and now, exhausted from sifting through the emotional duress of the past, she wanted to escape, even if temporary. She wasn't staying another day, so she said her goodbyes to Floyd, not making any promises. She strode to her sedan and her door squeaked again when she opened it, cutting a slice through the strain of leaving her father, a lonely abashed man. Willow's job was to help people pull themselves from the grips of whatever their despair may be, but for her father, she couldn't. She was still grieving for the father she lost so long ago. Floyd quickly ran into the cabin and brought out a bottle of lubricant to spray the hinges and now, the door didn't squeak when she closed it. Willow backed out and before she pulled forward on route 1008, she looked back at him on the front porch. With a longing in his eyes, he watched her leave with sorrowful intensity as if he wanted to call her back, but the words couldn't be said. He raised his hand and gave her one last wave, and Willow waved back as a tear dropped on her lap, feeling sad to leave her father alone on the porch. He didn't ask for another visit and Willow couldn't say she would have agreed yet the closure she expected was still unfelt but one thing she was able to do was put away the shame she held from this time of her life spent on Old Rock Road. The house no longer existed. Floyd had told her it was torn down, and her family, the people who once lived there, were now transformed into different versions of themselves, better versions.

#

The next part of the journey into the past edged closer as she trod along the road, winding about treacherous mountainsides, and crags. She made the left onto Marshland Road seeing the places that played a significant role during the summer of her ninth year. Miss Kora's cottage and the farmhouse, a tiny speck in an immense world but to Willow, it was once her whole world. Her trip would be complete if she knocked on the Murphys' door and found Bonnie. She was compelled to try. The possibility of her wish coming true was within her grasp, and she couldn't let it slip away.

Both trucks were parked in the driveway of the farmhouse. The immense field of corn was quiet and unoccupied with the sun blazing its fire directly above. She parked in a small space; the last space left on the smoothly paved driveway. She stretched her neck to search for the mailbox that Floyd said was still there but all she saw were a compilation of branches and greeneries intertwined as if they were linking arms together. Tufts of weeds spurted from the ground. Willow peered at the door of the farmhouse and thought about the first time she felt brave enough to knock. She searched for the same courage as she tried to quell the nervous thoughts that swirled in her head and flipped her insides. The steps leading up to the front porch were updated, and the porch was freshly painted a slightly darker color. The door, more modern, was a deep red with a gilded metal knocker attached to the middle just below a panel of windows. She rang the bell and waited patiently for an answer all the while becoming more nervous with each second, thinking maybe she had delved enough into the past. One more unanswered ring and that would be a sign that things were well enough to be left alone, an adage she sometimes shared with her clients. Light steps could be heard approaching the door and the person on the other side fumbled, opening a lock and turning the doorknob as she saw a crown of a head in the window. Finally, the door opened and there stood a small-statured woman, with a wrinkled brow, drooping mouth, and gray, thin hair that was carefully sculpted into a short bob. A pair of glasses sat at the tip of her nose. Her shoulders slumped forward over her thin five foot five frame wearing a white shirt with blue flowers that circled around the collar and a pair of navy Bermuda's.

"Can I help you?" she asked in a shaky voice.

"I hope so," she replied sheepishly. "Uh, are you Mrs. Murphy?" she bleated out stammering her question.

"Willow Hitchens, is that you?" The older lady's voice elevated in delight and a reverie washed over her face.

"Yes, it is," Willow remarked in relief.

"Well, what on earth. Come in. Come in." She repeated. "Is that really you? My, oh my, how you have grown up."

"It's great to see you, Mrs. Murphy, after all these years."

"And you also. I'm so glad things turned out well for you. I prayed for you all the time when you first left us. Joseph updated me from time to time and I was relieved to know that you and your mother were faring well and now look at you. You're an adult. Why don't you come back here in the kitchen and I'll get you some tea?"

"That would be lovely."

Willow followed Mrs. Murphy into the kitchen. The Formica table with the cushiony chairs was replaced with a rustic farmhouse set. The cabinets were updated, and a small island stood in the middle. She directed Willow to sit down as she got her a large glass of tea with a freshly cut lemon slice.

"Do you like sugar in your tea?" Mrs. Murphy asked and offered her a pink ceramic bowl filled with the white granules. The bowl was uniquely molded and didn't appear to be store-bought.

"Sure, I like a little bit of sugar in my tea. Not too much though. This is a beautiful bowl, was it made by someone?"

"Bonnie made that in high school. She took a lot of art classes, ceramics being one of them."

"How nice. Where are Bonnie and Jenny living now?"

"Bonnie lives in the mountains where we used to camp when the kids were young. She studied to be an archeologist in college. She works as a museum curator and makes pottery as a side business. Jenny lives right here with her husband, Cliff, and the children, Michael, and Marcy. She and Cliff run the farm. Jenny went to college to be a biochemist but when Mr. Murphy passed on, she moved back home and took over the farm."

"Oh, I'm very sorry about Mr. Murphy, When did he pass away?"

"Five years ago. He had a major heart attack, the kind that comes on suddenly and takes a life without warning. They call it the widowmaker, and that's exactly what it did. It made me a widow."

"I'm very sorry." Willow offered her condolences again.

"It was a daunting situation at first. I was afraid I'd have to give up this farm. Mr. Murphy and I, well we relished in making our lives here. I'm doing better now. It helped to have Jenny come home and the kids."

"How old are the kids?"

"They are both nine. Twins."

Nine, that's how old I was when I lived with the Murphys.

"They like to be out at the barn with their mom when she is working. They play with the animals. Cliff also works at the state park as a park ranger, so Jenny does much of overseeing the farm. With a farm this size, the work is unending, but, Jenny is assiduous at everything she takes on. She has the production of this farm down to a science."

"The farm has grown, and you have animals on the farm now," Willow noted.

"Yes, Jenny bought some pigs and sheep and the barn is full of kittens, now since the mamma cat had her babies."

"That brings back memories of Oliver. I suppose it would be a miracle if he was still around."

"Yes, it would be. Oliver unfortunately is no longer with us. I think he died of licking peanut butter," Mrs. Murphy joked.

"Mrs. Murphy that was never my idea," Willow alluded, "but I went along with Bonnie. Her unusual ideas captivated me."

"I know, Willow. That Bonnie she still carries on with the affluence of life, not money, but she is rich with experience."

"Is Bonnie married?" Willow asked.

"No, that girl has been all around the world on archeology digs, she hasn't had time to marry but I hope one day. Are you married, Willow?"

"Well my name is changed to Jones but not because I'm married.

My mom changed our names after we left here. You know so my dad wouldn't find us."

"Your dad lives not too far from here. I hear he's doing better, but I don't bother with him. What brings you to town?" Mrs. Murphy paused and took a breath as she realized. "You came to see your father, didn't you?" She looked concerned.

"Yes, I did. Sometimes a person has to face the past to put the bad things behind them."

"You're right, Willow. You know, you sound like a psychologist."

"I am."

"You are!" Mrs. Murphy's face lit up with admiration.

"Yes. I felt inspired after the struggles my mother and I faced. I wanted to help people overcome life's obstacles like we got help along the way. And my mother works in a woman's shelter. We live in Pequot."

"How 'bout that Willow the psychologist. I remembered when you struggled to read. You were so shy when you lived here with the weight of the world on your shoulders. You have come a long way. I have got to get your number for Bonnie. She would be thrilled to hear from you."

"That's one reason I came here. I would love to reconnect with her. She saved my sanity that summer. I was distraught and she was my light. Well, you all were my light, actually, but Bonnie and her adventurous spirit made me forget all my troubles when we were together."

Mrs. Murphy pulled open a small drawer on the end of the counter and grabbed a miniature spiral-bound pad of paper. She jotted down Bonnie's number and handed her the pad to write her number. She filled Willow's glass with more tea and fetched her fresh lemon wedge from the refrigerator. She continued to give more details about her daughter's lives and her grandchildren as Willow listened to Mrs. Murphy extoll the accomplishments her daughters made over the years. Jenny won several awards at her first job as a biochemist and then quit to take on the farm. She also has written articles for farm magazines. Bonnie traveled to places all over the United States where she, along with a crew, uncovered artifacts from the past, before working for museums.

"Why don't you wait a minute while I see if I can find Jenny?"

"Could I walk outside with you? I would love to look at the field again."

"It's not the sunflowers like when you were here. This year, Jenny planted corn. She used one of the other fields for sunflowers. You might be able to see them in the distance or if you drive down Old Rock Road, you can see the sunflower field."

"I'm not sure I want to do that. I'm not ready for Old Rock Road."

"Willow, I'm sorry."

"It's all right. Like I said, I have to face my past but seeing Floyd was enough for this trip."

A few minutes later a woman with long, dark-brown, hair came out of the barn. She had wispy bangs and the same build Willow remembered but taller. She moved vigorously, hauling materials as if she was intent on accomplishing a mission. She called on her children. Bonnie saw Michael and Marcy bounding out the barn door the instant their mother hollered for help. They both were about the same height and looked similar but not identical. Michael had short loose curls that covered his head. His hair was thick and dark. Marcy's hair was longer with spiral curls and the same ash brown as her brothers.

"Jenny. Jenny," Mrs. Murphy yelled. "Come to the porch for a minute. There is someone here to see you. Bring the kids."

When Jenny arrived at the porch, she widened her eyes in surprise. "Willow! I haven't seen you in years. In fact, I never thought I'd see you again. You look wonderful!"

A hug ensued and Jenny introduced Willow to her children, who were cordial and looked as astute as Jenny was and had the same sparkling blue eyes as their mother. They said hello, curling the ends of their mouths into polite little smiles and moments later excused themselves to attend to the sheep. Willow, Jenny, and Mrs. Murphy talked for another half an hour on the back porch catching up on the past twenty years.

"Jenny," willow addressed her. "Remember the night you showed us Leo the Lion. Ever since that night, I search for constellations quite often. I can't find them quite as well as you did but I find it to be a perfect way to unwind in the evenings. In fact, I have a telescope on the balcony of my condo."

"Ahhh, you remember that night, Willow. I remember it like it was yesterday, and I still search for Leo the Lion among other constellations when I'm not too tired from farming."

Willow told Jenny and Mrs. Murphy where she lived. They filled one another in on the past twenty years in a very condensed way while sipping tea on the back porch. After some time, Willow yawned, tired from a day filled with reunions, and Jenny seemed to get distracted by thoughts of farm tasks that waited.

"You must be tired Willow. All this catching up," Mrs. Murphy said.

"I am, Mrs. Murphy. I really ought to be going, but before I do, I want to thank you both for taking me in that summer. And thank you Jenny for helping me with my reading. I don't know if I ever would have found the motivation to overcome my difficulties if it wasn't for you."

"Your welcome. You have done quite well, Willow. I always knew you had it in you!" Jenny told her.

"It was great to see you, Willow." Mrs. Murphy said.

Jenny reached out embracing Willow before she went back to the barn. Then Mrs. Murphy walked Willow to the front door keeping her arm around her the whole way. The goodbye was more drawn out than Jenny's goodbye which brought back that arduous feeling she felt on the first encounter with Mrs. Murphy. She possessed that motherly love, the same as her mother. When Willow left the farmhouse, tears tickled her eyes again but as she pulled away, she thought of one more person she just couldn't leave the valley without at least trying to find her. She turned her car around and drove to where the entrance to Miss Kora's was located and parked on the side of Marshland Road. When she edged closer to the thick brush, she saw a metal lip sticking out. It was the mailbox. The handle was the only visible piece from her stance. It was held up by the branches signifying the entrance to Miss Kora's enchanted dwelling. Willow let out a loud gaggle. Some people have a gate, Miss Kora has a rusty old mailbox. After twenty years, that old thing remained, proudly holding on to its existence.

Willow walked past the thicket and found the driveway to the cottage which had become so dense it was more like a path. She saw it in a distance, the same cottage she ventured to twenty years ago. Its structure was the same, but it was worn. Willow knocked on the door, at first with a light tap but when the call went unheeded, she knocked a little louder, and finally, the third time she was forceful. Suddenly, the door opened. There stood Miss Kora. Her hair still long and gray but thinner. She was hunched over and held a cane in her hand. The handle of the cane had been carved into a tiger.

"Come in, Willow," she said as if she was expecting her and as if 20 years hadn't passed.

Willow hugged her. She felt a brittle body but the spunk and energy of a woman much younger. The cottage was still filled with rocks and minerals which lined along the walls on glass shelves. It even seemed as if her collection got bigger. The black dress that once aroused her and Bonnie's curiosity was still hanging on the same hook by the fireplace and every piece of furniture was the same. Willow felt as if she had been sucked back into 1976.

"Do you still have the moon garden?"

"Willow, how you loved that moon garden. We had some wonderful exchanges of knowledge there. Well, darling, the bench still exists, but I'm afraid my body won't let me keep up my gardens like it used to. It takes everything I have to keep my herbs growing. But come out back. We can still sit on the bench."

Willow saw that where there was once a magnificent garden of flowers was grown over into a thicket of plants blended as one; most were weeds but traces of the white flowers stuck out from the bush. The moon ball was dull and tarnished. It no longer reflected the sky like it once did. The bench was grey and weathered. It slouched as much as Miss Kora's shoulders.

"Come, let's go sit and have a talk," Miss Kora implored.

They sat on the bench and Willow not sure if it would hold her, eventually, felt herself relax. She had so much to tell Miss Kora, but now, her mind was quiet pausing to take in the forest around her. She heard the same sounds of bird chirrups. A hawk flew overhead.

"Ahhh, there he is," Miss Kora announced, and she commenced conversation as if she had to wait for the arrival of the hawk before she could begin. She still had her quirky ways. "You have made quite a life for yourself, you and your mother both."

"I'm a psychologist, and my mother runs a woman's shelter. We live on the coast in Pequot, east of Sol Valley."

"I know Pequot. It's a lovely place. My parents took me there as a child. Haven't been in years."

Willow told Miss Kora more about her life, but it was as if she already knew. It didn't feel like catching up like it did with the others. Miss Kora's life was the same. She tended her gardens and watched nature. She told stories of bringing healing medicines to Floyd. She said he was no longer a person to fear but that the spirits of nature had changed him.

"But he must always live alone." She told me. "You, darling, you must keep yourself out in the world. You have a different way of healing and people need you." Strange Willow thought, how Miss Kora felt an innate understanding of people. They talked for an hour, Willow revealing the events of her life and Miss Kora, listening with the adoring ears and eyes as if she were her guardian angel and had known the path of her life. Now exhausted, Willow decided it was time to head back to the hotel. She promised to keep in touch and Miss Kora replied with, "We will always be in touch." She was older and worn but still the same woman with an intuitive sense that seemed surreal. Willow hugged her goodbye and walked down the path to the road where her sedan was waiting for her. She opened the door and noticed again; the squeak was gone. She drove away leaving the radio off. In the silence, she was able to gather her thoughts. Although she never thought of it, Miss Kora called her a healer. Willow supposed she was, but as she vividly remembered, Miss Kora was a different type of healer. Willow suddenly got a craving for pot roast. She pulled off the highway and searched for a diner.

8

Chapter 8

Mamma's Roast

When Daddy walked in from work, he took me with him to Powel's Market for necessities, as he called them. They were the things like milk and bread and cans, food you just heat up, but nothing special like the cookies Mamma would buy, just the basics. He asked Willow to name the ingredients for her mother's biscuits, which implied that she was to make them for dinner. She rattled off the six ingredients: flour, sugar, baking powder, salt, butter, and milk. He dragged Willow around the store searching until every item for the recipe was in the cart. Along the way, he picked up a roast, some carrots, and potatoes and told Willow she was to make roast and biscuits for dinner in which she quickly complied with a nod.

When Daddy says he wants something done, you better go on and do it.

Joseph the preacher was standing in line when they arrived at the checkout. His cart was right in front of theirs and Floyd began to fumble through his wallet with his eyes fixed downward. Joseph turned and offered a kind greeting, first making eye contact with Floyd and then Willow. Floyd nodded and immediately drew his eyes to the cart and began rearranging the products. Then he pulled Willow by the hand and proceeded to another checkout line, one that he said would be quicker, but Willow knew it was to get away from Joseph. Willow's heart sank. She wanted to tell Joseph about Mamma but that was to be hushed. Willow remembered how happy Mamma was at church, and she shared the same feeling, but Floyd, week after week, rushed from the service as soon as it was done with the two of them following behind him, trotting to keep up with his pace. They never had a chance to talk much to Joseph nor the kind people that attended the service. Willow had wished it was different, she wanted to stay and enjoy the Sunday potlucks.

When they got home from the market, Floyd demanded Willow to put the food away and quickly vacated the house to fiddle with his truck. Willow did as she was told. When she unpacked the last brown bag, it was lined with four boxes of Barnum's Animal Crackers at the bottom, just like the cookies her Mamma would let her eat while they shopped for groceries. Funny, she didn't remember Daddy putting those in the cart, and she wouldn't dare have asked for them; she hid the crackers deep in the pantry for later.

#

Willow found the cookbook placed on the counter when she awoke the next morning. Daddy was already at work and the clock read somewhere around nine. One of these days, Willow would have to learn to tell time. She wasn't sure if she would be able to read the recipes but could picture Mamma in the kitchen putting the roast in a pan with cut-up vegetables. She reluctantly sifted through the sections of Better Homes and Gardens, relying on the photographs to locate the pages she needed, and finally, managed to find the biscuit recipe. Mamma's handwriting was scribbled in the column. *Bake ten minutes*, was written close to the typed time. Willow would have to forgo playing at Bonnie's today if she didn't want to make her father angry. It would take her all day to figure out how to make dinner. Willow spent the morning trying to read the recipes and formulated a plan.

Later in the morning, Willow began her task, which seemed arduous as she glanced through the cookbook, but as she remembered what Mrs. Twine would tell her at the beginning of a math problem, one step at a time. She managed to bake the biscuits, mostly relying on her memory, and using what she could decode, to read the recipe. After they came out of the oven and cooled, Willow tasted a sample.

Delicious!

She was rather proud of herself.

Next, Willow flipped to the meat section, where she carefully scanned until she located a recipe displaying a photograph of beef beside it which resembled the roast Daddy purchased. The words for this one seemed harder to read or maybe she was too tired to try. Willow thought hard about the steps Mamma took when she made this meal. She would cut up carrots and onions after lunch and they sat on the counter until it was time for them to be added to the meat and then off to the oven. It cooked for several hours and the house would fill up with the decadent smell of tender roast. After it was pulled back out, she let it settle in a covered pan while she made gravy. Willow had no idea how to make gravy. She knew Mamma mixed the juices with something but couldn't exactly remember.

The gravy, maybe, isn't going to work.

In the early afternoon, right about the time Mrs. Twine would read aloud to the class, Willow pulled the carrots and onions out of the refrigerator. She found a sharp knife in the drawer and went to work slicing the vegetables. The onions were easy to chop through, although they made her eyes tear, but the carrots took more effort to cut. She laid one of the thicker carrots on the board, and pinching it steady with the fingers of her left hand, she began to saw at it as if she was cutting a log, but the knife stubbornly stuck in the center. She pushed harder on the handle and after some brute force, managed to cut off a chunk. Blood appeared beside the knife and then she felt the pain. Apparently, Willow cut more than the carrot. She had sliced into the side of her pointer finger as well. She ran to the sink and held the bloody finger under running water and the coolness of the liquid offered a moment of relief.

Blood mixed with the stream and swirled in the bottom of the sink before it drained into the pipe.

Willow recalled times when Mamma would fix her up after she got a scrape of some sort. She would press a towel on her skin until it stopped bleeding. The hydrogen peroxide she used to clean the cut would bubble up into white foam, as Mamma would blow light puffs of air at her skin to take away the discomfort. Willow located the peroxide and poured the liquid on the cut. The pain was imposing, and she let out a whimper. She wished Mamma's hand was holding hers. Willow used several large band-aids to cover the laceration and when the bleeding subsided, she finished preparing the dinner, in a more somber manner but with a doughty persistence. Mamma would be proud of her if she could do this and she managed to complete the job.

When daddy came home from work, a roast, no gravy, with vegetables and biscuits was ready to be eaten. They sat together at the table in silence as Daddy sliced through his beef and Willow struggled to cut hers. The meat was chewy and tough, but the biscuits turned out just like Mamma made them. Willow noticed Daddy ate several helpings and, for the first time, he seemed to appreciate Willow's hard work. He smiled and thanked her for making dinner. Daddy was pleasant this evening, she noticed. It wasn't until the end of the meal before he commented on Willow's finger.

"Willow, what's with the Band-Aids?"

"I accidentally cut my finger when I was slicing a carrot," Willow replied.

"Take the bandages off and let me have a look," Floyd directed.

Willow did as her dad asked. He gingerly took her finger and examined her swollen, warm skin. A dark red line, about a half-inch long, started at the tip of her finger. The skin split showing a deep cut, like a crevice.

"Do I need stitches, Dad?" she sheepishly asked.

"No, you'll be fine, Willow. I don't have money to take you to the hospital, and I sure don't need anyone nudging 'round in our business.

You just make sure you keep it clean and bandaged. You hear me, Willow?"

"Yes, Daddy," Willow obeyed.

But Willow knew better. She remembered when Elizabeth, a girl from her fourth-grade class, sliced her finger on a broken glass window. She missed a day of school because she was at the hospital getting stitches and when she returned, her finger was wrapped in white gauze. Daddy didn't want people to know and that is why he didn't take her to the hospital. Willow felt uncared for and needed to hide this unpleasant feeling.

This means I can't go see Bonnie because she'll ask what happened.

She retreated to her room after the dishes were cleaned and sunk into her bed, steeped in melancholy. Her finger, now a deep red, felt puffy as if it was stuffed with cotton. She rubbed lotion on it, hoping to soothe the pain. Then she wrapped more Band-Aids around the cut. Willow, now exhausted, slumped back into bed, and mewled herself to sleep.

9

Chapter 9

The Moon Garden

Willow stayed true to her conviction that no one must see her finger and remained in the house for a few days, but then she became restless. Thinking she could keep her finger hidden in her pocket, she went outside, the allure of adventure too enticing to keep her home. *Maybe I can just walk along the field without the Murphys seeing me*, Willow thought to herself as she left the house about mid-morning, the temperature already humid and hot. She crept along the edge of the field but was careful to stay hidden among the trees. She noticed the sunflowers were just about as tall as her and the buds had become fuller. The field, sodden from a thunderstorm the night before, was plush with verdure and the flowers were still ensconced with a green bedding of leaves. The heads of the plants were pointing east, toward the town.

Willow's finger throbbed. She learned if she held it horizontally, it hurt less so she walked along pointing her finger toward the sky. She came to the edge of the tree line, close to Marshland Road, and could see the shanty. Peeking around the structure, she noticed the station wagon wasn't in the driveway. Then, she listened for the sound of a tractor or people talking in the field. She waited for Oliver to strut across the yard watching for birds in the sassafras tree, but he didn't show himself either. All was quiet at the Murphys' house. Bonnie wasn't there and neither was her sister or parents.

When Willow came out of hiding, closer to the farmhouse, she noticed a new coat of white paint on the front of the house. White paw prints stepped down the cement walkway that led to the front door. They were Oliver's paws.

Down the road, she heard the scrape of a mailbox lid opening.

She saw the witch.

A thin woman with long gray hair reaching to the middle of her back was retrieving envelopes. Willow concealed her presence behind a Rhododendron but the spaces between the branches were too wide to hide effectively. The witch caught Willow's eyes.

Startled, Willow wanted to run but was too fascinated to move. As if a force held her, her eyes stayed fixed on the woman and the woman stared back. She didn't look scary like a witch might. On the contrary, she was attractive with neatly combed hair and a flowery, flowing dress adorned her slim figure. She even smiled at Willow, who in turn, smiled back. Willow felt brave, and she wished Bonnie was here to see it.

Coming out from behind the tree, she saw her beckon-the woman motioning with her hand. Willow inched toward the woman, taking slow steps until she reached the mailbox. It was leaning a little further west now and slumped, like tired shoulders.

"What's your name?" the woman asked, her voice was inviting.

"Willow."

"Hi Willow, I'm Miss Kora."

"Hi Miss Kora," she said confidently. If Bonnie was here, she would come right out and ask her if she was a witch. Willow was not that brazen.

"And where do you live, Willow?"

"I live behind Bartholomew's farm on Old Rock Road."

"You must be Floyd's daughter," Kora mentioned.

Willow's eyes widened. She hoped Miss Kora didn't know about her life. "Yes," she replied and was relieved that the woman didn't mention anything else about Daddy.

Miss Kora looked down at the envelopes she was clutching with her fingers, "I hope this is all good news. I only check my mailbox once a week because I don't normally get a lot, but this is more than usual."

"We only get bills."

Miss Kora started looking at the fronts of the envelopes putting one behind the other when a large piece of mail slipped out of her hand and landed at Willow's feet. Willow reflexively reached down to pick it up and handed it to Miss Kora forgetting about hiding her bandaged finger.

"Oh dear, what happened to your finger?" she asked concernedly.

"I was slicing carrots and I cut my finger. Daddy, Daddy said I didn't need to go to the hospital," she stammered.

"Come with me and let me have a look. I have something to help it heal."

"I already put peroxide on it."

"Oh no dear, you shouldn't use peroxide. I have something better. Trust me, it will work like magic."

Willow didn't understand why, but she believed Miss Kora. She followed her through the dirt patch that led to her cottage and around the back, where several gardens with an abundance of plants grew. Willow was mesmerized by the beauty she saw before her.

"Oh child, you must like what you see."

"I've never seen a garden like this one."

"These are my healing plants. Each one not only has a natural loveliness but it also has purpose."

Willow's eyes were drawn to the garden on the left side of her, at the point where the bottom of the hill met the flat land. In the middle of the white flower patch, beside a bench, was a greenish, metallic ball. It reflected the sun and branches of the tall trees overhead. The tree displayed on the ball like a photograph.

"What is that ball over there?" Willow asked pointing in the direction of the unusual object.

"That is a gazing ball. It brings harmony to the moon garden by reflecting the day's energy and calms in the evening when the sun goes down."

"Moon garden?" Willow's voice elevated as if to ask what Miss Kora meant. She never heard of a moon garden. To Willow, gardens were for growing vegetables. She remembered Mrs. Twine explaining the process of planting a garden, but she learned that plants need sunlight, not the moonlight. The fettle confused her.

"Yes dear, a moon garden. It's the best way to calm the body and mind for a perfect night's rest. You see, the sun gives us energy, and the moon," Miss Kora's eyes twinkled, "is calming."

"Can I sit on the bench?"

"Of course."

Miss Kora is so friendly, Willow thought as she relaxed on the bench snuggled among the flowers of the moon garden. The lady whom she just meant, sat beside her, and Willow felt unusually comfortable. She enchanted Willow with explanations about the gardens growing in her backyard. The plants in the moon garden only bloomed white flowers.

'*White Climbing Roses, Four O'clock, which opened their flowers after the sun starts falling at four o'clock, Angel Trumpets, White Cleomes...*'

Willow couldn't keep up as Miss Kora was rattling off the names, like she was reciting the alphabet. She went on to explain that the plants were night pollinators. The only thing Willow knew was that bee's pollinated. She remembered Mrs. Twine showed the class a picture of a bee sitting on the center of a flower. The plants on the other side of the yard held a different type of garden and were for medicine. To Willow, medicine was when Mamma gave her a spoonful of bitter-tasting, syrupy liquid that was hard to swallow or a pill that had to be crushed up and put in her orange juice.

"Why are all the flowers in the moon garden white?" Willow asked.

"Because they shine better in the dark, as the moon shines in the dark."

"They shine at night?" Willow asked for clarity.

"Yes, you see as dusk turns to dark the leaves fade and the whites of the flowers stand out, like they are glowing. It's quite fascinating."

"I wish I could see the garden at night."

"Let me have a look at that finger, Willow."

Willow undid the bandages and showed the cut to Miss Kora. She inspected it meticulously from every angle. By now the cut was a deep burgundy and the skin around it was light red and warm to the touch.

"I have just the thing," Miss Kora said, as she disappeared into the herbal garden, and then returned with a bouquet of green plants. As Miss Kora walked closer, Willow could smell a fresh scent.

"What is that?" Willow asked with interest.

"This is Lemon Balm. Smell it."

Willow stood up to smell what Miss Kora held in her hand. "That's what I smelled. Lemon."

"Here. Eat a leaf." Miss Kora handed Willow a tiny, oval-shaped bumpy leaf, who thought of Bonnie eating the sassafras leaves, as she slipped one between her teeth.

"How will this help my cut?" Willow asked as she chewed.

"I'm going to crush the leaves and lay them on your finger."

"And that will heal it?"

"Yes, my dear. It's a remedy that's been used for thousands of years. My mother used to put lemon balm on all my scrapes. Works like magic," the woman paused. "I'm going in the house to fix up the medicine. I'll be right back outside when I'm finished. Wait right here in the moon garden," she instructed.

Willow waited on the bench observing everything around her. She was enthralled by Miss Kora's backyard. She felt as if she was in another land from a time century's old. When Miss Kora came out, she was crushing and swirling contents in a small acacia bowl with a pestle made of the same wood. The leaves she held in her hand, were crushed up and soaked in a liquid.

"Let me put this tincture on your finger."

Willow held her hand up to the same height of the bowl Miss Kora was clasping with both of her hands. She scooped out a clump of the leaves using the bottom of the tool and spread it carefully on Willow's finger, who instantly felt her pain soothe as the cool liquid seeped into the wound.

"That feels better," Willow said with a sense of relief resounding in her statement.

"Sit on the bench while the potion does its magic and relax my child."

Willow stayed with Miss Kora in the moon garden listening to the trees sway and the birds of the forest squeak. They watched a hawk glide above the trees, its wings spread at full span. Willow was comfortable with this woman and felt as if she was far away from the valley. The place had a heavenly, beautiful charm like no other place she ever experienced. This woman, who was deemed as a witch by her father, was not what would come to mind at the mention of the word witch. There was something angelic about her. Her voice was feathery, and her words seemed to float in the air when she spoke. Willow questioned in her mind if she ever left the cottage for there wasn't a car in the driveway.

Time seemed to stand still until they heard a window being opened at the top of the hill behind them. Willow and Miss Kora turned in the direction of the sound and saw Edwin Mann-incensed. Willow was afraid he would come down and yell at her again to go home, but he just stood like a statue at his window, staring, obviously irritated. Miss Kora seemed to notice the worry in Willow's eyes.

"Don't worry about him; my place is protected from his negative energy. He's angry at me because I live on his property and he can't make me leave."

"If you're on his land, why can't he make you leave?" Willow asked.

"My family has lived here for hundreds of years. When Edwin Mann bought the property, there was no deed to be had. All I know is that my great, great grandparents lived in this place since right before the Civil War began and we've been growing gardens of herbs ever since. The Adverse Possession law says if you use someone else's land for a long enough time, you have the right to stay there. Edwin Mann can't kick me out as much as he wants to."

"How is it his land then?" Willow asked.

"Like I said, child, there is no original deed to this house that I know of, so when he bought the estate from the previous owner, this part came with it."

"So, a deed belongs to the person who owns the property? I heard my mamma and daddy talking about that. I'm glad you're here Miss Kora. Your place is so pretty."

"Yes, child, and thank you, my dear. You are a very intelligent little girl. How does your finger feel now?" She asked affectionately.

Willow paused for a moment to make sure she understood what she heard. *Did Miss Kora call her intelligent?*

"I forgot I had a booboo," Willow chortled. She took off the tincture of Lemon Balm, and to her surprise, the cut had a different look. Her hand was no longer red and warm around the laceration and a scab tightly brought the wound together.

"Now that looks better. Next, I'll give you some lotion to rub on it. You won't have any more pain."

Miss Kora went inside the tiny cottage and brought out a vile of a clear salve. She popped off the lid and rubbed a thin layer over Willow's wound.

"Now that should do it, Willow."

"Thank you, Miss Kora." She gazed into the woman's sparkling eyes. Her eyes were two different colors, blue like a tropical ocean with a light brown, glassy center. Willow had never seen such a thing.

"I better get home now," she panicked.

"Is everything all right?"

"Yes, it's much better. Thank you for fixing my cut but I'm not really supposed to be out right now. Bye, Miss Kora."

"Bye, Willow."

Willow felt Miss Kora watch her as she skipped along to the road-on her way home. With a lifted spirit she ran with an extra step in her stride and couldn't wait to tell Bonnie about meeting Miss Kora, who wasn't a witch after all. She thought about how Miss Kora called her intelligent. No one had ever said that to Willow before. Mamma always encouraged her, helping her sound out words and giving her practice spelling tests the night before, but when she came home with another E, Mamma would look at Willow sorrowfully and say, 'maybe next week'. Willow wondered what Miss Kora meant when she said her land was protected from negative energy. She wondered how she could protect herself from Daddy's negative energy.

Daddy came home from work, grumpy again, yelling about the shirts that blew off the line.

Doesn't he realize I'm not tall enough to clip the clothes to the line?

When he went into the house and slammed the screen door, it broke the rusty hinge on the bottom. Now the door is hanging crooked and it banged the door frame when the wind blew. It kept Willow up half the night. Every time she heard the squeaky sound, she knew the loud thud was next.

#

Willow trekked to Bonnie's house each morning over the next several days hoping to find her in the tree or behind the house, but still, there was no sign of her. The house was quiet, the sunflower field was untouched, and even Oliver was nowhere to be found, so she stayed home trying to read the recipes from Mamma's cookbook. After Miss Kora put the lemon balm on her finger, the pain subsided and the skin healed to a barely-noticeable scar, but it didn't make her want to cook. The food in the pantry was dwindling again and the cookies she hid were long gone. Willow would have to find the perfect time to ask Daddy to take a trip to Powel's or maybe if she was lucky, she could get him to take her to Lucille's for a home cooked meal. She would even be satisfied with a takeout bag.

Daddy left early to go fishing. She said a prayer that he caught *the big one* because that would increase the chance of him being in an agreeable mood when he returned home. By four in the afternoon, Daddy had yet to return to the house, so Willow resigned herself to the fact that she would have to forage for something herself. She tugged the handle of the refrigerator listening to the door squeak as it opened. Willow spotted the egg carton and came up with a plan. She pulled out the sugar, baking soda, a half-filled bag of flour, chocolate icing, and some cupcake liners from the cupboard where Mamma kept the baking items. A memory of her last birthday arose.

Mamma used those liners to make treats for her party-well it was supposed to be a party. She wanted to invite Joseph and Mr. and Mrs. Timmons, a couple from church that had brought casseroles to the house when Mamma was sick. She wanted me to invite a friend or two from school and maybe Grandpa. Mamma was hopeful when she broached the subject with Daddy, but he turned her down. Willow overheard the discussion when Mamma thought she was outside.

'We can celebrate Willow's birthday with just the three of us. She doesn't need a party. Willow felt Daddy's austere response tighten her heart.

Willow dragged out the Better Homes and Garden book and found a recipe for vanilla cupcakes. She read it slowly, her voice puttering out the words like someone kept hitting the brakes of a car. She gathered ingredients on the counter. The only one missing was vanilla, she noticed, but continued with her plan. Willow measured and added items one at a time to a large, amber mixing bowl that splayed wheat designed across the front. When she opened the flour, Willow discovered it was speckled with tiny pieces of brown dots and as she looked closer, she noticed the pieces were wriggling. *Bugs*, she finally realized, had made their way into the bag. She remembered Mamma storing the flour in the refrigerator during summer, when the weather was hot and humid. 'It prevents bugs', she heard Mamma say in a serious tone. Disappointed, Willow stared into the bowl. How she longed for something sweet.

I wish Mamma was here to make cupcakes, with icing and sprinkles.

Her desires were implacable, so Willow picked out as many bugs as she possibly could before measuring two cups, then inspected what had been added to the bowl to make sure it was clear of those tiny creatures. When the batter was ready, she noticed it was thicker than what she remembered but continued, determined to have a dozen or more. After scooping the mixture into the accordion liners, she slipped her creation in the oven. The timer sounded twenty minutes later. Wearing Mamma's blue quilted oven mitts, she pulled the cupcakes from the oven and was extra careful not to burn her arms on the hot racks. She spread a thick layer of chocolate icing on the top of each one. What would Mamma say if she saw what Willow accomplished all on her own, she prided herself.

T*ime to taste.*

She peeled back the foil and took several large bites. The cupcake was dry and had an odd taste, like the time she ate stale bread at Grandpa's house, but she liked the icing. She took several cupcakes and licked the sugary delight off the tops, leaving the mounds of cake bare. Afterward, her stomach felt sick and she burped, a sour taste lingered on her tongue and in the back of her mouth.

"These cupcakes are horrible," she said in a huff as she felt anger ooze from her insides and her face flush with tears.

"Why can't Mamma be here?"

Willow took a fork from the counter and began stabbing at the cupcakes, marring each one until they were nothing, but a heap of crumbs held together in clumps with the sticky icing. She cried on the stoop. The same place where Mamma cried the last night she was there.

"Where is Mamma?" She asked herself, repeating the words as she cried. When the tears dried up, she went back in the kitchen and looked over the mess. She stuffed the cupcakes in the garbage and cleaned every part of her chaos so Daddy wouldn't know what she had done.

10

Chapter 10

Bonnie's Back

On Monday, Daddy went to work at the usual time, when Willow was still sleeping. She woke to a sticky heat that engulfed her body. Today was a humid day, typical for mid-July. She was determined to venture to Bonnie's house and find her at home. She couldn't wait to tell Bonnie about Miss Kora's backyard and how the lemon balm cured her finger but then she remembered, she wanted to keep that a secret. She wanted to tell her how Mr. Mann was trying to kick Miss Kora off her land and how creepy he was spying on them in the moon garden. These thoughts swirled in her head as she left out of the side door.

When the screen door closed, she noticed it was fixed, secured on both hinges. It no longer tilted toward the other side of the doorframe. Then it dawned on her, she hadn't heard squeaking and banging last night. *Daddy*, she wondered, but he had fallen asleep on the couch when he got home from fishing and as far as she knew, hadn't budged till morning when he woke for work.

She left the stoop, feeling the excitement of adventure ahead of her, as if she had been caged and was finally able to leave. She carried herself along the field and the dewy grass brushed her ankles leaving remnants of moisture and making her legs itchy. She stood at the corner of the field staring at the shanty, thinking about what that old thing was used for. Maybe it was a house where the original landowners lived before, they built the farmhouse. She remembered Mrs. Twine teaching the class how Abraham Lincoln lived in a log cabin. But this wasn't a log cabin. It was made from wooden planks and seemed even smaller than Abe Lincoln's cabin. She recollected the importance of the lesson that day while a few of her classmates raised their hands to ask silly questions and Mrs. Twine had to remind them to behave or they would be inside for recess.

She glanced toward the driveway and noticed the station wagon parked in its usual spot with the driver's door right next to the sidewalk. Her heart leaped. Willow knocked on the door. When she heard the television, she pictured Bonnie and her sister, sprawled on the couch. Mrs. Murphy answered. She wore gingham shorts with a white sleeveless top. Her hair was in a bun with wisps of hair falling around her face. A blue apron contoured in rickrack trim covered the front of her body. Willow hoped she was making chocolate chip cookies again.

"Hello, Willow. Come in. Bonnie and Jenny are watching television."

Willow followed Mrs. Murphy in through the front door and saw the two girls sitting on the floor, their backs leaning against the couch. Jenny was weaving pieces of fabric on a small square loom and Bonnie was working on a latch hook rug. She saw a start of what would become a kitten when finished. When she saw Bonnie's head, she was befuddled. Bonnie had white pieces of cloth tied around bits of rolled-up hair.

"Hi, Willow. I'm doing latch hook. It's going to be a kitten."

"What do you have in your hair, Bonnie?" Willow asked, her eyes fixated on her head.

"Rags."

"Rags?"

"When I take them out, my hair will be curly."

"Really? I've had curlers in my hair but never rags." Willow remembered going to sleep with curlers in her hair the night before picture day. The tiny needles poked into her head and she never slept well when she wore them.

"Well rags don't hurt like curlers do," Bonnie stated and took one out of her head. A strand of hair bounced as it fell into a windy spiral. Then she rolled the same piece of hair around the cloth and tied it to show Willow how it was done.

"Can I take the rags out? I want to see what your hair looks like."

"Sure."

Willow sat beside Bonnie and untied all the pieces of cloth. Her hair bounced in a bonnet of spiral curls. Bonnie slid her hands up the sides of her head, running her fingers through the strands.

"It looks so pretty," Willow told Bonnie.

"I can put them in your hair if you'd like."

"OK."

"I'll go get my brush. Hold on a minute."

Once Bonnie came back downstairs, she rolled Willow's hair around each piece of rag and tied the little slips to hold the curls in place. When she finished, Willow's hair was pulled up off her neck and away from her face. "There you go. Give it a few hours and you will have curly hair."

"I have to sit like this for hours?" Willow asked.

"Yeah. We can go outside while your hair is setting."

"I shouldn't go outside with these pieces of cloth in my hair."

"Why not? Nobody is going to see you and besides who cares if they do."

"I suppose your right. We are out in the middle of the country."

Willow and Bonnie went out front and sat under the sassafras tree. Oliver came along and stepped on Willow, kneading her legs with his paws. They began to laugh. Then he stepped closer to her face; his tiny feet moved with precision. He rubbed his head against the ties on the side of her head. Bonnie laughed out loud while Willow sat motionless, snickering in gulps, feeling as if she was unable to move. Then, Oliver nestled in Willow's lap and fell asleep.

"He really has takin' a liking to you," Bonnie said.

"I like him too. I missed him and I missed you, Bonnie. Were you away?"

"We went camping in the mountains for a week."

"What did you do there for a week?"

"We jumped on a huge trampoline and went on trails to see beautiful waterfalls. We also played mini-golf and sat by the fire every night roasting marshmallows and singing campfire songs."

"I've never been camping. I'd like to go someday but Daddy doesn't like to leave home. Hey, I have to tell you about Miss Kora," Willow said purposely changing the subject.

"Who is Miss Kora?"

"Miss Kora is the witch. Well, if she is a witch, she is the nicest witch I ever met. She helped me fix my finger with her plants."

"What happened to your finger?"

"I cut it ...and she has these big gardens in her back yard. One is called a moon garden. It is like magic." Willow went on and on telling Bonnie about her time with Miss Kora. Bonnie was engrossed in listening to what Willow was explaining.

An hour slid by as they played in the sassafras tree, untrammeled by distraction and following their whims. They climbed up to the lowest branch and watched Miss Kora's house looking for a sign of the woman. They looked up the hill to Mr. Mann's house. The curtains were open, and the grounds were manicured into a perfect specimen of a maintained estate. The bushes that stood in the front of the house, were cut into rounded carvings. They saw Edwin Mann step out of his front door and scowl at the cottage. They made a spectacle of themselves waving at him as he slammed the door, retreating into his mansion.

"Let's go see the witch today."

"She's not a witch," Willow said, "well, not a bad witch."

The door of the farmhouse swung open. Mrs. Murphy shouted for Bonnie to come in for lunch. Willow hadn't had Mamma call her for lunch in several months.

"Can Willow eat lunch with us?" Bonnie shouted. The sound of her voice seemed to shoot through Willow's ear and out through the other side.

"Of course, but you have to eat at the table in the kitchen."

After lunch, Bonnie took the rags out of Willow's hair. She had a mane of bouncy brown curls. When she shook her head, she could feel an airy space between her neck and where her hair touched her skin. Bonnie brought her a handheld mirror and Willow was delighted at the change in her appearance.

"I love it, Bonnie. I've never seen my hair so beautiful. The plastic curlers could never make curls like this."

"You can take these rags home."

"Are you sure?"

"Yeah. They're just old towels cut into strips. I can make more." Bonnie put the rags into a brown paper bag and rolled the top to the middle of the sac. "Are you ready to go to the witch's cottage?"

"Let's go."

"Mom, mom," Bonnie yelled. Her voice took up the whole downstairs.

"Yes Willow," Mrs. Murphy said from the top of the stairway.

"We're going outside."

"Don't go too far."

Willow and Bonnie zealously left the house, the door slamming behind them. Oliver moved out of their way as they ran down the porch steps and skipped out of the yard.

#

They arrived at the mailbox, which was now leaning in the opposite direction. Willow gave the rusty figure a second look.

"That mailbox is leaning different every time I see it."

"It is old," Bonnie commented as she led Willow onto Miss Kora's cottage.

When the girls stepped on the porch, they paused debating what to do next and came to the accord that knocking on the door, like most folks do, would get Miss Kora's attention. They gently tapped on the wooden door which was painted a hue of blue Willow had never seen on a door before. The sapphire color, different from the last time she was here, was freshly coated. When the knock went unanswered the first time, they knocked more fervently the second time. Mr. Mann must have heard it because he came running down the hill and stood at the side of the house starring at Willow and Bonnie with an angry glare that shot right through them. The girls, disconcerted by his ambush, stood stiffly like statues, too scared to move.

"Why are you snooping around here? I told you to stay off my property." Mr. Mann, a hefty fellow, was furious, more so than last time. He squelched his brow line and a droplet of spit popped out of the side of his mouth when he spoke. He stood staunchly, waiting for an answer, like one would placate him enough to make him back off from his reprimand.

"We're here to see Miss Kora," Bonnie spoke up.

"Well she's not home!" he huffed.

Suddenly the door opened and there stood Miss Kora, dressed in a long flowing blue skirt, the same color as the door, and a white peasant top. She peered outside as if to take inventory of what was happening on her porch.

"I am home," she answered in a lifted sweet voice as a bird warbled in the distance. "These girls are welcome to visit me, Mr. Mann."

"Very well then. But remember Kora, this is my property," he said, with the airs of a rich, arrogant man and plodded back up the hill.

Kora watched him struggle when he reached the steepest part, his feet slipping on a slick spot. He had to hold his arms out for balance as he wobbled to catch himself. "Serves him right," Kora dauntlessly expressed. "He can't get me off this land. I have the law and the spirits on my side. This land is protected."

"Do you have guns?" Willow asked. She thought of Daddy sitting on the edge of his chair, cleaning his gun with a rod. It seemed to energize him as he went through the ritual of taking out the bolt, checking that it wasn't loaded, and pulsing the brush up and down the barrel. Then he would move a piece of cloth through the tube until it came out clean. He did this with such precision and always made comments while he went through the process. 'Yeah, this gun here will keep us protected. Anyone who tries to get in this house will be looking down the barrel of this gun.'

"I don't need guns. I buried amethyst crystals on the corners of my yard and along the side of the house. It brings me good luck and dispels evil. It has worked for hundreds of years since my family has lived here. Would you like to see my crystal collection?"

Just as Willow was about to object to the idea, Bonnie spoke up, "Why yes. I'd love to see your crystals."

Kora opened the blue door and invited them in her cottage. When they stepped on the threshold to enter, something crunched under their feet.

Willow looked down expecting to see some crumbs of some sort but instead, she saw flecks of a white, shiny substance. "What is that?"

"That is salt. Salt keeps out evil spirits and demons. You are perfectly safe in my house."

Bonnie didn't seem phased by Miss Kora's unusual ways. The woman led them to shelves that lined an entire wall of the front room of her cottage. They were filled with rocks. Rocks of different magnitudes, varying in size, color, and shape. Some were exquisite, resembling crystals and diamonds, or had smooth surfaces with rich colors of green and purple while others were heavy in appearance with grotesque shapes and dark colors. The girls gawked in wonder at the magnificent collection. Kora scanned the rows counting her precious stones, making sure they were all accounted for as if they were her children.

"Why do you have all these rocks?" Bonnie asked, focused on the crystals.

"These are more than just rocks," Miss Kora began emphatically. "They are minerals of the earth, earth's energy which can heal us and bring us to a more fulfilled life."

Willow wondered if one could bring her mother back. She looked at Bonnie, who was still inspecting the rocks. "I like this one." She said and grabbed a rock that was contoured by red, white, and orange lines. Willow thought it looked like a piece of taffy.

"That is carnelian. It brings courage," Kora paused for a moment. "That piece I want to keep but I have more of that kind." Kora scanned the shelves and found a group of Carnelian rocks. She carefully plucked two rocks off the shelf and handed one each to Willow and Bonnie. "There. Now you have the mineral of courage."

Willow and Bonnie each clutched a rock in their hand and thanked Miss Kora. They turned their attention to the sound of a crackling fire. It was a hot afternoon, yet this woman was burning wood. A black iron hanger held a pot attached to the fireplace. It looked like a scene from an 1800's cabin when people cooked over a fire. It made sense since Kora didn't have electricity. The black dress was poised on a hook which hung next to the fireplace.

"What is the black dress for?" Willow asked.

"That is my dress for Samhain."

"What is that?"

"Samhain marks the end of the harvest season. It's celebrated every year halfway between autumn equinox and winter solstice. For my ancestors from Ireland, it was the largest celebration of the year. I keep the tradition going."

Willow knew the end of the harvest season to be when Bartholomew's fields were barren. "What do you do for Samhain?" Willow asked.

"I burn candles, make pumpkin soup and burn a big fire. It's quite a spectacle. Makes Mr. Mann angry," she remarked, as she let out a bubble of laughter.

"Can we go outside and sit in the moon garden?" Willow asked remembering how relaxed she felt the last time she sat in the moon garden.

"Of course." Miss Kora was always genial, the opposite of Daddy, Willow thought.

Outside, Miss Kora showed them around the herbal garden explaining the names of the many plants and how each was used, going into deep explanations of their healing powers. Then they sat in the moon garden, talking, and listening to the chirps of birds and squirrels jumping from trees and running along branches. A hawk circled above them, and Miss Kora explained that when a hawk flies over your land it's like the spirits of nature giving a blessing. She seemed to have an explanation for everything, and Willow and Bonnie listened attentively. The moment seemed ethereal until Willow heard the purr of a truck motor and it reminded her that the afternoon was slipping by too quickly.

"I have to go. Daddy will be home soon, and I still have chores to finish." Willow brought her mind to reality. The reality that life was real and if only these rocks and plants that Kora possessed could fix everything that was wrong. She clutched the carnelian rock and stood to her feet.

Miss Kora looked at her. "Don't fret child. Troubles do pass."

If only, Willow thought but she wasn't sure what to think next. Willow could tell Bonnie didn't want to leave but she followed her friend to the end of the dirt where the mailbox stood on the side of Marshland Road. They waved bye to Miss Kora as she stood on the porch, the blue color of the door leaving a sensation of calm around the lithe woman. Willow hurried past the farmhouse and ran along the field. The sunflowers, towering over the dirt, seemed to be a foot taller and the bristly leaves were bold in the daylight. It won't be long, she thought, when they open their centers.

11

Chapter 11

Fire

Willow awoke, with fullness in her heart after leaving Miss Kora's the day before, to the engine of Daddy's truck stalling out. It replicated her plummeting mood thinking about not being able to see Bonnie today if Daddy couldn't get to work. He turned the ignition to restart the motor but the sound that followed was a raspy, elongated cough and then a clunk. He tried at least six times, but Willow stopped counting after that. Each try was accompanied with a cuss word that Willow would get her mouth washed out with soap if she said it in front of Mamma. She went to the window of her bedroom and watched Daddy get out of the truck, open the hood, and inspect the intricate configuration of machine parts. He fiddled with wires and took off caps to check fluids. After his unaccomplished attempts to find the problem, Daddy slammed the hood and slogged the center leaving a slight indentation in the metal, deep enough to hold a splash of water. Willow shuddered and ran back to bed, hiding under the covers. She heard Daddy leave, trudging down the driveway. Each footstep scratched the pebbles as he walked and eventually the sounds tapered to nothing but the sough of the wind.

Willow was home alone at last, but not knowing if Daddy was on his way to work or to get help with his truck, she decided she had better stay home. She slumped under the covers, disappointed. Later in the afternoon, a bulky work truck drove down the pebbled driveway and parked under the oak tree. A man got out and worked on a wire that extended from a metal box attached to the side of the house. Later in the day, about the usual time he arrived home, Daddy was dropped off by a man in a light blue pickup truck. He hurried inside to the hallway, close to the kitchen, and plugged a phone cord into the wall. He called for a tow truck to hall his truck to the garage in town.

"I think it's the transmission," he told Willow somberly. The sound of defeat vibrated in his footsteps as he mulled around the house. "It's going to cost me a pretty penny for this one." Then, he ordered Willow to make dinner.

Willow opened the refrigerator, looking for something that would please her father. The milk was low already, about an inch from the bottom of the jug, a tub of butter was almost full. There were leftover sausages and some potatoes that had grown eyes, the chutes poking out from the skin like skinny fingertips. A few apples and oranges remained in the bottom drawer. There was more meat in the freezer, but it wouldn't thaw in time for dinner. Willow went to the pantry, finding a few cans of green beans. She wished she could get some fresh ones from the Murphys' garden but was relieved she had enough to scrap together supper.

Willow went to work peeling and cutting potatoes. She boiled them until they were soft. After draining the water, she mashed them with butter and milk, leaving the jug almost empty. She thoroughly heated the sausage in the oven until the skin was tough and crisped when it was poked with a fork. She set a pot of beans on the stove to heat. Dinner was complete.

Willow, quite proud of what she was able to put together in a short amount of time, stood back to look at her creation for an instant and hurried to set the table before the dinner cooled. She set up two plates with silverware, putting a folded napkin under each knife, like Mamma taught her. Then she went to the living room to let Daddy know dinner was ready, hoping he would be happy. She found him slumbering on the couch with the television blaring the evening news. She turned the tube off and woke Daddy, gently nudging his shoulder till he came out of his sleep. She looked at his bloodshot tired eyes, noticing a different daddy she remembered before Mamma left. He seemed sorry about something. Willow could never remember Daddy ever being sorry, but Mamma was always sorry, even if it wasn't her fault.

Daddy sat quietly, cutting up his sausage before eating the meal. They usually never spoke more than a few words if they ate together but today would be different. After Daddy was finished with his food, he laid his fork beside the plate and contemplatively leaned back into the seat, his balled hands resting at his sides. He began to talk slowly as if he was scrutinizing his choice of words.

"Willow, this town is full of self-righteous, do-gooders and if you're not just like them, they don't like ya, and your mother has turned into one of them. That's one reason she left."

Daddy's words covered up any sorrow he might have been feeling. Willow could tell, he wanted to try and make her feel as if Mamma leaving was a good thing, like her life was better off because of it. But Willow couldn't be convinced. Still, she sat quietly as Daddy went on about his disdain for the people in the valley, and she should just keep to herself because *ain't nothing good gonna' come out of trying to take up with people 'round here.*

"Have you finished, Daddy? I'll clean up the dishes."

Willow learned a long time ago that when Daddy is complaining about everyone around him, you just be quiet. Daddy liked to keep to himself. Willow never remembered her parents having friends like she saw other families at church have. On the few occasions when they stayed for the potluck Sunday's she remembered multiple families sitting together, laughing, and engaging. But her family sat alone, Mamma looking around like she wanted to talk with other people, but too nervous to do so, and Daddy either watching her or looking down into his food as he ate, careful not to make eye contact with anyone. The tension Willow felt kept her quiet and close to Mamma, where she felt safe. Now the only time she felt that kind of security was when she was with Bonnie or Miss Kora. She didn't believe what Daddy was telling her. She knew there were nice people in this town.

That evening, a storm blew into the valley like a thunderous train. The wind was howling and a tree branch, from the oak tree, repetitively hit her window keeping her awake. Lightning shot through the window, making the room electrified with a bright white light for a few seconds at a time. She tossed in her bed and closed her eyes tightly, thinking if she could shut out the light, she could fall back asleep but it was of no use. She shuffled out of bed to the window and watched the rain slap her window like buckets of water were being thrown against the house. She heard Daddy talking on the phone, but she couldn't decipher the conversation, so she went to the door and opened it slightly, and poked her ear into the hallway.

"...someone's been snooping around this place."

Pause

"I don't know who it is. It might be her and if..."

The next part became muffled by a wind gust and rain dropping on the roof. Willow strained to hear what Daddy had told the other person on the line. The next thing she heard was the slam of the receiver, as if he smashed it into the cradle, and then the sound of his footsteps inching toward the staircase. Willow, frightened, shut the door and ran back into bed.

"Willow," he shouted.

She didn't respond.

"Willow! You better be in bed."

Willow pulled out the carnelian stone and rubbed it, hoping for courage.

#

The next day, the same man in the blue truck picked up Daddy for work. Willow spent some time with Bonnie in the morning but came back to the house by noon just in case Daddy would get home early with his truck fixed. She pondered about the phone call she overheard. Daddy was worried about someone coming to the house, Willow was not. Intuitively she felt a presence had been here to help her, which gave her hope that she would see Mamma again.

The house was muggy and damp from the wetness-remnants of the rainstorm. The afternoon sun was drying up the last of the water, making the humidity soar. She went outside to sit on the stoop hoping to find a breeze. The rain had done wonders for the plants. The daises were extra perky and so had been the sunflowers this morning. At the edge of the yard, just where the forest began, she heard a crackle of branches. She turned in the direction of the noise, but she saw nothing, taking note that there wasn't an ounce of wind to move any branches.

The early afternoon sun was infusing its stagnant heat in Sol Valley. It was going to be a long, hot afternoon, Willow thought. The sound grew louder. Willow looked again in the same direction and the subtle movement of branches rose to a clatter. A second later, Oliver emerged, like he was making an appearance on a stage. He sauntered over to the stoop observing and sniffing the grass along the way. Willow watched him as he climbed the steps and sat at her feet.

"Oliver, you found me." She retorted.

Oliver was a safe visitor, she thought. He could take off, out of sight, as quickly as he came. Willow patted Oliver on the head as he put his front paws on her thighs and rubbed his nose on her cheek. Then he stepped forward bringing his back paws onto her legs and ensconced himself into her lap. She heard the branches move again and turned her attention back to the forest. A second later, Bonnie walked through the trees and stood at the edge of the woods.

Willow's spirits lifted but sank just as fast like she would finally be found out. This lonely house is where she lived, and she didn't want Bonnie to know. It wasn't full of neatly placed knick-knacks on end tables and pictures of family hung on the walls. It lacked the smell of homemade chocolate chip cookies and dinners being made by a loving mother or friendly greetings from a father coming home from work. It wasn't clean or pretty or comfortable with the love that Bonnie's house had, now that Mamma was gone.

"Hi Willow. Is this where you live? I followed Oliver through the woods, and he brought me to your house. He's a smart cat."

Willow stared at Bonnie. "Bonnie! Yes, I live here."

She wanted to tell her that it wasn't safe to stay, but Oliver, comfortably curled in a ball, was purring and content. Bonnie skipped through the grass and sat on the stoop next to Willow. For a moment, peacefulness seeped into her body as if she slipped into a warm bubble bath. It was like Bonnie brought all the comforts of her home over to Willow.

"I had to get out of my house. My mom is putting up wallpaper in the hallway and my sister is helping. She kept telling me I was getting in the way, so I left. Mom keeps complaining because of the heat but she is determined to get that wallpaper up before my dad comes in from the fields."

Willow didn't have fancy wallpaper in her house. All her walls were a dull white, except for the kitchen which Mamma painted bright yellow last summer before she hung the sunburst clock.

"What kind of wallpaper is it?"

"Oh, you should see it. It's a fancy design of orange flowers with a silver background."

"We don't have wallpaper in our house but my Mamma..." Willow paused. She couldn't bring herself to talk about Mamma. She was afraid she would cry.

"What about your mom?"

"Never mind; let's go get Oliver some milk."

The two friends went into the kitchen and pulled the jug of milk out of the refrigerator. Even though she knew it hadn't expired, Willow sniffed it like she always did since Mamma's been gone and made sure it wasn't soured. She poured what was left of the milk into one of the bowls she used for cereal and set it on the floor. Oliver lapped up a portion of it and then circled through the legs of the table making a figure-eight path several times. His tail stuck straight in the air as it always did when he walked. Curiously, he tiptoed into the living room with soft, soundless steps. Willow and Bonnie followed behind him.

"Let's play school," Bonnie implored.

Despite her difficulties with learning, Willow liked school and sometimes pretended to be a teacher when she was bored and alone in her room, but she had never played school downstairs in the living room. "Let's pretend the wall is our chalkboard. You can teach over there on that side of the couch and I can teach on this side."

"Good idea," Bonnie replied. "Do you have any hair ties? We should put our hair up into a bun like a teacher."

"I have yarn." Willow went to fetch the yarn from her bedroom that Mamma used to tie her hair into pigtails for church. She remembered how good it felt when she shook her head and the pigtails swished back and forth, the tips patting her neck.

After they tied their hair up, they went to each end of the couch and pretended to be teachers, talking to their class, and using their fingers as pieces of chalk. Some minutes later, Bonnie began to look around.

"What are you looking for?" Willow asked.

"Do you have any magazines? We can pretend they are books."

"We have newspapers." Willow pointed to the stack of papers in the corner near the fireplace. Mamma read the newspaper and daddy used it to start fires when the temperature was cold, which hadn't occurred in months, so the newspapers stacked about two feet high.

Bonnie grabbed two bunches of newspapers giving one to Willow. She opened it and read the weather section, then announced the forecast to her class according to the Sol Valley Press.

Willow turned the pages pretending to look for an interesting article.

Bonnie began to read a story to her class about the Public Library being renovated. Bonnie was a good reader. She didn't stumble over her words like Willow.

Willow continued to thumb through the paper, her eye being drawn to photos. She saw a photo of a house with a burned-down garage. The article was circled with a red ink pen which drew her attention. She tried to read it, but when the words started flipping and the letters appeared to her as a jumble of straight and curved lines, she decided to show it to Bonnie and somehow get her to read it in a way that wouldn't reveal she couldn't.

"Bonnie, I read this exciting article," she fibbed. "Why don't you read it to your class?" She handed the paper to Bonnie who quietly examined the piece for a few seconds.

It piqued her interest. "Listen up class. Miss Willow shared an interesting story with me. Pay attention while I read it to you."

Suspect Denies Involvement in Fire

A man from Sol Valley allegedly started a fire that burned the detached garage at the home of Jerome and Mae Ferebee. The Ferebee's recently moved into Sol Valley with their family. The fire department detected the use of an accelerant that is believed to have started the fire. Floyd Hitchens was brought in for questioning but denies any involvement in the incident. The incident is believed to be racially motivated. His father, Robert Hitchens, who was a rabble-rouser during the Civil Rights movement, led a group protesting the integration of schools in 1965; he has also been questioned and denies any involvement. There were no injuries and the loss of possessions was minimal, but the family is saddened by the incident. Pastor Joseph and church members are assisting the family. If you have any information about this, please contact the Sol Valley Police Station.

Bonnie showed the photograph to her imaginary class. Willow was speechless. She wanted to shrivel up and sink into the cushions of the couch. The article was about her Dad. She knew he didn't like certain people, but he wouldn't do this. The article said he was a suspect and Willow understood that meant it wasn't certain that he is guilty. She watched Bonnie closely to see if she made a connection to the name. She hadn't told Bonnie her father's name as far as she could remember.

"Now class," Bonnie continued, "Who can tell me what you should do in case of a fire?" Pause "Yes that's right stop, drop and roll."

Bonnie didn't notice. In fact, she seemed to miss the whole point of the article. Willow was relieved but she couldn't go on playing anymore. She needed to be alone. She wanted to cry and not in front of Bonnie.

"Bonnie," she interrupted her lecture to her imaginary class about fire safety, "I need to get some chores done before my dad gets home from work, so you better go."

"I can help you. Gosh, you always have a lot of chores."

"No, it's boring. Why don't I come by your house tomorrow? Maybe we can go see Miss Kora and I can't wait to see the wallpaper your mom is putting up."

"Ok Willow. Let me get Oliver." Bonnie found him in the corner sleeping peacefully. She picked him up and carried him out the door yelling goodbye as she disappeared in the woods. Willow watched her friend leave, saddened that their day ended this way yet relieved that Bonnie hadn't found her out.

12

Chapter 12

PPD

After visiting with her father, Willow left the valley with a deep-set emotional exhaustion that lasted the entire day. When had she left Pequot, the anger Willow held was a nagging part of her life for many years and she fully expected to unleash it on her father but for some reason, she couldn't bring herself to let him know how much she detested him. Maybe it was because she finally saw the pitiful lonely man he's always been. It wasn't something she felt when she lived with him nor did it come to her when Willow and her mother left the police station that day. The repugnance took a while to penetrate her awareness. It happened slowly as she realized what it was like to live in a normal house where she was free to laugh, free from being sent away to her room at a moment's notice, and free from a fractious father who yelled unpredictably. Her mother told her bits and pieces of the abuse along the way. Her stories would come out at unexpected moments. She would be in a fine mood and then all the sudden it was as if a light switch had been flipped. Something would set her off into a crying spell, and she'd shake all over unable to calm down until she described the memory that was causing her breakdown. Like when Daddy threw a hot pan at her because she burnt dinner. Luckily, the pan missed her, but it scattered dinner all over the wall. Her mother was frying chicken for dinner in one of the skimpy apartments they lived in, the evening that memory came to the surface. The pan must have reminded her.

Willow remembered her father's paranoia. She learned about Paranoid Personality Disorder when studying Intro to Psychology, course 1201, and thought of her father when the professor lectured about its symptoms. Floyd always thought her mother was cheating on him and he never allowed her to talk to anyone, especially males. If he felt someone wronged him, he would go out of his way to get back at the person in some misanthropic way.

Once, a man who worked at the gas station filled up another customer's tank first. Her dad had been waiting but the attendant didn't notice him on the other side of the gas pump, the side closer to the road. She recalled him shouting to the attendant, 'Listen, pal, I was here first, so get on over here and pump my gas'. The other man must have known him by name because he answered Floyd from his car window, 'Floyd you just calm down. The gas ain't goin' nowhere'. Those words didn't sit right with her dad.

Barbara tried to explain to Willow after the incident, making excuses for his erratic behavior. He chased behind that man and almost pushed him off the road. Mamma was scared. Willow had felt her tension when she tightened her arms around her and asked him coolly to slow down. Willow's eyes were watching the taillights of the man's car as she sat on her mother's lap. He finally let the man get away. Willow knew her mother wanted to scream but that would have only inflamed Floyd's anger even more. Her mother always had to keep her emotions quelled. The day Bonnie read the newspaper article aloud came to her memory and she felt hollow. The embarrassment of the incident was never far from her mind.

13

Chapter 13

The Buick

Willow couldn't stop thinking about the article in the newspaper. Daddy couldn't have done that. She knew the Ferebee's. Rhonda Ferebee was in her class. Daddy told Willow she wasn't allowed to play with black children, but Mamma said people shouldn't be judged by the color of their skin, although Daddy wouldn't believe that so keep it to yourself, she had said.

In church, Willow remembered preacher Joseph talking about Martin Luther King. Daddy didn't like that. Willow contemplated about the red circle around the article. The paper was dated April 10th, 1976, right before Mamma left and she could have circled it.

Was that what they were fighting about?

Willow continued to glower over the newspaper article over the next few days, and it made her uneasy about venturing beyond the boundaries of her yard. Eventually, the longing to see her friend and the obsessive speculation about the appearance of the sunflowers compelled her out the door. She left for Bartholomew's farm, dressed in baby blue terry cloth shorts and a tank top. Her favorite pair of striped knee-high socks was finally clean.

She traversed in and out of the trees as she jaunted to the edge of the sunflower field. The decrepit shanty, that sat unchanged, contrasted the growth of the sunflowers. Today they looked more alive than ever, she noticed. The buds were now a lighter green and a bright yellow center, barely noticeable, was emerging. The plants were proudly tall, and she imagined she could magically open the petals into a flower with the wave of her hand. Willow caught the deep stench of miasmic manure in her nostrils and it knocked her back into reality.

She noticed Bonnie was near the field where Mr. Murphy was working to lay the fertilizer. Willow watched as she went to the side of the porch to fetch a ball and heard her ask Jenny if she wanted to play Seven Up.

"No Bonnie. I'm reading and I can't play in my clogs."

"Why don't you take your clogs off? Mom said you can't wear them for play."

"That's why I'm not playing. I want to wear my new clogs."

"Please," she heard Bonnie beg.

"No Bonnie. Not right now." Jenny got up from the chair and clomped into the house. Her feet sounded like horse hooves on a paved road.

"I'll play." Willow had walked closer to the porch.

Surprised, Bonnie turned to face the sound of Willow's voice and released a startled cry that mimicked a high-pitched bird call.

"I'm sorry, Bonnie. I didn't mean to scare you."

Placing her hand on her chest, Bonnie sighed.

"I didn't know you were here," she said lifting her voice. "You must not have chores today, so can you play for a while?"

"I can play till my dad gets home."

"You never talk about your mom. Does she live with you?"

Willow, too frightened to tell the truth, scrambled around in her thoughts trying to think of something to say. Finally, she spoke. "She is gone to visit my grandmother who is sick. But she'll be back soon."

"My grandfather was sick before he died. He had trouble breathing. We had to give him a lot of medicine."

"My grandma too."

"My mom says I can't come to your house anymore because no one is home to watch us. You're so lucky you're allowed to stay home by yourself. Mom says when Jenny is another year older she might let us stay home by ourselves for a short while."

Willow wished she could feel lucky about being home alone. *If Bonnie only knew.*

"How do you play Seven Up?" Willow asked.

"First of all, let's play on the driveway. We need a hard surface and a wall to bounce the ball on. You start with sevensies. You bounce the ball seven times against the wall and catch it on the seventh time. Then you do sixies. This time you let it bounce once before catching it. After you do it six times, you go to fivesies..." Bonnie explained the game as they walked to the driveway, talking the whole way.

They stayed in the driveway for a while and when they grew tired of Seven Up, Bonnie suggested they go inside for lemonade. Willow readily obliged. A cool drink was the perfect reprieve from the heat.

"My mom finished the wallpaper. It's so pretty." Bonnie was eager to show Willow the completed wallpaper project.

She led her to the stairway and gestured with her hand as if the wallpaper was making a debut. Along the steps was the boldest pattern Willow had ever seen. Its flowers were bright shades of pinks, orange, and greens with metallic hues intertwined between the petals. Mrs. Murphy was standing at the bottom clutching a laundry basket.

"Hi, Willow." Mrs. Murphy smiled.

"I just wanted to show her the wallpaper," Bonnie stated.

"Do you like it?" Her mother asked.

"Yes, it's so pretty. I wish we could have that in our house," Willow said. Willow's wish wasn't just about having pretty wallpaper but rather her mother at home to make her house pretty.

"Willow's mother is taking care of her grandmother who is sick. That's why she isn't at home," Bonnie explained.

"I'm so sorry, Willow. Would you like to have dinner with us this evening?"

"Thank you, Mrs. Murphy, but, but, I'm not sure my dad would let me. He wants me home for dinner." Willow stammered.

"I see. Well anytime you need anything, you be sure to let me, or Bonnie know."

She wanted to ask Mrs. Murphy to help her with her chores. She wanted to ask her to help her read better. She wanted Mrs. Murphy to make her dad love her and her mother, like Mr. Murphy loves his children and wife. She wanted Mrs. Murphy to bring her mother back. These desires Willow couldn't express. She didn't even know they existed in words, but she felt the aching in her heart every day. Mrs. Murphy couldn't ameliorate her life at home, but her generous invitation made her feel welcome at the Murphys' household.

"Willow, let's go up to my room and play school."

"Ok," Willow agreed. "Do you have any books?"

"I have a whole shelf of books, every book since I was born."

The two thumped up the steps. Bonnie dragged her hand along the newly decorated wall as she ascended. At the top, she paused and called out to her mother. "Mom," she yelled loudly, her shrill voice shot in Willow's eardrum.

"What?" Mrs. Murphy's voice boomed from the kitchen.

"Can we make lunch up in my room?"

"NO!" Her response was swift.

Willow was in awe as she entered Bonnie's room. There was a colorful rope rug on the floor and stuffed animals covered half of her bed. A furry lamb was laying on the pillow with the sheets pulled up over it like it was tucked in for a nap. Some of the small stuffed animals had tissues configured around them as clothes. Across from the bottom of the bed was a backless three-tiered bookshelf painted a matte plum color. The room also contained a white dresser and a matching side table that held a butterfly lamp. Willow frowned when she thought of her nicked dresser and bed with springs so worn, she feared sinking to the floor as she slept at night.

"Let's use the stuffed animals as our students," Bonnie suggested.

They both started collecting stuffed animals and after choosing different corners of the room, they sat their animals up like a class gathered around the teacher, listening attentively. Bonnie gathered some books and brought them to her area. Willow searched carefully to find titles of books she was familiar with. She found one of her favorites, *Bears in the Night* by Jan Berenstain.

In first grade, she checked this out from the school library and her mother read it to her repeatedly until she could read it herself. She checked it out in second grade and in third grade but this past year, Miss Everton, the librarian, told Willow she was too old for this book and must check out the chapter books like the rest of her classmates.

Willow and Bonnie became engrossed in playing school again, and this time, Willow felt safe. There were no newspapers around that could let out secrets. After playing for a while, they grew bored and started drawing figures using her Spirograph. Soon Mrs. Murphy called them to the kitchen for lunch. She set out bread and peanut butter and jelly at the kitchen table where she could keep an eye on them making lunch. This time they put the peanut butter where it belonged. After lunch, they played outside on the back porch. Mr. Murphy was fooling with the irrigation sprinklers in the sunflower field when suddenly, water spewed everywhere.

"Ahh crap," he yelled as a stream of water shot in his face. "A line must have ripped."

Willow and Bonnie giggled at Mr. Murphy's flustered response to having his face doused. He turned in the direction of the girls, who were laughing at his expense. Not looking so pleased, he asked if they would like to be drenched in water. Wrong thing to ask children on a hot summer day, he soon found out. Bonnie shouted to her father that yes, she wanted to run in the sprinkler. Mr. Murphy gave up his fight with the mechanism and set the hose in the yard for them to run through. Bonnie didn't hold back. She took off running across the spray with all her clothes on.

Willow reluctantly joined in after about a minute of watching Bonnie's joy. Her inhibition seeped away after the cool liquid hit her body. She ran back and forth over the shoots of water, in the opposite direction of Bonnie. They slapped hands as they passed each other, back and forth, back, and forth. Then they stopped in the middle, flattening out their hands and pressing them together at shoulder height as the water sprayed upwards between their bodies. Mr. Murphy was just as amused as they were, and the liveliness stirred up quite a commotion. It brought Jenny outside to investigate. She sat on the porch watching but too prudent about keeping her outfit intact to join in.

The amusement went on for a while but then, their attention detoured to a black Buick that pulled in the driveway. Mrs. Murphy went outside to greet the person who sat in the driver's seat. A man's voice spoke but a dark shadow was cast over his face from the sassafras tree and they couldn't see who it was. Willow looked at the position of the sun. It was getting close for Daddy to return from work and she would have to change before he caught her soaked in her clothes. Mr. Murphy had gone around front to see who was in the driveway.

"Bonnie, I really ought to go."

"Are you sure you can't stay a little longer, Willow?"

"Nah. My Daddy will be home soon, and I have to get out of these clothes and get them into the dryer before he notices."

"All right. Will he let you come this evening?"

"Probably not. I'll see you tomorrow, Bonnie. This was really a lot of fun," Willow said, and she ran off past the shanty house to her pathway home. She followed a squirrel, maybe the same one from the first venture to Bartholomew's farm when she met Bonnie. He led her home.

When Bonnie got back to the stoop, there was a note taped to the door. Someone was here again. She took the note and stared at it for a long time. The letters looked like a bunch of lines jumbled on paper. Willow was scared and her head pounded. She didn't have the courage to try to read this but she remembered the rock Miss Kora gave her and began to cry. A teardrop slid onto the paper and landed on the word dad. She put her finger under the letters and sounded out the words as best as she could and read it out loud.

Willow, if you get home without talking to Mrs. Murphy you must go back to their house. Your Dad will not be back. Pack some clothes. You will need to stay at the Murphys' house.

It took Willow three tries before she was able to fully understand what the letter said but somehow, she managed, then stood on the stoop and looked around.

"Who put this note here?" she said out loud. Then she remembered the Murphys talking to the man in the Buick. Maybe he had something to do with this. At once, she ran to her room and stuffed clothes into a paper bag from Powel's grocery store, and ran off to the same path along the sunflower field. Willow stood at the edge and stared at the farmhouse, the house where her best friend lived.

Willow was greeted by Mr. and Mrs. Murphy who stood in the door frame of the front entryway. Mrs. Murphy was holding the door open with her left hand and Mr. Murphy was standing by her side. The atmosphere was tense, not the usual easiness she felt at the Murphys' house. Bonnie and Jenny were not in the living room, and there was not a hint of them being nearby. With sober actions and sorrowful faces, they sat her down on the couch and looked upon her with pity in their eyes. She had been found out. Boxed in by her ignominy, she felt as if Daddy's words were true. She wasn't good enough for people in this town.

"Where's my dad?" Willow asked, frightened by the apprehensive faces of the adults. Their furrowed brows told her it was bad news. Was she in trouble? Daddy told her to stay around the house, but she blew it. He was going to be so angry. Her fears were coming to fruition right here in the Murphys' house.

"Willow," Mrs. Murphy spoke softly, "You're Dad is at the police station. Now, you don't need to worry. They just want to ask him some questions, but he won't be home this evening. Well," she sighed and paused. Willow sensed her reluctance to continue. "He might not be home for a while, but you will stay with us until this is all worked out."

Willow thought about the article in the paper. "Is this about the fire?" She asked.

"We don't know honey. You don't need to worry yourself. You are safe with us until we find out more information." Willow believed that Mrs. Murphy was telling the truth, they didn't know anything.

"Where will I sleep?" Willow inquired.

"You can sleep on the couch if you'd like or in Bonnie's room. I'm sure Bonnie would love to have you sleep in her room. We have a cot you can sleep on."

"OK," Willow agreed shamefacedly.

"Willow this is not your fault and we are happy to have you here. Aren't we honey?" She turned to her husband for reassurance.

"For sure, Willow. You let us know if you need anything."

Willow noticed how Mrs. Murphy called everyone honey. It made her feel welcome. Her own mother called her '*her little strawberry*'. How she missed that affection.

"Bonnie is upstairs in her room if you'd like to go see her while I make dinner. We are having hamburgers tonight with corn on the cob."

"Thank you, Mrs. Murphy."

Willow left the couch and headed for the staircase that led to the second floor. The steps creaked when she placed her foot on each board. As she ascended, she looked at the wallpaper Mrs. Murphy so meticulously put up. Oliver was standing at the top of the steps as if he was waiting for her arrival. She could see the outline of his pointy ears and oval-shaped head. He stared at her with the intuition of a cat. It was like he was saying you'll be with us for a while, welcome. She walked into Bonnie's room and found her lying on her bed reading a chapter book. She turned her attention to Willow.

"Hi, Willow. Mom says you'll be staying here for a little bit. She said your dad had to go somewhere."

Willow's face flushed with warmth, and she placed her hands on her cheeks as if she could stop her embarrassment. "Yes," she said shyly. "Your mom said I can stay in your room on a cot."

"Where do you want to put it? Maybe right beside my bed or at the bottom of the bed. Do you get scared at night?"

"Sometimes, especially if it is storming. I think I'd like the cot beside your bed in case I get scared."

"Good idea and if I get scared, you'll be right there beside me."

Willow liked the idea of having someone to sleep beside. Bonnie's room was bright and filled with fun. She had stuffed animals, books, crayons, coloring books, markers, and paper — all the things that girls their age love. The rope rug in the middle of the room was an array of colors like a 48 numbered crayon box. Her bedspread was a quilt that resembled the collection of colors in the rope rug; it wasn't dingy like her own room. Her mamma had said she was saving money to get her a new comforter and sheet set with pretty flowers, but then something happened to the money. Willow recollected a jar hidden in the pantry where her Mamma started hiding change and bills.

Willow went to the bookshelf and perused through the chapter books, none of which she could read, but she didn't want Bonnie to know. She found the book Mrs. Twine read to the class, "Tales of a Fourth Grade Nothing" by Judy Blume. This one, she knew the story. She could fake her reading as she did so often in school.

"I haven't read that book yet. That was Jenny's book. She gave it to me because she is too grown-up for those types of books now."

"It's one of my favorites," Willow said as if she read it herself.

"What's it about?" Bonnie asked.

"It's about a boy in fourth grade whose little brother is a pest," Willow stated, looking at the summary as she fiddled with the worn corner of the back cover.

"Maybe I'll read it before I start fourth grade. Read me the summary on the back to see if I'll like it."

Willow stared at the words and just like the note left on the door, the lines jumbled. It was like the pieces of the letters were pulled apart, thrown into the air, and dropped onto the paper. She put her finger under the first word. *In*, she recognized, and she knew the rest of the title. She conjured up every bit of confidence thinking about the carnelian rock and began to read. "In Tales, of, Fourth, Grade, Nothing," she said slowly, pausing between each word.

"The mis, mis, mis," she repeated. Her voice tremored and quivered and her palms began to sweat. She fiddled again with the corner of the back cover that had been bent over and creased from wear and tear. If Mamma was here, she would have helped her sound out that word, but it was too long for Willow to decipher the sounds the letters made. In school, she was able to blend into the class. Teachers stopped calling on her to read aloud after they realized how slow and broken, she read but Bonnie, her friend, was unknowingly waiting.

"Go on," Bonnie inoffensively urged Willow.

"I can't, Bonnie. I can't. I just can't."

"Why not?" She asked.

"I can't read too well." Exasperated, Willow's eyes dropped a stream of tears. She put her head down in defeat. The cornelian rock didn't do its magic this time, but then she realized it had been left at home.

"It's all right, Willow. I don't care if you can't read."

"You don't?"

"No. You'll get better. My sister Jenny loves to read and study. She helps me with my homework. Maybe she can help you."

"She can?"

"Yes!" She assured. "Hey, Jenny can you come here?" Bonnie pierced Willow's ear again.

"What do you want?" Jenny yelled back.

"Just come here."

"You don't have to bother your sister." Willow desperately tried to avoid a spectacle about her poor reading skills.

Jenny's door opened and her clogs heavily thumped down the hall. She stood at the doorway of Bonnie's room, seemingly bothered by the interruption.

"Can you help Willow with her reading?"

Jenny's mood shifted to pleasant when she looked at Willow. "Sure, I can read with you. What would you like to read?"

A moment later, Mrs. Murphy called for dinner.

"We can start after dinner, Willow," Jenny stated.

For the first time since Mamma left, Willow didn't feel ashamed about her lack of ability. She didn't have to hide it from Bonnie or Jenny, and they didn't look at her differently because of it.

#

The dishes were cleared from the table and the girls shared in the chore of washing and drying. This evening's tasks went faster with Willow's help, Jenny noted. When the last dish was left to drip in the drying rack, they made a dash for the porch, lugging a basket filled with reading material.

Jenny sat patiently beside Bonnie with a stack of picture books, helping her through each one. Some were familiar to Willow, and she was able to sound out many of the words except the long ones, that's when Jenny helped. She pointed her finger underneath and told Willow what sounds to make. It almost felt the same as Mamma reading with her. They read together until the sun dipped below the horizon and the fireflies started their nightly dance, sprinkling dashes of light in the darkness. The books were dropped hastily on the floor of the porch and the girls ran off in pursuit of the creatures flashing throughout the yard.

The sunflowers stood beyond them in rows only showing the silhouette of their bold, lofty figures. Mrs. Murphy came out holding a jar with holes in the metal lid. Jenny opposed the idea. She explained that the insects ought to be free in their natural habitat and not cooped up in a glass *cage* as she called it. She tried to convince Bonnie, but Bonnie's incorrigible insistence on keeping the fireflies in the jar left Jenny frustrated.

Jenny retreated to the porch to read by the light of a flashlight, while discreetly eyeballing the girls in the yard. They picked grass and dropped it in the jar then added the tiny bugs as they caught them. Soon they had a jar full of lights flashing sporadically, but then dimming to nothing, like silence. Jenny stomped from the porch and emptied the jar.

"What did you do that for?" Bonnie screamed at her sister.

"Bonnie. The bugs will die in the jar."

"No, they won't. That's why mom put holes in the lid. So, they can breathe."

Mrs. Murphy came outside to settle the argument. Jenny huffed. "I'm going to watch television," she shouted and stormed off to the living room.

Bonnie and Willow continued catching fireflies. Some they added to the jar with more grass, others they let go and some they held in their cupped hands which they shaped like a clam shell to keep the tiny insects enclosed. When the thrill of catching fireflies wore off, they ran around the yard with their arms in a t-shape, flying and buzzing like the bugs. They ran in circles so much they became dizzy and fell to the ground with laughter. The air was cooler and as they settled, they stared up at the translucent night sky, freckled with stars.

"The stars look like the fireflies we were catching," Bonnie said.

"Let's try to catch them too." Willow reached in the air and pretended to pull them out of the sky. Bonnie followed her lead. Willow felt as free as the fireflies this evening. Her troubles were as far away as the stars and her heart glowed, just like the fireflies and the stars.

14

Chapter 14

The Message

Often, when Willow visited her mother, the sounds of the drills and hammering pushed them to the outdoors to converse without noisy interruptions. The evenings were growing cooler as the end of summer approached. Willow wore a sweatshirt and long pants to have dinner with her mother. She had stopped at Cinnamon, a restaurant on the south side that is known for its deli sandwiches and delectable desserts. She had been there on a date when she discovered it was a quaint and cozy place to eat a quick meal while having a clear view of the lighthouse and water. The date failed, but the eatery became one of her favorite casual places to dine-in or order take-out. She had asked her mother to meet her for dinner, but Barbara wanted to be at the house to oversee the work being done. '*Just in case Mr. Keller has any questions for me*' her mother had told her. Barbara's contractor was willing to work into the evenings and today they were starting to close in the second floor with drywall. Barbara was meticulous with the details of the renovation. After all, this was going to be her forever house, she had expressed.

Willow carefully pushed the door shut with her shoulder, her purse swinging against the door as it closed making it difficult to juggle the three Styrofoam boxes of food she was clumsily gripping. Lately, she seemed to carry everything from her cosmetic drawer in her purse since she spent more time with her mother overseeing the renovations, which were now steadily transforming the house. The pull of her heavy purse reminded her that it needed to be shed of all the unnecessary items. Barbara was sitting at the table with envelopes stacked beside her checkbook. Willow noticed that familiar worried expression on her face she had seen so many times when Barbara paid bills.

"Mom, is everything all right?" Willow asked.

"Ahh," her mother instinctively let slip from her mouth. "Willow, I didn't hear you come in."

"Oh, I'm sorry Mom. I didn't mean to scare you. I suppose I should have known you couldn't hear the door open with all the noise."

"How did you get in?"

"I used the key you gave me."

Since the renovations started, Barbara had given a key to Willow and the contractor, Mr. Keller, whom she eventually trusted to let come and go as he needed. Barbara now kept the locks secured only at night. Ever since Willow told her mother of Floyd's improved civility, she no longer feared his release from jail as fierce as she once had.

"I would like a little warning when someone sneaks up behind me."

"I wasn't sneaking. You were deeply engaged with your checkbook."

"Yeah that. Don't remind me," Barbara said sounding frustrated.

"Is everything all right? Mom, do you need help financially because you know I can help."

"No, you keep your money, Willow. I never want you to have to worry about money like I had to."

"Mom, I make a decent salary. I can give you some money."

"Willow, you've helped me enough already by feeding me almost every night. I don't want to take any more from you."

"Mom stop letting your pride get in the way. You always told me we're in this together right," she said hoping to remind her mother of the sinews they drew from one another. Ever since they lived on their own, Willow found strength in her mother's nurturing yet firm determination to succeed. She encouraged Willow through every challenged she faced with learning, never letting her believe she couldn't overcome and achieve, and Willow consistently supported her mother's wishes and followed her rules. There was never a time when Barbara couldn't rely on her daughter to do the right thing. They were a formidable team since the day they reunited and ventured away to a new, yet unknown life.

"Mr. Keller has been more than agreeable and kind enough to keep working even though I'm late with the second payment. I'll think about it, Willow."

"All right. You just let me know," Willow said, but she wouldn't let her mother think about it. She would privately talk with Mr. Keller and make the next payment for her mom. "Are you hungry? I brought you your favorite sandwich from Cinnamon, a Reuben, light on the sauerkraut." Willow opened the lid to her mother's meal and placed it in front of her, hoping to entice Barbara to take a break from her finances.

"That smells wonderful. You even got me the homemade garlic chips."

"Wait till you taste what I brought for dessert."

"Is it the chocolate lava cake?"

"You'll have to stop working to find out."

"All right, Willow," Barbara said and begrudgingly pushed her papers aside.

"Trust me. You'll be happy you took a break. In fact, why don't you put it away for the rest of the evening? Tomorrow might bring a clearer picture of the situation."

Barbara contemplated her daughter's supposition for a moment. "I think you a right, Willow. These bills can wait. Mr. Keller has been patient and understanding. I'm sure he's not going to quit working. Putting this off another day or two won't make a difference. Let's eat. I'm starving."

"I knew you'd see it my way."

Willow retrieved the napkins and Barbara brought out a pitcher of water with lemons. They sat at the table and ate while Mr. Keller and his two workers continued the toil upstairs. The noise of the drills and hammering had slowed but then started up again and became distracting, so they took to eating their sandwiches on the patio. The wind blew offshore from the east and the fresh air, although somewhat chilly for outside eating, was a welcome change to the noise that sputtered throughout the house. The sun had dipped and almost met the landscape. The yard was covered in a shadow except for one last beam of sunlight that connected to the Azaleas which lined the back of the yard, a plant ubiquitous in Pequot. Barbara remarked at how sprightly they'd become since she fertilized them.

"Willow, have you heard from your father again?"

"Not since I last saw him at his cabin."

"I know we've talked about this, but you don't think he'll try to find me, being that the restraining order has lifted. I trust what you tell me but it's always in the back of my head that he would follow through with his threat."

"Mom, he seemed different. Now that does not promise he'll never want to try to see you again but my experience with him those two days gave no indication that he would seek to harm you. He was more despondent than threatening and he seems to have a good support group now."

"Willow, I might have seemed overly sensitive today because I got a call from him at the women's shelter."

"You did!" Willow exclaimed. "Why didn't you tell me?"

"I didn't talk to him. Brandy answered the call and left a message for me."

"Is Brandy that woman with the nasally voice that calls everyone dear?"

"Yes, that's her."

"She is, well, different."

"I know, she's a bit gregarious but she works hard and is very dependable. So, what does that man want? I spent many years healing from that marriage."

"Yes, you have, and I don't blame you for never talking to him again.

You have every right to be angry but also know that maybe you need closure too. You haven't talked to him since you disappeared from his life. I'm not saying you should start some sort of reconnection but maybe you ought to tell him how his actions impacted your life so you can let it go once and for all."

"I am angry at him and rightfully so." Barbara implored.

"Yes, rightfully so, but maybe you need to close this with forgiveness. Forgiveness doesn't mean to forget but it just might let you end this chapter in your life. I feel different since I visited Floyd. All those years I wondered what happened to him and wanted to know why."

"Have you forgiven your father?"

Dusk rolled in, making the backyard a dim blur. "Another night, Mom. Just like the bills, some things need to be put aside for the time being. The sun is gone, and we still haven't had our lava cake," Willow noted.

"So, it is lava cake!"

Willow shivered. The air was cooler than it was last night. When she slid the sliding glass door open to step inside, the construction noised had stopped. They saw Mr. Keller's two helpers leave but Mr. Keller had stayed longer tonight. Barbara explained to Willow how each night he meticulously inspected the work that was completed and cleaned up thoroughly before leaving. He appeared at the bottom of the steps just as Willow went to get the dessert from the boxes. He was a tall man with a thin physic and white hair. His glass blue eyes were noticeable against his dark skin tone. The cordial way he addressed Barbara, made Willow feel comfortable approaching him with a payment.

"That will be all for this evening, Ms. Jones. We should finish the drywall tomorrow and then we'll start on building the closets."

"I told you to call me Barbara."

"Do you have any questions, Barbara?"

"No, I don't. You've been very thorough with your explanations, Mr. Keller."

"Call me Bill."

"All right Bill," Barbara acknowledged his request.

Willow was heating up the cake and had placed a piece for herself and Barbara on two plates when she realized the deli gave her an extra one.

"Mr. Keller, would you like to stay and have some cake with us?"

"I shouldn't. I wouldn't want to impose."

"You're not imposing Bill," Barbara added.

"Well, I don't have to meet any clients this evening. Sure, why not."

Mr. Keller decisively chose a chair directly across from her mother, Willow noticed, and her mother seemed quite comfortable having him there. While they were eating, she saw how Mr. Keller set his eyes on Barbara as if he were admiring a fine piece of art. She seemed to welcome these secretive glances, and her smile widened considerably when she caught him looking at her. Barbara had kept up her appearance over the years, not looking a bit her age. She highlighted her hair with an auburn shade and her cheeks were plump with a soft rose coloring against her milky skin. She worked to keep a slim figure with regular exercise and consistent healthy eating. Lava cake was a rare treat.

After dessert was finished, Mr. Keller recapped what he would be working on next before he left. Willow said goodbye to her mother. She gave her a tight hug and Barbara returned the same affection. When the door shut, she heard the clinks of the three locks. Willow hurried home, for she wanted to bask in a warm bath and snuggle into her comfortable bed. She noticed the blinking light of her answering machine as usual and thought it could wait till the morning to be listened to, but for some reason, she felt an urgency to hear her messages.

The first message was a call from her car insurance company. "Hi, Miss Jones. We were reviewing your file and wanted to go over the current policies you have and see if we could better serve you. We would like to offer you a car insurance and rental insurance combination policy that could save you money. Please give us a call back at your earliest convenience. My name is Juanita. You can call me at 1-800-555-5467.

The next message was from a neighbor. "Hi Willow, this is Sammy. I'm leaving out of town next weekend and I was wondering if you could feed Coco for me and clean out the litter while I'm away. Just give me a call when you get a chance. Thank you, Willow."

The third message played. "Hello, Willow. This is an old friend. Someone you haven't seen or talked to in a very long time. My mother gave me your number. I've been thinking about you all these years and I would love it if we could reconnect again. This is Bonnie by the way if you haven't already guessed. I'm living in the mountains on the other side of the valley. Call me, but not tonight because I have a date. Call me tomorrow if you can at 412-555-6971."

#

The reunion with Bonnie was unexpectedly an easy transition from childhood playmates to an adult friendship. Their cadence seemed to pick back up as if they were never apart. Awkward silences and grabbling for words were nonexistent in their phone conversations and they both knew that an in-person visit was exactly what they needed to reunite the bond that had formed so long ago, a bond they had been forced to break at no fault of their own.

Willow took vacation time and drove to the mountains. When she started her drive, she took delight in noticing the landscape along the way. The smooth flatness of the land turned into arduous ups and downs and twisty mountain roads that put a strain on her car, but she welcomed the picturesque sights of the journey. Willow meandered through the last stretch of the trip tracking her mileage while corroborating it with the written route Bonnie explained over the phone a few days before her departure. Willow had difficulty reading her own handwriting because Bonnie was late for a pottery class and talked quickly, spewing out the directions. It was just like her to be dashing off to another engagement. Since the day Willow received the message from Bonnie on her answering machine, they called each other at least once a week. Catching up was effortless as if time hadn't passed.

Bonnie's house was set back off the road, and her property was carved out by tall pines. The white modular home's rectangular shape resembled a shoe box with a roof. It was simple yet interesting with all the objects that were scattered around the house. There were ceramic pots of different colors and sizes scattered on a deck that jetted from the front of the house and was protectively covered by an awning. Her dogs were barking at Willow pulling into the stony driveway and ran toward the car as if giving their welcome. Bonnie, unheeded by the sound of the dogs, did not come outside to find the reason for the barking. She was probably distracted by some impetuous idea and didn't realize a visitor had come to the house, Willow surmised. The side of her house was lined with sunflowers, withering, and slumped forward, obviously at the end of their cycle. Willow rang the bell and peered inside the door, her eyes searching for her friend. She was sure she'd recognized her from the senior picture her mother displayed on the wall alongside her sister. Bonnie had long wavy reddish-brown hair. It was cut in long layers and the bangs were puffy and fanned out, covering her entire forehead. She was draped in a black velvet cloth with small beady pearls around her neck. She had a pretty smile that bared a perfectly aligned set of unblemished teeth. Willow rang once more, and Bonnie appeared almost instantaneously before the door as if she had been there all along. Her face held the same youthful beauty of her senior picture, but her hair was longer and straight. Her bangs were flat against her forehead.

"Willow Hitchens," Bonnie announced with the same robustness she portrayed the day she beckoned her to climb the sassafras tree.

"Bonnie Murphy," Willow replied. She felt a poignant sense of excitement rise through her chest.

"Come in, come in." Bonnie reached out and hugged Willow and in return, Willow held onto her as if stretching out one of life's momentous moments. Her eyes watered for the happiness that had filled this longing sensation of seeing Bonnie again.

"Bonnie. I love your place and you have quite a few dogs." She wiped the wet from the corner of her right eye with her finger, hoping Bonnie didn't notice.

"Just four. The golden lab, I found at the shelter, and then she had puppies. I kept two and gave away the rest. Then the shepherd, collie, whatever mix, he wandered into my yard one day and never left, so I just kept him."

"What are their names?"

"The mother is named Sara and her two girls are named Sadie and Sunny. The male dog is Sam. It's easier for me to remember if I start them all with the same letter."

A cat sauntered into the room to greet Willow. Bonnie noticed and picked her up, pecking her cheek. The cat squeaked and squirmed, trying to wriggle out of Bonnie's grip. Bonnie held onto her and the cat submitted, relaxing in her friend's arms.

"This here is Sassy cat. She doesn't like to be picked up but loves to cuddle with me when I sleep. She only likes affection when it's on her terms and only when it's me. When Scott comes over, she hides under the bed."

"Scott is your boyfriend, I presume."

"Yes, he's a drummer in a band. We are on again and off again. That's how it goes with a musician."

"All these S's. How do you keep from twisting your tongue when you're calling your pets and your boyfriend?" Willow asked.

"You can include him with the pets," Bonnie jested. "I get them mixed up all the time, but all my dogs stick together so it doesn't pose a problem when I call the wrong name. When I call one, they all come. And the cat, well she does her own thing, so the names don't really apply around this house."

"How was your ride?" Bonnie asked. "I hope my directions were right."

"Yep, mostly. I did have to stop once at a gas station and ask for clarification, but I think that was because of my bad handwriting. Should I get my bags from the car?"

"Of course. Make yourself at home. I don't have much in the fridge but help yourself to whatever you like."

"I noticed the sunflowers growing on the side of your house," Willow stated.

"I planted those in late June. They grew tall this year. I think as tall as the crop that grew when we were kids. Amazing! I always have to pick a flower that needs full sun and weirdly enough, this is the first summer I decided to plant sunflowers and then you reappeared in my life."

"That is strange. It's like it was meant to be," Willow grinned. "You know I never got to harvest the seeds that summer. How did that go?"

"That was quite a time. At first, it was fun but then my fingers bristled from the dried-up edges of the plant. I wanted to quit but my dad kept pushing us to keep going. He kept us harvesting until we had buckets full of seeds."

"I would have loved to have been there."

"Well, you're in luck, Willow Hitchens. I started pulling some seeds from the flower heads yesterday but there's more to be done. We can do it tonight after you get settled. Why don't you get your things and I'll show you to the guest room?"

Willow retrieved her items from her sedan and settled them into a small bedroom next to Bonnie's, the second of only two bedrooms. Bonnie's house was tiny and simple but filled with eclectic pieces of her life. The dogs loyally followed Willow along the way and saw that she settled into the guest room, crowded with boxes, apparently the room was also used as storage. Willow found a place to put her bags and joined Bonnie in the living room where she was sifting through packages of clay and sculpting tools, on a mission.

"Are you looking for something?" Willow asked.

"I'm trying to find a particular tool I need to finish off a pot."

"Do you sell your pottery?" Willow asked.

"Most of it, I try to sell at a few local tourist shops. It goes better during peak tourist season which seems to be growing. I moved to these mountains because as a kid, we came here at least once a year to camp, and I fell in love with the area. Now it's overrun with tourists; however, it keeps me working, so I'm not complaining."

"Tell me about your work. Your mother told me you are a curator and you sell pottery, which is obvious."

"Yep, that is exactly what I do. Tomorrow, I'll show you around and take you by some of the museums I work for."

"That sounds great."

"And you'll have to tell me more about your job. What you told me so far is interesting. I don't know how you listen to other people's problems all day, but you obviously have the patience."

"I just do. Haven't I told you enough about my job over the phone?" Willow joked. "I'm so happy to get away from it."

"We don't have to talk about it." Bonnie smiled and changed the subject to dinner. "I don't have that much food in the house, but I have a package of hotdogs. Why don't we make a fire and roast some hotdogs and drink a few beers a little later?"

"That sounds like a wonderful idea. I'm going to change out of these traveling clothes if you don't mind."

"I'll get the firewood ready for our bonfire. When the sun goes down, we'll sit outside."

Willow agreed and went to the guest room to change and rest before the evening's fire. When twilight appeared, Bonnie and Willow went outside and set chairs beside a stone firepit. Bonnie carried a tray of hotdogs and chips, and two poker forks for roasting. The wood Bonnie stacked in her yard was a rather large stack for one person, and Willow suspected making fires were a regular occurrence. The fire that evening roared with heat and accompanied long conversations between friends while picking seeds out of sunflower heads. They swapped stories of college and failed relationships. Bonnie listened with compassion as Willow revealed the struggles, she and her mother had after fleeing Sol Valley. Bonnie told stories of her adventures into some of the most beautiful state parks in the country. She worked long, demanding hours, but it was well worth the effort when a piece of history was unearthed. Eventually, she grew tired of living in tents and jetting from one site to another without a day off. Her body longed for the comforts that one would find in a home, so she applied for a job working for the state parks and a month later, she was living in this house. This was her third year here. The catching up led to a late evening and it was one in the morning before they crawled into bed.

After a breakfast of toast and coffee, Willow and Bonnie ventured among the mountains, visiting the museums, scattered on the edges of the park, where Bonnie worked. She was responsible for keeping records of the collections and organizing exhibits. She led tours and had to learn a plethora of information about the acquisitions brought to the museums. Their jobs were opposite, Willow noted. While her job took her to one place and one task, to help people work through problems, Bonnie's led her to delve into the past. Each day for her was different and every day for Willow was the same office, although different people and problems. A picnic lunch in the forest ensued after visiting the museums. After several hours of eating and relaxing, they regained their energy and ventured on a trail to one of the waterfalls. Willow and Bonnie lived in two very different places, but each had its own niche in the world of tourism and a reason for visitors to leave with a sense of being whisked away to a unique place. Willow told her friend about the town she lived in and invited Bonnie to visit her in Pequot one day.

That evening, they dined in a restaurant in a small bustling town nestled among the mountains. Scott showed up after dinner for drinks just before his next gig. He was polite, engaging in conversation but seemed rushed. He commented that Bonnie had told him stories of her summer when she met Willow. He had the same reddish-brown hair as her friend and almost the same length, but it made them fit snuggly as a couple. He seemed to be attentive in her presence, but it wasn't long before he excused himself and before he left, he invited Willow and Bonnie to see his band play. When the waitress came with the check, Bonnie offered to take care of the bill and before Willow had a chance to reach into her purse, Bonnie took out her cash and placed it on top of the check for the waitress to collect.

"You can get the next one," she slipped in before Willow could disagree.

"Thank you, Bonnie. I could get us some drinks tonight while we watch your boyfriend's band."

"Are you ok with going? I've seen him play many times so if you want to go home, we can."

"No, I think it sounds like a blast. It's been a while since I've been out. What does he play again?"

"The drums. But I must warn you, it's a heavy metal rock. Some of which is extremely loud. I'm sure I've lost some of my hearing since we've been dating," Bonnie teased.

"I'm ready for a change of pace. I don't go out much in Pequot besides work. My life is busy helping my mother right now." Willow explained the house renovation that had her so engrossed in her mother's life.

The reunited friends were peppy as they left the restaurant, excited for what the night may bring. Willow was out of her comfort zone, for it had been years since she went to see bands playing at bars, but she reveled in the change of pace. Hours sitting in an office day in and day out, and the reunion with Bonnie left her with a need to unleash something pent up, something she couldn't quite put her finger on. Perhaps she slipped back into the way she felt when she and Bonnie were playing in the sunflowers, climbing the Sassafras tree, or visiting Miss Kora's cottage. Whatever it was, it felt freeing, as if she was experiencing that summer again.

Bonnie was right, the band was loud, but Willow didn't care. She danced, bought drinks, and met the other band members on a break. Bonnie declined another drink after two since she was driving, but Willow had more. She felt relaxed. Bonnie danced with her and after the night drifted into the morning, men sent secretive glances her way, all of which she ignored. Experiences of meeting a man in this type of place never turned out well and besides, she was here to be with Bonnie. They rocked out to grunge and punk rock covers that Scott's band played. By two A.M., they were tuckered, and their bodies hurt. When the band played the last song on the playlist, they re-entered the stage at the urging of the crowd who was shouting *encore, encore* and when the playing finally ceased, Bonnie made a beeline for Scott. She hugged him and kissed him goodnight. On the drive back, they complained of ringing ears and sore necks but laughing all the way home. Back at the house, Bonnie checked that her animals were safely inside, the doors were locked, and Willow was set to sleep for the night. And two minutes after she laid her head on the pillow, she felt tiny paws stepping on the side of her body. Sassy settled in the curve of Willow's body. She felt the soft fur of the animal and its vibrations when it purred and remembered Oliver.

#

I heard people say if you see a friend you haven't seen in a long time and you pick up right where you left off, that's a true friend, which is exactly what happened with Bonnie and me. The fact that she had sunflowers growing in her yard and I showed up just in time to pick the seeds was like magic. We literally picked up where we left off in the cycle of the sunflowers. I noticed how Bonnie's boyfriend learned about me through her recollections of the summer we spent together. She thought about me too over the years. We'd been apart but our bond was never broken. I've read bits and pieces of information over the years about various flowers, trying to learn how to garden. I had the idea that I would grow flowers to make our rundown homes look beautiful, but my mother and I would have to move to another place before my notion could come to completion. Somewhere along the way, I learned that sunflowers represent loyalty because of their devotion to the sun.

Bonnie once again brought out a different side of me. I was free again. It seems as if every decision I made since stowing away with my mother was judicious, well thought out, and done with precision. I never allowed myself to throw caution to the wind as they say, like I did with Bonnie. The week in the mountains was filled with the wonder we captured as children. Hiking the trails along rushing water swept me back to the day I almost fell through the suspension bridge. I was scared but it was well worth the effort to keep going for what awaited us at the top of the hill. While the picture in my mind has faded a bit over the years, the solace in my heart never will. I was safe again with Bonnie.

15

Chapter 15

Be Not Afraid

Willow had been with the Murphys for almost a week and Daddy still hadn't come home. The Murphys haven't mentioned another word of his whereabouts, except for what they told her on the first night she stayed. If Daddy did set the fire at the Fereebe's place, then maybe he did something to Mamma. Mamma had a bruised eye one time, Willow remembered. She told Willow she walked into a door, but now Willow wondered if that was a fib. When her dad became angry, the kind of anger that would cause Mamma to send Willow away to her room, Willow would cover her ears and sing that special song from church. The song that gives you courage, Mamma always said. "Be not afraid, I go before you always, come follow me and I will give you rest." Willow sang this every night in her head since she'd been at the Murphys.

Willow, lying on her side, was awoken to Oliver walking on her. His tiny paws pressed into her skin as he crept delicately along the edge of her frame and stopped when he reached her head. Then he draped his body over her back. His head faced hers and he poked the tip of his nose into her cheek a few times to wake her up. She was tickled by his whiskers. She laid still, relishing the feel of his soft fur on her neck and shoulders, and the calming effect from his purring. Bonnie still slumbered in bed next to her cot. She usually slept later, and Willow would not go downstairs alone, where she could hear dishes clinking and food being prepared, so as per usual, she waited patiently, thinking about Mamma, and praying for her to come back.

Today was Saturday. Mr. Murphy had tested his crop of sweet corn Friday for the milky secretion that came when it was ripe and discovered it was ready for harvesting. He was going to take a trip into town this morning for supplies, and he invited the girls to ride in the back of the truck. Willow had a sense of stirring anticipation waiting for this. It wasn't often that a joust to town presented itself, especially in the back of a truck. She had ridden in the bed of Daddy's truck before and recollected the exuberance she felt when the wind blew through her hair as the truck sped along the highway. Today she would get to do that with Bonnie.

Moments later, Mrs. Murphy poked her head in the room, summoned them to breakfast, and left as hastily as she came. Bonnie groggily told Willow good morning as she reached for Oliver, who was still lying on the cot. Oliver, being an agreeable cat, did not object. She lifted him above her, leaving his limbs and head dangling over her body. He started batting in the air with his paw like he was shooing at some dangling object and subsequently, wriggled out of Bonnie's hands to pounce on her chest. He continued batting at the ripple in the cover in a playful manner. Willow lifted sideways, supporting her body with her elbow, and craned her neck to watch. The door opened again.

"Bonnie, didn't you hear mom? It's time for breakfast. Now get up," Jenny succinctly commanded. She was still in her pajamas but had a flowered pinafore tied around her waist and was holding a metal spatula in her hand. She looked as if she wanted to swat her sister with it. She left the door wide open as she plodded downstairs. Oliver jumped off the bed and followed Jenny out the door.

"She thinks she is the boss of me," Bonnie replied disconcertedly. "Today, Willow, we are going to town with my dad. I can't wait. Can you?" Bonnie's capricious flip in manner befuddled Willow.

"What?"

"We are going to town today with my mom and dad. Are you as excited as me?" She asked again.

"Oh, that yes! I can't wait Bonnie. It's been a while since I've been to town or have been anywhere besides Old Rock Road or Marshland Road."

The girls climbed from their beds and found the rest of the Murphys in the kitchen, sitting at the table. It was set with dishes, utensils, and amber-colored glasses filled with orange juice. Mr. Murphy was at the table with the rest of the family; he was usually out in the fields by now. A stack of pancakes, eggs, and bacon was in the center of the white oval Formica topped table.

Willow liked the comfortable, vinyl upholstered, bucket seats that went with it. She noticed the way the seats let out a puff of air each time she sat on the cushion. After a prayer of thanks, the family dug in filling their plates with breakfast. Willow waited. She didn't feel it was her place to take the food before everyone got their share but as always, Mrs. Murphy told her not to be shy and eat.

When breakfast was finished, Jenny implored Bonnie to help with the dishes. The routines of the meals remained constant since she had been with the Murphys. They prayed, ate and Jenny and Bonnie had to help with the clean-up. It was a routine she was unaccustomed to, but one she began to anticipate with delight. She hadn't had to worry about where her next meal was coming from or the tumult that would stir up in her stomach right before bed or searching through the kitchen for a morsel of fresh food. She wasn't inundated with chores or fears or loneliness.

Breakfast was cleaned and the girls promptly dressed in their play clothes putting on shorts, T-shirts, and sneakers with tube socks. Jenny took time to curl her hair and apply blush, mascara, and lip gloss. She wore a blue shadow that almost matched the color of her eyes. Mr. Murphy started up the engine of his truck and saw that the girls were seated in the bed, leaning against the sides, before he latched the door of the bed that had the letters FORD all in capitals. Mrs. Murphy sat in the cab. Oliver watched them from the front porch as they backed down the driveway and turned on Marshland Road, heading in the direction of town.

As the truck accelerated, the girls gripped the handles that were attached to the sides of the bed. The opaque sky shielded them from an overbearing heat, and the wind blew their hair back, surrounding them with a tunnel of cool air. Mrs. Murphy fiddled with the knobs of the radio, to tune in a station. The sound of an electric guitar and singing were sonorous, but they couldn't tell what the words were saying. Still, they bobbed their heads in beat with the music. Today, Willow felt rid of the tarnish that had painted her life.

When they arrived in town, Mr. Murphy's first stop was the hardware store. A man named Pete worked at the counter, who seemed to personally know the Murphys. He greeted them and they conversed for a few minutes before Mr. and Mrs. Murphy indicated they were ready to shop.

" Whatcha lookin' for, Murphy?" Pete inquired.

"I need some parts for my tractor and grain bags. The sweet corn is ready for harvesting and it seems my Dad's tractor needs a new latch for the mounted corn picker. He had it girded with a belt when I found it in the barn. And I need a new gas can."

Mrs. Murphy politely interrupted. "Pete, do you have canning jars in stock? Sorry to interrupt." She added.

"No problem. Yes, we just got a load in. Look on aisle five, near the back." Mrs. Murphy thanked him and left on her quest for the jars. Jenny followed her. Willow and Bonnie stood by Mr. Murphy looking at the prizes in the gumball machine.

"I just sold you a gas can when you were planting the corn."

"I thought so, but I seem to be missing my five-gallon can. I will need one during corn pickin'. I don't want to be in the middle of a job and have to run to town for more gas."

"Follow me and I'll fix you up with what you need."

They finished at the hardware store, and their next stop was the gas station where Mr. Murphy had the attendant fill up the truck and the gas cans, the one he brought with him as well as the new one. Willow and Bonnie watched the man clean the windshield of the truck with the squeegee. Then they were off to Powel's market for groceries. The cart was full of fruits and vegetables, milk, boxes of cereal, and meats. Willow had never seen a shopping cart so full, and she thought it should last a while.

When they were leaving, they spotted Joseph pulling out of Lucille's as they were loading the supplies into the bed of the truck. Mr. Murphy watched as he quickly crossed the road and pulled up next to them. He had a Buick that looked exactly as the Buick in the Murphys' driveway the night Daddy was taken into custody. He sat in the parking lot idling his car as he talked with the Murphys. Willow noticed he kept glancing at her during the conversation. When they finished talking, he waved at her and then at Jenny and Bonnie.

#

The trip into the town tired them out. Willow, Bonnie, and Jenny spent a few hours under the shade of the sassafras tree reading with Oliver, who was taking turns sitting in their laps and looking at the pages of the books as if he was reading too. Mrs. Murphy stayed in the house sterilizing the jars she would use to store corn that they weren't selling, and Mr. Murphy had disappeared to the barn. The time came for dinner. Jenny once again helped her mother prepare the meal. Bonnie and Willow set the table. Dinner led to a conversation of the sunflowers, started by Jenny, who always had an inquisitive mind.

"Dad, how long will it take the sunflowers to develop their seeds?"

"It will be a month or so. They haven't reached their full height yet."

"When will that happen?" Bonnie asked.

"My girl, that will happen within the next two weeks. We are nearing August and soon the sunflowers will be at their tallest height; the flowers will be wide open and swarming with bees."

"Why will the bees swarm the flowers?" Bonnie asked.

"Bees are part of the pollination process and will fertilize the seeds,

Bonnie," Jenny chimed in as she was so often inclined to show off to Bonnie her propensity for knowing scientific facts.

Bonnie retorted with, "You think you know everything." She stuck her tongue out at Jenny when her parents weren't looking.

Mrs. Murphy told her to shush and Mr. Murphy assured Bonnie that her sister was right. Bonnie quailed at her parents' response but quickly shrugged off her irritation.

"So, after the pollination, the seeds will grow Dad?" Bonnie asked.

"That's right, Bonnie. You are a quick learner."

Bonnie turned to her sister and flashed a curt smiled as she tilted her head. A loud ha would have erupted out of her mouth if Mr. and Mrs. Murphy weren't at the table. Jenny rolled her eyes in return.

Mr. Murphy continued, "When the flowers are ripe, we will cut the heads and can harvest the seeds."

"Will the seeds spit out a milky white liquid like the corn when it's ripe?" Bonnie asked.

"No, Bonnie, this isn't corn," Jenny barked at her.

This time Mrs. Murphy told Jenny to shush.

Mr. Murphy answered her question. "When the flower begins to droop, we will check the back of the flower head. When it starts browning and the petals are drying up, then it will be time to harvest the seeds."

"Will you use the tractor to cut the plants like the corn?" Willow asked.

"No, Willow. Good question. You cut the stalk about eight inches from the flower. Then you scrape off the dried flower structure and the seeds easily come out. You can pull the seeds out with your finger or cut the flower head and scrape them out into a bucket. It's easy. You girls will be able to do it by yourselves once I cut the flowers."

"I can't wait. I love to eat sunflower seeds," Bonnie exclaimed as she elevated her voice with excitement.

Willow didn't' know if she'd be here for this event. If Daddy came back home, he wouldn't let her out. She wished deep in her heart she could see this part of the cycle. She wished she could have a family like Bonnie's.

#

Dusk arrived on time at the farmhouse. This evening, the Murphys would relax with music as they continued their Saturday evening tradition of listening to albums on the record player. The record player was its own entity, a cabinet in the corner of the living room, next to the new television. The wooden rectangular box that sat off the floor on top of four wooden legs had a door in the center that could be lifted and propped up with a metal arm. Underneath that door was the turntable. The speakers sat evenly spaced on both sides, with a line of knobs in front that could tune in radio stations. The front was covered with a porous screen to release the sound of the tunes being played. Tonight's selection was a mixture of Elvis, The Mammas & the Pappas, and Neil Diamond. The Murphys kept a collection of albums and 45's stored in their cabinet and often picked up new selections when they went to Powel's, which had a portion of the store that sold vinyl records. Today, before checkout, Mrs. Murphy had found a new one that she was anxious to listen to this evening.

Willow, Bonnie, and Jenny were playing card games lying on the living room floor with Mrs. Murphy. She taught Willow how to play solitaire. Bonnie watched over her shoulder, offering her hints as she flipped the cards and moved them into descending stacks. Mr. Murphy was picking vegetables from the garden. He brought a colander of fresh green beans and sat it on the kitchen counter. Mrs. Murphy left the card games in the living room to inspect what he gathered. Willow heard the water gush from the faucet. Soon both parents were back in the living room pulling the square, thin cardboard albums from the cabinet. Mr. Murphy gently slid one out and held it in place between the palms of his hands careful not to touch the smooth surface with his fingertips.

"Put it on darling," Mrs. Murphy urged.

Willow's parents didn't own a record player, but she knew how they worked because Mrs. Twine would play music after reading. She always noticed how carefully Mrs. Twine would set the needle on the edge of the round disc. She would hear a few scratchy sounds before the music started. Mr. Murphy took the same care when he slipped the album on the machine and set the needle in place. Music filled the room. The girls continued playing cards and Mr. and Mrs. Murphy went to the dining room table to play a different game with each other. The daylight dimmed and the dark sky made the inside lights brighter. Jenny, in search of celestial displays, suggested they go out on the porch to look at the sky. The clouds in the sky broke in the late afternoon and this evening was clear and peppered with stars. They sat on the steps. Willow had to keep swiping her arm to swish away mosquitos. The sound of the crickets filled the air and they could hear the music playing from inside the house. Jenny intently inspected the sky.

"There it is!" Jenny yelled.

"What?" Bonnie inquired.

"Leo the Lion." Jenny's head was tipped, and her eyes were fixed on the sky.

"Leo the Lion?" Bonnie asked.

"Yes, the constellations. I've been looking for that one," she replied and ran in the house, the screen door slamming behind her. Moments later with a book in her hand, Jenny was back outside, flipping through pages. She searched the details on the page then poked at the dots in the sky with the tip of her finger.

"Is it Leo the Lion, the one you've been looking for?" Willow asked moving herself next to Jenny, peering at the page.

"Yes!"

Willow and Bonnie joined Jenny in viewing the patterns of stars. Bonnie said she thought she saw Leo the Lion but was unconvincing with the way she softly spoke. Willow had no clue. All she saw was a random order of stars. She tried looking at the example in the book, but she couldn't make sense of it. What she was able to distinguish was the word ***Constellation*** in bold print. She read it out loud, **Constellation Guide**. Jenny instantly retracted her attention from the sky.

"Willow, you read that long word. You can read Willow."

Willow was not sure she wholeheartedly believed the words Jenny just spoke, but she did read, probably the longest word she ever read, without stumbling. She felt her heart twinkle like the stars of Leo the Lion.

Moments later the music turned louder, and its sound waves traveled through the screen door and vibrated the porch. Mrs. Murphy had finally put on her new Neil Diamond album. Bonnie and Jenny looked at one another like they were embarrassed of the loud music blaring from the house and after they glanced around the front yard to where no one except Mr. Mann or Miss Kora would hear the loud display of music, they laughed.

"Mom and dad are blasting their music again, "Jenny spoke loudly.

Bonnie started dancing and singing with the music. "She got the way to move me, Cherry. She got the way to groove me." And she added her own "yeah" to the end of the lyrics. Bonnie grabbed Willow's hands, pulled her to the yard, and twirled her around. Their hands stayed glued together while they circled, and their arms twisted with each turn. Willow moved her body in time with Bonnie, spinning and turning, spinning, and turning under Leo the Lion.

16

Chapter 16

The Second Floor

The summer tourist season in Pequot dwindled and visitors who came to the area this time of the year, were there to visit the museum. The beach was empty, except for occasional fishing and people strolling along the shoreline. Willow welcomed the quiet and settled atmosphere and found herself spending more time near the water, looking up at the constellations. Every Saturday since visiting Bonnie, she had lunch at Cinnamon, the deli where she could indulge in tasty food while watching the rhythmic motion of the water. Occasionally, her mother would meet her, but Barbara was spending most of her time at home watching the renovations of the second-floor morph into a spacious and livable area. Other times a friend or co-worker would be available but when no one was, Willow didn't mind going alone. So, by one in the afternoon, after reading some new research from Psychology Journal, she ventured from her cozy condo to the quaint hamlet of shops near the coast and had lunch once again at Cinnamon. Today she was alone but brought the notes she took from her morning of reading. Wanting to keep her new discoveries fresh in her head, she planned on studying while eating. After ordering and settling into an unnoticeable seat in the corner of the restaurant, her phone rang. Willow had finally bought a mobile phone and had found it useful for her job when she needed to answer an emergency call from a client. Today's call was from Barbara.

"Willow, this is your mother. Where are you, sweetie? I just tried your condo phone." The line was slightly static, and she had to push one ear close to understand her mother's words.

"I'm at Cinnamon. I come here most Saturdays for lunch."

"Oh, of course. Well, uh umm," Barbara cleared her throat. She sounded raspy like she had a touch of something. "Can you come over when you are finished? Bill is just about done wrapping up the final touches on the second floor and I want you to see it."

"Are you ok, mom? You sound like you have a cold."

"Yes, with the weather change, my throat has been sore and I'm starting to sneeze. I do think a cold is coming on but I'm fine. Can you come over?" She asked again.

"I'll be right over after I finish up here. Do you want anything? I can bring something over for you and whoever is working."

"It's just Bill and me. And no, we already had lunch."

"We," Willow noted. "This is getting a little bit beyond being your contractor, I've noticed."

"Willow stop."

Barbara's futile attempts at dating gave Willow little hope in her mother's romantic life. If she ever got close to a man, Barbara would find a reason to break it off. *It wasn't the right time*, or *we're just not compatible*, she would say, and usually by the second date, she found faults that carved doubts in her mind. Willow understood the caution she took each time a man showed interest but hoped that one day her mother would allow herself to be loved by a man who would treat her the way she deserved. Her protective nature of her mother was innate so of course, willow would have to approve, and she had become fond of Mr. Keller's genial nature toward her mother. His furtive way of bringing her gifts led Willow to believe he must have sensed that she was strongly adamant about being independent. When he brought her something, he did it in such a way she couldn't refuse, and she was always delighted. He would bring her a cup of coffee and say they gave me the wrong kind so I got this extra and I thought you would like it. He finished the new bathroom ahead of schedule because he heard her say her lower floor bathroom was uncomfortably tiny. Willow didn't know any contractors that worked as late as he did, and she suspected it was because of Barbara that his day ended at eight or nine in the evening. Willow smiled as she thought about all these kind gestures.

"I'll be there as soon as I'm done."

"Thank you, sweetie. Bye now."

"Bye, mom. See you soon."

Willow shivered as a gust of wind blew against her body when she pushed the door open. The car engine rattled after she turned on the heater to full blast. She drove away from the bay, passing the lighthouse along the way, and wound around Pequot Avenue. The air blowing from the vent had barely warmed her hands when she arrived in the neighborhood. She delighted at the sight of a group of children playing in the leaves, it reminded her that images like that from her childhood were almost nonexistent. She parked in her normal spot in the driveway next to her mother's car, the Honda Civic and she noticed Mr. Keller's work truck parked in the street. The sign on the door read Keller Designs of Pequot and included a lighthouse symbol beside the phone number. The truck was quite polished for being a work vehicle, an indication of Mr. Keller's work ethic Willow concluded. She was finally warm before she stepped out of her sedan. When Willow unlocked the door with her key, she heard voices coming from upstairs.

"Splendid!" She heard her mother belt which piqued Willow's excitement about seeing half of the project done.

"Mom, I'm here."

"Willow is that you? Hang on a minute. Bill needs to finish something before you see it." She called from upstairs.

Her voice widened as she spoke, and Willow heard her scampering down the steps. Her mother was dressed fancy for a Saturday afternoon. Not like she was attending an evening event, but her khakis were ironed, and she wore a cashmere sky blue sweater with boots. Her make-up and hair, styled in loose curls, were fixed as if it were a weekday. She looked attractive.

"I'm so glad you came. I can't wait for you to see it. Can I get you something to drink?" She hugged Willow affectionately.

"No thank you. I just came from lunch."

"I know."

"Ok ladies. You both can come up now." They heard a deep, eager voice call from upstairs.

"We're coming," Barbara answered back with the same enthusiasm.

They are acting like two people who have become quite comfortable around each other, Willow thought. She followed her mother up the maple wood steps. The white clapboard walls of the stairwell and hallway were lit with pendant lights. The once small upstairs that felt closed in by slanted walls was erected into a three-bedroom and one-bathroom floor. Two of the rooms were spacious, while the third one was a bit smaller and could be used for an office or reading room if a third bedroom was not needed. In Barbara's case, she announced that it would be used as an office, a perfect place to put the new computer she planned on purchasing. The wood flooring extended in the hallway, but the bedrooms were covered with soft, beige carpeting. A similar-sized crown molding was paired with the baseboards. Every detail of the renovation was completed to perfection and every line of flooring, baseboard, and paint was seamless. In the smallest room, on the east side of the house, there was a round window. It was the one salvaged piece that didn't quite fit the style but added an eccentric charm. Mr. Keller had sanded it down to the bare wood and painted it a cotton blue. The same blue as the lighthouse and it resembled the round window of it as well. There were two panes that latched in the center where it could open, and Barbara made it a point to show Willow. She sauntered to the window and pulled the latch. A cool breeze wafted inside and refreshed the air. Barbara motioned for her to peek outside. The water and the lighthouse could be seen in the distance and the ocean pervaded her sense of smell. She could picture her mother working at a desk and taking a break to gaze out the window. What a lovely place to work, Willow thought.

"This is a nice sentiment to put this window here and seeing the lighthouse in the distance is like seeing your beacon of hope in the night. How clever! Where was it before?" Willow asked.

"It was in the gable above the front door," Barbara answered.

"Funny, I didn't remember it."

"Maybe because it was so weathered and dull," Mr. Keller stated.

"Bill revitalized the window," Barbara added.

Willow, intrigued by her mother's quick response to complement Mr. Keller, was distracted by her thoughts and didn't notice the two of them descending the steps as they engrossed in discussion. Willow followed behind their path to the kitchen, where they were now unraveling the blueprints of the bottom floor. She saw her mother point out something in the plans and remark that she would like to have a doorway put in between the kitchen and front room so she could turn it into a formal dining room.

"I think we can do that. Let me get in touch with Marybeth Dawson."

"Thank you, Bill"

Willow was inclined to ask what had been shared but that too, she would save for later. Mr. Keller asked Barbara if she needed anything else and she assured him that everything was perfect. She thanked Mr. Keller and walked him to the door, while Willow stayed tucked away in the kitchen not wanting to interfere with possibilities. Moments later, Barbara returned to Willow.

"What do you think, Willow?" she asked her daughter.

"It's lovely and spacious but not overwhelmingly big. Perfect for you."

"I'm delighted. Now to get my furniture out of storage and move it back in and I must start thinking about buying more furniture to fill up the other two rooms. Unless, perhaps you would like to move into the additional bedroom." But Barbara quickly changed the subject after Willow threw a grimace her way. "I'm having Bill over for dinner to celebrate. What shall I cook? Any suggestions?"

"Oh, you are." Willow flashed an animated smile in her mother's direction. "Your chicken. Definitely, your baked chicken."

"It's not what you think. It's a way to thank him for his persistence. He got this project done ahead of schedule and I want to thank him for the extra efforts. I really hope he gets the bottom floor done just as fast. I do not want to wait long to have this project wrapped up. Anyway, I would like you to be here to celebrate too, that's if you don't have other plans."

Willow knew better than to think this dinner wasn't just about thanking Mr. Keller but recognized her mother was not quite ready to admit she may be falling for him. In time, Willow thought.

"I'll be here, mom."

#

Dinner was being prepared and Willow offered to take charge of the dessert. Barbara took Willow's advice and decided on making her delicious roasted chicken. Willow hadn't met anyone who could prepare chicken the way her mother did. She even tried ordering from reputable restaurants and still, Barbara's was the best. It was moist with just the right flavor, and she was sure it would dazzle Mr. Keller. Willow was working carefully on an apple pie with a crumbled topping when an unwanted memory surfaced at the sight of the knife she was using to cut the apples. She recalled the time she sliced her hand and Floyd neglected to take her to the doctor. A vision of the blood swirling down the drain enveloped her mind and the knife slipped from her hand. When she realized, Willow quickly shook off the bad feeling before her mother had a chance of noticing. The last thing she wanted was to ruin the evening and besides, she knew how to shift her thoughts to happier memories at times like this. The weekly sessions of counseling that she and her mother participated in, taught her to cope. In fact, it was what inspired Willow to be a psychologist. Willow was pleased when she turned around to see her mother working diligently and as serene as a gentle warm breeze.

Mr. Keller arrived with a bouquet of fall flowers attractively arranged in a basket. "I thought this would look good in your kitchen," he said, gently handing the gift to Barbara.

As Willow set the table, she contemplated getting out candles but then figured she may be pushing the dating idea a tad too far. Besides, she didn't know much about Mr. Keller, except that he wasn't married, which was a very important detail. The romantic notion would have to wait, she thought as she centered the basket in the middle of the table while Barbara took his coat.

"Would you like a drink?" Barbara asked.

"Sure, what do you have."

She rattled off the choices and he chose a beer. Barbara got herself and Willow a glass of wine. The three of them settled around the table and conversed about the renovations. Then Mr. Keller announced he had some news that would delay the next phase. He had to leave for Florida on Monday. His mother was sick, and he needed to be there to see that she got the proper care. It was going to take some time, he announced, but he could send another crew to begin the work. Barbara rejected that idea. Her reasoning, plausible only to someone who didn't see the way her eyes lingered on Mr. Keller, was that she wasn't in a rush. Willow knew better. From the beginning, Barbara vehemently expressed her wish to have the renovations completed as quickly as possible. She dreaded having these changes linger on too long.

"Whenever you're ready Bill. This can wait," She insisted when setting the dinner food on the table.

Willow tried to hold back a smile but couldn't. Barbara nudged Willow's leg with her foot. The dinner ended and after the table was cleared, Bill offered to help with the dishes, but Barbara was adamant to leave them until later. They engaged in several games of Rummy and after more conversation, the evening had slipped by and Bill announced he had better get going. Barbara walked him to the door while Willow stayed behind to begin cleaning up. She tried to eavesdrop, but the noises of the dishes prevented her from hearing their hushed conversation. The door closed. Barbara secured the locks and came back to the kitchen to her daughter.

"The renovations can wait?" Willow laughed. "That's not what you wanted before. I think you like Bill. And, mother, Bill seems very fond of you."

"Oh stop, Willow. Let's get these dishes done."

17

Chapter 17

ADVENTURE

With Mr. Keller gone and the renovations halted, Willow wasn't at her mother's house as often, so she filled her time catching up with Bonnie. They spent evenings on the phone laughing and telling stories about their lives. Bonnie's job whisked her on adventures to places far from the valley, where an archeological dig would dredge up relics from the past. Most sights were out west in Idaho, Wyoming, Nevada, and California. She had a base camp in Northern California near the Redwood Forest. Her team found artifacts from the gold rush she exuberantly rambled on about one evening explaining how finding these buried treasures: clay pipes used by the Chinese to smoke opium, chamber pots made from ceramic or pewter, sterling silver and glass perfume bottles, bronze jewel boxes and toothbrushes made from animal bones, were a remarkable and rare discovery. She chuckled about the clamor a badger made on one of the campsites. Its head got stuck when the creature was eating cereal out of a plastic storage container because some idiot probably left it open, she alluded. Willow laughed for hours thinking about Bonnie's bumper story. It fell off in the Shoeshine Mountains when she parked too close to the brush. A branch got stuck underneath her front end and when she pulled away, it tore the thing completely off the front. She needed to be at an engagement and with no time to delay her trip, she tied it to the top of her car and drove all the way to Vegas. Some lady told her it was a nice canoe. She dropped her car keys in The Fountain of Youth which delayed her crew getting to a dig on time in Yellowstone. My archeology mates weren't too happy with me she had remarked with a long-drawn sigh. Bonnie divulged about her travels on the east side of the United States. She stayed in Acadia National Park and had been chased by moose on a few occasions. Apparently, they didn't like humans camping in their territory. Those territorial little buggers, she stated. She snickered about how one tripped and toppled during the chase. The most relaxing place she ever worked on a dig was near Hot Springs Arizona in the Ouachita Mountains. She worked at a site near bathhouse row and spent many evenings healing her overstrained muscles relaxing in the naturally heated waters. She dreamily expressed her knowledge about the claims of those waters being of a healing kind, a legend she believed in. Out of all the places she ventured to, she found the mountains next to Sol Valley to be home and that is why she settled there.

When it was Willow's turn to talk about her life, she confessed it wasn't as interesting. She explained to Bonnie how the therapy she and her mother went through to overcome the effects of living with Floyd, inspired her to become a psychologist. Willow recollected the difficulty she had with reading and explained that it was eventually found that she had a learning disability when she was tested in middle school. The testing revealed that her intelligence was in the gifted range but her ability to perform lacked because of a reading disability called Dyslexia. It was the therapist who noticed her gift and encouraged Willow to study in advanced classes in high school. Eventually, Willow grew confident as she was able to overcome her reading difficulties. Her grades in high school soared and she graduated in the top ten of her class, winning a full scholarship to college. Willow's story was remarkable, people would tell her. She learned then she wanted to put her energies into helping others who struggle, enrolled full time in college, and then continued to obtain her masters.

#

Willow could hear fainted screams and shouts in the distance of children playing kickball or some other sort of outdoor game. She never had experienced that kind of fun as a child, except for the summer with Bonnie. So, Willow called her friend late one Friday evening and asked her to meet at the beach over the summer. It turned out that Bonnie was going to Buxton Island, a small vacation area just off the Atlantic Coast, on an assignment for the month of July. Her boyfriend, who wouldn't be able to get away from work commitments, would stay behind to care for her house and pets. She suggested for Willow to vacation with her while she was there. Willow wouldn't be able to take a month away from her patients, but this was the adventure that Willow had been longing for, and it would be with Bonnie. She had a moment of déjà vu as if she was back in the house on Old Rock Road, trying to figure a way to venture to Bartholomew's farm to see Bonnie. An organic smell came to her and her body seemed to inhale the freedom she felt when she stole away to her friend's house. She felt a sense of urgency as the familiar feelings enveloped her and right away, she began to formulate a plan to take time off. She managed to get three full weeks of vacation.

#

Willow parked in front of a tiny cottage. Its surroundings were sandy and marsh grass grew making the lot spotted with spikes of green. There was no driveway, so she parked next to Bonnie's Subaru right beside the cottage. Bonnie, who had arrived the day before, ran outside to meet her. The sweltering heat beaded up drops of sweat on her arm. The island was swarming with mosquitos. They swatted their arms and batted the air to thwart off the pesky creatures as they walked inside.

"I hope the mosquito truck comes along this evening," Bonnie said.

"What's the mosquito truck?" Willow asked.

"They spray to get rid of these irritating bugs. I heard they even spray by plane. The island is known for its mosquitoes. I'm sorry I didn't mention this before, I didn't want to scare you off."

"Bonnie, I'll be fine," Willow said as she itched the tiny bumps penetrating the skin on her arm.

Bonnie smirked when she noticed Willow itching. "I've been exposed to so many mosquitos, I think I'm immune to being bitten."

"Lucky you," Willow replied as she grabbed her bags and carried them into the second of a two-bedroom cottage.

She had a look around which took about two seconds, but the cottage had the essentials: two beds for sleeping, a kitchen, a bathroom, a stacked washer-dryer unit, and a couch with cushions covered in a soft velvety sand-colored material. She felt enclosed, but Willow hoped to be out of the cottage more than in. From Bonnie's explanation, there was much to do on the island: the beaches, the wildlife park, hiking trails, shopping areas, and restaurants. Willow unpacked then spent time talking to Bonnie and when the sun started dipping, the change of light in the room moved them to make dinner. Bonnie made spaghetti with items she had purchased from the general store next to the cottage rental office. They filled up on the pasta and after dinner, while Bonnie started a fire in the pit on the rear side of the cottage, Willow cleaned the dishes. By the time Willow made it outside, the fire was crackling, and sparks were spitting, the flames dancing as tiny specks of ash rose in the night sky. The disappearance of the sun and the island breeze cooled the temperature enough so that the fire felt pleasant. They talked late in the evening until the fire muffled its roar and coals were simmering on the ground.

Early each morning, Bonnie left for the island's county building to catalog artifacts which would be placed in a museum that would soon stand at the entrance to the island. The Parks and Recreation department were hoping for this project to increase tourism and subsequently more revenue. Most people came to the Island to fish and relax on the beaches. The locals of the island came to accept tourism because it brought in money, but people were slow to adapt to new changes. They were drawn to the old lore of the island, the lore that Bonnie hoped the museum would capture but still, some weren't so happy about another building going up. Some of the local folks called it an eyesore. Bonnie had become privy to this information from working at the county building and filled Willow in on the local's gossip. Willow kept herself busy hiking or shopping when Bonnie had to work in the mornings and, on most days, when she returned home, they carried themselves straight to the beach. There were some rainy days when they stayed tucked inside playing cards or ventured around the island to explore some of the many antique shops. And, like clockwork, every evening presented a bonfire. There had to be a torrential downpour for Bonnie to forgo the evening fire and tonight was no different. Willow put away the dishes and Bonnie piddled with the kindling until the flames caught the wood, the routine they had unconsciously established. Willow shifted her seat to get out of the way of the smoke. Night hadn't yet made its darkest arrival when a man appeared on the other side of the flames. He was wearing a floppy brown hat, a hat one would use to shield the sun if they worked outside all day. Bonnie was preoccupied with poking the fire, but Willow noticed him. He stood staunchly, his eyes fixed on the fire, staring. His presence unnerved Willow.

"Hello," Willow called out to the stranger.

Bonnie turned away from the fire in the direction of the man. He didn't answer Willow, but Bonnie recognized him.

"Hello, Mr. ahh," Bonnie stuttered.

"Clyde Weiss." He nodded.

"That's right, Mr. Weiss. I met you at the county building. Um, you were speaking to..."

"Dwight Ward, city council member, the one who has taken charge of the project."

"What brings you here?"

"I'm from the Buxton Historical Guild. We work hard to preserve the history of this island. There are generations of families that have lived here for some time before it became a tourist spectacle."

"So, what's your business with the council?" she asked.

"Miss Murphy, I know you are here to do a job and I just want to remind you to stick to your job. The locals are none of your business."

"You are correct, Clyde Weiss. I'm here to do a job. I would think being from a historical guild you would be pleased that my job is to preserve history. I get the sense you are not pleased."

"Good evening, ladies," Clyde said in a deep voice. Then he tipped his hat and disappeared into the shadows of twilight.

Willow and Bonnie immediately turned to each other.

"That was creepy," Willow stated.

"I'm not quite sure but I think he's one of the people protesting the establishment of the museum."

"Bonnie, it sounded like a warning."

"I just want to do my job and enjoy our vacation. I'm not going to let him rattle me. You know. He reminds me of Mr. Mann. Remember that arrogant man who wanted Miss Kora off his property."

"He was creepy too."

"But a harmless, angry man."

"The picture of him stomping up the hill and slipping just came to my mind," Willow said, and she laughed at the memory. Bonnie joined her.

#

Willow and Bonnie put aside the afternoon to explore the wildlife refuge. Willow had spent some time in the mornings hiking a portion of the park, where she watched the wild horses graze on cordgrass. This afternoon, they were eager to hike the longest trail. The overcasts skies and spitting rain made the day contrastingly cooler than the usual. They doused themselves in bug spray so much so that Willow thought she may choke. With a day pack filled with water and lunches, they started out on a short trail that connected to the largest path, Sandpiper Trail. It started in a wooded area and connected to marshy land where a wooden walkway was necessary to allow the trail to continue and eventually, it snaked around dunes. Willow and Bonnie took a side path that led to the beach area. The beach was empty but what a magnificent sight, willow thought as they stepped between the mounds. The sand was white and the windswept dunes that lined the shore were taller than herself. Seashells washed ashore and speckled the sand. Pieces of driftwood were deposited on the beach by the currents that pushed it to shore. The ocean was roaring louder this afternoon and waves broke sharply, clapping the shore in a rhythmic pattern. Out to sea, the water was choppy. The two women paused and gazed at the scene.

"The public beach must have red flags up today. Looks too dangerous to swim." Willow commented.

"But a surfer's delight," Bonnie added. "I'm hungry and need a rest. Would you like to park it here for lunch?" She asked Willow.

"Yes, I'm famished. This is a perfect spot."

Two seagulls flew overhead and landed near where they were picnicking. Bonnie tore off bits of bread and threw it toward the gulls who quickly pattered to the food and ate it. Willow did the same. The birds hopped closer and stood waiting for more.

"One more piece each and you two go away." Willow threw more bread and watched the birds suck it into their beaks. Eventually, they hopped along searching for more but with no other humans on the beach eating, their luck was grim, and they flew off.

Down the shoreline, they saw a tiny speck of a person in the distance walking in their direction. As he encroached the area where they were sitting, Willow noticed it was a young teenage male. He was tall and slender, maybe about five-nine, and was clutching a metal detector in his right hand. The ease in which he handled the contraption, waving it from side to side in slow careful motions, made it look as if this was one of his typical pastimes. Willow and Bonnie stared in his direction until he was close enough for them to see the contours of his square-shaped jaw and deep-set eyes. His wavy black hair was uncombed and lifted from the wind. When he saw them, a look of recognition swept his face and he started walking toward the dune.

"Do you know him?" Willow asked Bonnie.

She squinted as she carefully studied his presence. "As a matter of fact, I do. He comes around the county building asking questions. He seems unusually interested in what I'm doing for a teenage boy. Most boys his age sleep late and stay home playing video games during the summer days."

"Hello," Bonnie said as the young man stopped in front of them.

"Hi. What are you doing out here on the beach?" He asked.

"I do get breaks from my work," Bonnie replied. "This is my friend Willow. I don't believe I ever caught your name."

"Rock. It's short for Rockford."

"Did you find any treasures today Rock?" Willow asked.

"No luck today. But my uncle, he uncovered some Native American spearheads yesterday."

"Is that so? Does he find them often?"

"Oh yes. He has a stash. He makes a lot of money off this stuff. That's why I'm out here. He'll pay me if I find something good."

"Who is your uncle?" Bonnie asked.

"Uncle Clyde. Clyde Weiss."

Bonnie and Willow turned to each other. Willow, unsure if she should say anything, noticed the startled expression on Bonnie's face.

"I may have met him. Does he live in town?"

"Yes, the white house next to the Dairy Queen. Do you know him? He's the coolest uncle. He drives a mustang."

"Ahh actually, that was a different person I was thinking of. I don't know him."

"It was nice meeting you. I got to scram. I need money desperately for a keg party tonight."

"You have fun Rock. Bye." Bonnie said.

"Bye," Willow said.

Rock ambled on waving the metal object over the ground as he moved along.

"His uncle is the strange man that came by the fire the other night. Why didn't you tell him we met him?" Willow asked.

"Something weird is happening on this island. I really just want to do my job and stay out of it but I'm afraid I suspect something."

"What do you mean?" Willow asked.

"This guild that Clyde mentioned the other night, if they are for the historical preservation of the island then I can't understand why they wouldn't be in favor of the museum that will preserve the history, unless..." her voice trailed off and her mind drifted.

"Unless what?" Willow asked.

"Remember I told you how a man on one of my digs was caught keeping an artifact, the old French jewelry box."

"Yes."

"That is against the law. He didn't get much but a fine and he lost his job but if it were a big operation, that would be different. A museum would cut into Clyde's business. Oh, I'm presuming and maybe I'm getting carried away. It's just that things I've heard."

"What did you hear?" Willow asked.

"Town gossip or so I thought but I've heard there's a group running a bootleg operation and a museum would cut into their profit. The thing is, it's hard to prove which artifacts were obtained illegally. I'd like to find out if Clyde is the leader of this operation. That would explain his urgency for me to mind my own business." Bonnie's mind seemed to be turning with ideas.

#

Bonnie had her camera ready with a flash attached. Both wore a comfortable pair of jean shorts and a dark T-shirt with tennis shoes ready to make a run for it if needed. The fire this evening would have to wait or be rescheduled until tomorrow depending on what they found. Dusk had already taken over when they ventured outside. The crickets were starting their evening musical concert and the lightning bugs winked flashes of light.

"Bonnie, I feel like I'm back in time when we ventured to Miss Kora's place for the first time. I feel nervous."

"Willow, don't be. Remember our excuse. We thought we saw the house for sale in the Real-Estate Magazine and we wanted to have a look. We must have gotten carried away," Willow emphasized changing the tone of her voice.

"Let's just get this over with."

They jumped in Bonnie's Subaru and jetted over to the other side of the island where Main Street encompassed most of the marketplaces and entertainment options. They passed the mini-golf, the Dollar Store, and the Dairy Queen sat at the end of the street where the retail shops ended, and the residential area began. Right next to it was a white house with a blue mustang parked in a paved driveway that stopped about 10 feet from the curb. The front porch was enclosed with muted windows and the white paint was chipping off the wooden panels. There was a small dormer with a window in the top center of the house which glowed with a yellow light. The rest of the house was dark. Bonnie pulled in the Dairy Queen.

"Let's get something from Dairy Queen while we wait." She suggested.

Bonnie ordered fries and Willow ordered a hot fudge sundae. They sat in the car listening to a CD of Bob Marley while they staked out Clyde's place. Bonnie seemed confident while Willow felt out of place. If her patients saw what she was doing, she would lose all credibility to her profession, however, Bonnie was fearless, and somehow, that put Willow at enough ease to carry out the plan. Was this the adventure she wanted, Willow asked herself as they staked out Clyde's place?

Suddenly, the mustang revved up its engine and backed out of the driveway. Its taillights lit up in red before it sped away. The light in the dormer was now off and the house sat quiet, empty, and dark.

"Let's go!" Bonnie commanded.

The plan was in motion and Willow couldn't turn back. They parked across the street and ran to the house. They began to walk around the exterior, peeking in each window with a high-powered flashlight, and then circled to the back of the house. Three cement steps led to a stoop and a back door and two windows sat on each side. Willow spied in one and Bonnie in the other.

"There it is. I got him." Bonnie whispered loudly sounding as if she were an investigator.

Willow focused her vision inside and concentrated on the shadowy lines she saw, then adjusted her flashlight giving the beam a different angle into the room. She saw it too. The space was filled with objects: shiny pieces of glass, pots, pewter, and metallic items that she couldn't quite tell exactly what they were but nonetheless were vessels of the antique kind. There were boxes stacked as if they were going to be shipped out or were just received. Bonnie snapped her camera continuously, the flash cutting away the dark each time the camera clicked. Willow hoped if anyone saw the light, they would think it was lightning.

"Let's move along to the other side." She pulled Willow's arm.

They snooped in the windows on the opposite side of the Dairy Queen but didn't find any more suspicious objects. All the loot was contained in the back room of the house.

"I think we're done." Bonnie decided. "You ready?"

"I've been ready," Willow answered.

They ran from the property like ninja's tiptoeing as if it would make them unseen, jumped in the Subaru, and sped off, making a left on the first cross street. When they got back to the cottage, they stumbled in the door and slammed it shut as if they were being chased. Loud bursts of laughter erupted as they slapped hands and breathed in heavy gulps of air trying to calm themselves.

"Bonnie, I can't believe you got me to do that like we are a couple of detectives or something. I have to say, that was the most invigorating thing I've done since you saved me from falling in the water."

"Willow, I'm not sure it was my place to snoop around trying to catch a man stealing but I'm sure glad I had you to do it with."

Their breathing returned to normal and they slumped on the velvety couch exhausted.

"What will you do with the pictures?" Willow asked.

"You know I really don't want to get into this mess. I'm not sure. I'll decide when I get them developed," she stated as she pulled the 35-millimeter cartridge from the camera. "Maybe I'll show them to Dwight Ward, but I'll have to explain how I got them. Or, I could send them to him anonymously in an envelope. After I leave of course."

Willow and Bonnie talked a while longer before turning in for the night. Tomorrow hopefully would be uneventful with a relaxing fire. Feeling the excitement of the day wane, Willow fell right to sleep into a needed rest.

#

Willow and Bonnie sat on the beach in low seated chairs, and sipped rum drinks, while they gossiped about people from their hometowns, complained about long days at work, and commented about beachgoers as they watched them walked by. Bonnie had the radio tuned into a station that played a mixture of grunge and classic rock tunes. The noon sun grew stronger and they edged closer to the water to cool off.

"I wonder if Clyde or Rock will be here," Willow questioned. "Did you ever send the film to be developed?"

"No. I haven't thought about it. While I do want antiquities to have their rightful place, I'm not willing to get involved while I'm working here. Enforcing the law is thankfully not my job."

"It sure was a thrilling night if anything. You know, I was thinking about Rockford. He's oblivious."

"Rock is a good name for him," Bonnie replied.

"I agree," Willow returned.

They relaxed on the beach until they grew hungry. For dinner, they ate fried shrimp baskets at the beach stand before going back to the cottage. Tomorrow, Willow would be leaving; Bonnie was staying another week and her boyfriend was coming Monday. This was the last evening with Bonnie and one last fire. Willow put some beers on ice in a cooler while Bonnie did her magic and it was once again a roaring spectacle. They sat their chairs on the opposite side of the smoke and relaxed into the evening roasting marshmallows, drinking, and reminiscing about their time together. They vowed to meet again next year, and Willow looked forward to a summer tradition.

"I have one more thing to tell you before you leave." Bonnie's tone became somber which was unlike her. Willow never heard this side of Bonnie and her heart felt hardened in her chest.

"What is it?"

"I found a lump in my breast the day before I was leaving to come here. I called my doctor and she suggested that I delay my trip to have a mammogram. She told me that it was most likely benign based on my age, but it was imperative I have it checked. I decided to wait until I get back home to have the mammogram but it feels bigger. I'm a little worried."

"Oh Bonnie, you need to get that examined right away."

"I have an appointment next Monday."

"What does it feel like?"

"A hard gumball, here feel it." She pulled Willow's hand to the top area of her left breast. Willow flattened out her hand as Bonnie laid it against her and she felt the outer part of a hard lump.

"Bonnie, I'm so sorry."

"I'm trying not to think about it until I have to. I'll worry next Monday. Until then, let's enjoy the night."

"You know I'm here for you, Bonnie."

"Yes, I know that Willow. Cheers." Bonnie held up her beer bottle. Willow reached out her beer and they clinked their bottle tops letting the worries billow away with the smoke and stayed up several hours past midnight enjoying their time together.

18

Chapter 18

The Murphys' House

The Murphys' house was different than her house. Willow always slept soundly, especially last night after the Stargazing, and dancing in the yard. She loved being outside on a summer's night and Bonnie made it that much more thrilling.

Mamma and I used to sit outside at night, but she would always be called in by Daddy because he needed something. Mamma used to say, 'Daddy wants me at his beck and call'. Willow didn't understand it, but she knew Mamma always hurried when he called for her. Sometimes he would start yelling at her and then she would call Willow in and send her to bed.

When they came in last night to get popsicles, Mr. and Mrs. Murphy were still playing cards and the records continued to turn on the player.

Willow wondered what Joseph said to Mr. Murphy in the parking lot of Powel's Market.

Was it about Daddy?

Willow thought about the gas can. Her daddy had a gas can that he used to fill the lawnmower. He also used it once when Mamma's Gremlin was out of gas. He was not happy with her that she let it get so low, but she didn't have money for gas she explained to him. Then he got angry with her and swiped a glass off the counter with the side of his arm. It broke into pieces on the floor.

I've never seen Mr. Murphy get that mad.

#

Willow was awakened as usual by Oliver tiptoeing on the cot as he settled comfortably, coalescing his body alongside hers. She scratched his belly and he purred, the sound she looked forward to every morning. Bonnie roused and rolled over to her side, which must have startled Oliver. He sat up to inspect the noise and leaped to the bed, pouncing at Bonnie's feet. She picked him up and dangled him over her body, his face meeting hers.

"Good morning Oliver. How are you? Are you going to go outside and scratch in the dirt today or find a mouse?" Oliver unresponsively stared at Bonnie and she continued talking to him as if he could understand. Then she suddenly dropped the plump cat and sat upright to express her thoughts.

"Willow, we should go to Miss Kora's today."

"I hope we don't run into Mr. Mann. He's scary."

"When we get to the end of her driveway, let's run really fast behind her house, so he doesn't see us coming."

"And if he spots us, maybe we can hide in her garden," Willow added.

It wasn't but several hours later and they were sprinting down Marshland road, halting at the mailbox. The appearance of the upright post contradicted the last memory Willow had of its stance. Although the box was sturdy, it looked haggard and rusty pieces of metal hung from the underside. The door was hanging open, so Bonnie reached over and pushed it shut. Willow noted that the mailman wasn't due to come until later in the afternoon, and maybe Miss Kora had mail piling up in her box. She remembered that Miss Kora had little contact with what happened outside her cottage and gardens which meant she didn't often care to check the mailbox. The last time she fetched her correspondence, she had an abundance of envelopes. Willow opened the door and peered inside.

"Nope, nothing in the mailbox, except dirt."

"Come on Willow," Bonnie motioned for her to proceed down the driveway, hurrying to be hidden from the likes of Mr. Mann and hoping to avoid another confrontation.

They crept along the side of the house, hearing the bubbling of the water as they ventured into the backyard. The moon garden quickly came into view. A little kitten was sauntering along the edge of the plants, weaving in and out of the bench legs. To the right, the tall stalks of the herbs swayed side to side in bunches; the movement trailed in a path and crept closer to them every few seconds. Finally, the brush parted, and Miss Kora came through an opening in the garden. She was carrying a wide saucer-like basket with an attached handle that arched widely over the vessel. It was filled with long-stemmed plants whose flowers dripped over the edge. Miss Kora clutched the handle with the inside of her bent arm. She was oblivious to the presence of the young girls until Bonnie called out.

"Hi, Miss Kora." Her voice boomed.

Miss Kora jumped back and pressed her hand on her chest as if she was keeping her heart from leaping out of her body. "Aaah," she let out a sharp, pithy cry as she noticed her guests. "You children scared me. Oh my. Don't sneak up on me like that. I wasn't expecting company but now that you are here," she changed her tone. "why not look at the fresh herbs I picked from my garden. They are quite a glorious bunch."

Willow and Bonnie eagerly followed her suggestion. Behind her stood plants of various sizes. Some of which looked like weeds but obviously to Miss Kora, they were prized possessions. When she lowered her basket to share her findings, Willow noticed how she beheld the contents with the utmost adoration. The girls gazed over the basket and Bonnie impulsively reached for the stem of one of the cuttings.

"Not just yet my dear. The stems are armed with sharp prickles. I would rather you not cut your finger," Miss Kora warned. "Let's go sit on the bench and have a look."

Kora sat in the middle of the bench with the girls on either side of her. One by one she handed over a flower, directing them to hold it between the prickles, where they wouldn't be stabbed. The statuesque stem of the plant was sturdy and held jagged leaves with white mottling surrounding its veins. The leaves were as attractive as the pink ball that topped the stem. The flower held slender ray-like petals making it resemble the fine bristles of a brush.

"What is this, Kora?" Bonnie asked.

"This is Milk Thistle," she replied.

"Milk thistle? Why is it called Milk Thistle?" Willow curiously asked.

"You ask such good questions my little one." Miss Kora glanced adoringly at Willow.

That was the second time someone told Willow she asked good questions. She never had been told that in school. Other kids asked good questions but never Willow.

"Legend says that Mother Mary's milk once dropped on this plant. The milk was drawn from the root and traveled to every pathway in the plant. And," she emphasized, "from that very day, the leaves and stem of this plant grow with white markings surrounding the veins. Have a closer look."

"I see it, Miss Kora. I see." Bonnie remarked.

"It's so beautiful," Willow added.

"Not only does Milk Thistle shine with loveliness, it is healthy for you. You can eat every part of this plant."

"Are you going to eat this Miss Kora?" Willow asked.

"Yes, these leaves will be part of my salad this evening."

"Bonnie eats sassafras leaves," Willow remarked.

"Well, be careful my dear, sassafras leaves can be harmful if you eat too many. But I don't believe a little girl like yourself would eat that much."

"No, I won't," Bonnie replied. "Miss Kora, can you eat as much Milk Thistle as you'd like?"

"Oh, yes child. In fact, it will cleanse you if you eat Milk Thistle."

The girl's attention was drawn to the meowing of a tiny kitten. It came out from the moon garden and nestled at Miss Kora's feet. She bent down and lifted the creature, cupping it in her hands. It was gray with striped black lines. Its face was the size of Willow's palm. Miss Kora lightly brushed her fingertips over the back of the kitten's head and down his spine, repeating the motion as she spoke.

"I found this little darling behind the Moon Garden crying in anguish. I suspect its family was taken by a predator. Perhaps the owl I've been hearing at night."

Willow and Bonnie fussed over the kitten with Miss Kora. She let each girl hold it, gently placing it in their laps. The docile animal, comfortable being held, seemed to welcome the extra attention. After a bit, he wriggled, wanting to get back on the ground.

"Is it a boy or a girl, Miss Kora?" Bonnie asked.

"He's a male."

"Sad he lost his family."

Bonnie's comment stirred a familiar emotion in Willow. She felt a pull in her heart. She was orphaned like the cat and like the cat, was being taken care of by someone who was not her family. How kind Miss Kora is Willow thought. She felt as if Miss Kora loved every living creature. She was even kind to Mr. Mann. She had seen her taking plants to his house and leaving them in front of the door.

"I lost my family too," Willow sadly stated, surprised that the words came out of her mouth. "I don't know where Mamma is, and I think Daddy is in jail."

"What?" Bonnie asked, startled at her friend's belief.

Willow began to cry. Miss Kora wrapped her arms around her as if she was draping a shawl over her shoulders. Willow relaxed in her embrace. Miss Kora patted her on the back and suggested that Bonnie take the cat inside for milk. She explained that the milk was in the icebox and there were toys that he liked to play with near the couch.

"Willow, dear. It's going to be all right. Something tells me your Mamma is okay. Your father, well, he is different. Maybe he is in the place he needs to be right now."

"You know something about my father, don't you? There was an article in the paper accusing him of starting a fire at the Ferebee's house."

"I don't know where he is now, but I know of your father. You are just a child, but you deserve to know the truth if it's for your safety."

"Miss Kora, what do you know about my father? Please tell me. Something has happened and no one will tell me."

"I can tell you what I know of your father but I'm not sure it will help you feel better."

"Tell me. I'll be brave," Willow implored as she remembered the cornelian rock Miss Kora gave her.

"Your father, well your grandfather, Floyd's dad, whom I've known since I was a little girl, he was never that nice of a man. He was harsh. Harsh on your dad when he was a child, I saw him get whipped in town. It scared me. I was just a young girl, too young to witness such an act of brutality," Kora paused. "Floyd's father, Robert Hitchens, was vehemently against the integration of schools after the Civil Rights Act was passed. Do you know what that law is Willow?"

"Well, I remember hearing my teacher talk about the law, when black kids were now allowed to go to white schools and that some people were against it."

"Your grandfather led a movement against black and white children going to the same school. That Mr. Hitchens, he was a formidable man, a rabble-rouser. People who were against him were afraid to say so, and then some were right there with him caught up in his ire. He stirred up the community quite a bit with his verbal outbursts and letters to the editor in the paper. After the integration finally happened, there were unexplained happenings in the community like..."

Miss Kora ceased her explanation and seemed to drift off a bit into the past forgetting that Willow was sitting there, forgetting that she was talking to a child, while Willow was quiet and attentive taking everything in that Miss Kora was telling her.

"Like what?" Willow asked.

"I'm afraid I spoke too much, Willow. What I'm getting at is I'm not sure that you're safe with your Dad, but I know your Mamma is a sweet person who would never hurt anyone. You just stay put with the Murphys until we can locate her. You are safe for now but don't leave the Murphys."

It sounded to Willow like a warning, and she felt a sense of peril. Willow needed to know if this was really her father. A bad man, a man who was imprecated by his father's misanthropic deeds. A man who did bad things. Not her father she wanted to believe. He was the man who went to work every day. He was the man who bought her food. He was the man who she heard on the phone late that night. Willow couldn't think any further. She wasn't sure who her father was anymore. Maybe he wasn't who she imagined or wanted him to be.

Willow didn't want to believe what Miss Kora was revealing. She wanted her Mamma back. She wanted to be at home with Mamma and the unbroken jars of strawberry jam. We should be eating the sweet stuff that Mamma canned every year, Willow thought. She had to give it one last fight. She would run home and Mamma would be there admiring the daisies that bloomed, hanging laundry on the line. Daddy would be at work.

Willow immediately rose from the bench and took off running beside the house and off toward the mailbox. Miss Kora called for her to come back. She pleaded to no avail. Bonnie heard the commotion and came outside. She too ran after Willow, but it was of no use. Willow was far down Marshland Road.

Too far to catch.

Willow ran faster and faster. Her adrenaline carried her to the house on Old Rock Road. She ran up the concrete steps, opened the screen door, and twisted the doorknob, but the wooden door behind it wouldn't budge. She rattled the handle again and again, but it was locked solid. She kicked the door and banged on it over and over, her fists pounding out exasperation with every strike.

"Mamma, Mamma," She yelled repeatedly. Finally, with her energy drained, she turned her back against the hard, wooden door and slid down letting her bottom fall to the porch. She sat with her head in her hands crying and the screen door was held open by her stiff body. Just like Mamma, she remembered, crying on the stoop. When her sobs subsided, she heard birds in the distance. It soothed her to listen to their chirrups. The anger quieted and now, all she heard was the sound of nature but then, something rustled in the garage.

She saw a pair of eyes looking out of the window next to the door. The eyes connected with hers for a moment and her heart pothered in fear. When the door drifted open, she noticed an older man with a grizzled beard, and he moved with a limp. His nose was slender and elongated as if it split his face in two and pointed at the end. Although she couldn't see from her point of view, she knew he had a tooth missing in the upper row.

Grandpa.

He held in his hands, two red metal cans with a spout on each, jetting from the basin. *Gas cans*, she said to herself. She hadn't noticed his vehicle in the driveway until now because its view was obstructed by Daddy's truck, which was sitting closer to the house. Grandpa's truck was parallelly parked next to the garage.

He noticed Willow but pretended as if he didn't see her and quickly turned away from the stoop. He hurried to his truck, plopping the cans in the back, before he got in the cab. The engine sounded and he backed away over the gravel. When he turned on Old Rock Road, his wheels scraped, and it made a screeching sound as if it tore up the ground below.

She heard the motor travel toward Marshland Road and soon was out of range. Grandpa was gone. She slumped her shoulders and her body went limp from exhaustion. She melted into the porch and the rhythmic breaths of her despair, put her to sleep.

#

Willow woke up on the stoop with Miss Kora and Mrs. Murphy towering over her with inspective eyes as if she were a specimen under a microscope. Neither woman wanted to speak first, seeming unsure of words that would remedy the situation. There were none; Willow had to accept her plight. Finally, Mrs. Murphy spoke softly as she held Willow's hand and explained that she was unable to stay at her house by herself. Miss Kora reached for Willow's other hand and pulled her to standing. With the women at both sides, she walked to the station wagon, dragging her feet as if she couldn't get them to move, her shoes scraping the stones with each solemn step. The look of pity on their furrowed faces made her cry once more, but this time, just a soft whimper and tears that slid slowly over the bumps of her cheekbones.

Willow sat in the back of the station wagon with Mrs. Murphy in the driver's seat and Miss Kora in the passenger seat. A police car, with two male officers, pulled in the driveway and parked beside the station wagon. Mrs. Murphy glanced out her window before she opened the door and stepped to the driveway. The officers approached her and as much as Willow wanted to know what they were saying, she couldn't hear anything but muffled voices and low tones, one of those adult-talks that children weren't to be involved with.

Mrs. Murphy finished the conversation and returned to the driver's seat. She backed up with caution and Willow saw the police walking around the house. Before Mrs. Murphy pulled out onto Old Rock Road, Willow noticed the officers kicking in the door. Mrs. Murphy assured Willow she would get her back to their house where she could rest. Willow wondered why Grandpa just let her cry on the porch as if she wasn't there.

19

Chapter 19

Like Sunflowers

Several weeks later, Mrs. Murphy sat Willow down at the kitchen table with a tall glass of lemonade. Miss Kora came over too. The women had become acquainted after rescuing Willow from her distress that afternoon. Miss Kora was even kind enough to bring over some herbs from her garden to share with the Murphys. One of which was Kava tea. It would induce calm and a state of relaxation. Mrs. Murphy made the tea every morning since the incident and everyone enjoyed indulging in the Kava. It was a new routine for Bonnie and Willow. They began their morning drinking tea on the back porch watching the sunflowers sway in gentle breezes with the sun sitting low in the sky, ready to make its daily journey.

The weather was usually hot and dry but a few of those mornings were clouded with rain that pattered the back porch leaving streaks of water and droplets on the edges. The rain never kept them inside the house for breakfast. They stayed dry sitting on the floral cushion of the wrought iron couch. They felt like adults drinking coffee since the tea was taken from a mug and it made them pretend. Bonnie was the president of the Cheerio company and Willow was the vice president. They drew pictures of newly designed cereal boxes and made jingles to go along with the illustrations as they ate their bowls of cheerios and sipped tea. On one morning, Oliver knocked the box of cheerios that Bonnie left sitting on the floor of the porch, and the cereal scattered all over the porch. They gathered up the tiny circles and used them to create designs on paper. Their musings went on for an hour or so after breakfast and tea each morning then Mrs. Murphy, after several requests, would implore them to get dressed. Willow had seemed to accept her circumstances as they were and living with the Murphys became a new normal. She never tried to go back to her house again.

As Willow slumped in the seat at the kitchen table, she heard the puff of the cushion below the vinyl covering like she did every time she sat down. Mrs. Murphy was across from her and Miss Kora was right beside her. Miss Kora had brought over a fresh hank of thyme from her garden. Their manner was solemn when they broached Willow with the news. Miss Kora held her hand, squeezing it snuggly to give her comfort.

"Willow, Miss Kora, and I have to tell you the truth about what has happened to your father. We have found out more information and although this will be a lot for you to take in, you have to know."

Willow, finally acquiescent to her circumstances, was ready to hear what they had to tell her. She had been disappointed repeatedly since Mamma left and this was merely another obstacle, nothing that could surprise her. She had been able to pioneer her way through the chaos so far and had no choice but to face what was about to be thrown her way.

"Your father has been arrested and is awaiting trial for setting the Ferebee's garage on fire. He won't be coming home unless he is cleared."

"Where is my grandpa? I saw him at my house the day I fell asleep on the stoop."

The two women threw each other a disconcerted glance raising their brows at the new information they were just learning.

"Your grandpa is being questioned. He is a suspect and the police are searching for your mother," Mrs. Murphy continued.

"Why is Grandpa being questioned?"

"Willow," Mrs. Murphy said softly, "he is suspected to be a part of the arson. That's all I can tell you. That's all I know right now. I'm so sorry."

"Willow dear," Miss Kora beseeched, "Do not give up hope. There is pain in this world, but the light shines bright in the darkness."

Willow was not quite sure if she understood the advice that Miss Kora was giving her, because light doesn't shine bright in the dark, and with Mamma gone and Daddy in jail things seemed awfully dim, but the tone of her words gave Willow hope. She knew it was meant to be encouraging. Miss Kora handed her a crystal. It was translucent with a trace of pink winding throughout the grain of the rock. She placed it in her palm with deliberate intentions and folded her small fingers back over the stone to convey the specialty of the gift. "Hold on to this talisman, Willow, and your luck will change."

Mrs. Murphy appeared worried at Miss Kora's lofty idea as if a rock would change circumstances for this young, dejected child who couldn't possibly handle yet another disappointment, but Willow keyed up at the sound of Miss Kora's request. Mrs. Murphy, with her mouth agape, appeared to have left the words she wanted to say unspoken.

Willow opened her hand to view the object that was given to her. She saw its shiny exterior resting in the center of her palm as if it held the answers to the longing that had been eating at her since that night; the same longing she felt the day when Mamma's Gremlin puttered over the gravel stones of the driveway, tumbling away and out of her life. Willow didn't cry, and she didn't worry anymore. She had found safety at the Murphys' house and a friend who accepted her. She felt protected and hoped that Mamma felt the same wherever she may be.

Shortly after the conversation ended, Miss Kora left the farmhouse. Mrs. Murphy went about her daily chores and had just begun ironing clothes in the living room, when Bonnie hurried downstairs, dressed, and ready to venture outside. The breakfast dishes were cleared and washed. Jenny was watching television in the living room. The soap opera, General Hospital was playing, and Jenny couldn't take her eyes off the screen. Mrs. Murphy continued ironing clothes and watching the show at the same time.

"Willow," Bonnie yelled with the zest she always barred. "Let's go outside and climb the Sassafras tree."

Willow, who was walking toward the steps to go upstairs and change into her play clothes, answered Bonnie immediately welcoming the distraction from the news she had just been given. "All right. Let me get changed first."

When Willow was ready, they went to the tree. Oliver was running around the old shanty and it appeared that he was chasing a mouse or some other miniature creature. It was common for Oliver to leave a mouse or two on the porch. He even sometimes left birds around for Mrs. Murphy to find. Bonnie noticed and decided that she wanted to seek out what Oliver was finding. They scurried over to the decrepit structure and found him digging at the dirt. He pulled out a mole with the claws of his right paw and began to bite at the tiny mammal. It struggled to get loose but soon went limp. Oliver fondled it with his paws rolling it in circular movements on the ground. Bonnie shouted for Oliver to leave it alone, but it was too late. The creature was dead.

"Oliver." Bonnie scolded leaving him with his prize. Then she changed the subject and spoke about the people that may have lived in this tiny shanty long ago. "My Grandfather Bartholomew told me it used to be a house for slaves back in the mid-1800s when slavery was legal."

They peeked inside. There was nothing but a fireplace a room and a loft. "I can't imagine. They must have cooked their meals in the fireplace. Kind of reminds me of Miss Kora's cottage."

"Do you ever play in it? Like a clubhouse."

"Jenny and I did when we first moved here but we eventually got scolded. The floor is unsteady, and we could fall through, my dad told us. Besides, Jenny charged me a quarter every time I wanted to come in and I ran out of money. Daddy says this must come down. It is too old to let stand unless the county wants to restore it as a historical place."

"What does that mean?" Willow asked.

"I'm not sure. I just heard my sister talking about it with my dad. He is not sure if he wants to tear it down or leave it. It's so old. But I guess if they make it a historical place, they'll fix it so visitors can come. Maybe like a museum."

Down the road, they heard metal scraping. Their heads turned in the direction of the noise and noticed Miss Kora was shutting the door to her mailbox, jamming it a few times to make it stay in place. Mr. Mann was standing on his front doorstep beholding the view in front of him. His piece of property was superb and served his arrogance perfectly. When he saw Miss Kora at the box, he shook his head with scorn.

Willow and Bonnie took off running toward the woman. Now that Mrs. Murphy met Miss Kora, Bonnie was confident her mother would not be amiss if she found that they wandered off to her place. By then Miss Kora had already made her way back to the cottage. They could see the top of her head in the kitchen window as they brushed past her house.

Overcome by the moment, they kept running past the cottage and past the gardens. Their feet pitter-pattering the whole way to the edge of the river and stopped in a split second at the edge of the riverbank where they heard water passing in swallows. They cautioned at the celerity of the stream and steep gully that had formed from the repetitive flow. The soil was moist, and one slip of the foot could send them dangerously into the water. Up ahead they spotted a bridge that led to a path ascending the hill across the water. They edged closer and saw that it was a swinging suspension bridge, secured snuggly over the water with cables. They had never made it this far before. Rope strung along the sides of the bridge and served as handrails. There were about twelve to fourteen boards evenly spaced across with a gap separating each one. They ran further along and stopped at the beginning of the bridge.

"Should we go across?" Bonnie asked turning to Willow for an answer.

Willow, who normally would be cautious, felt as if she had nothing to lose today. "Let's go. Let's go to the other side," she vivaciously leaped to the first board and to the second. When she leaped on the third board, her foot slipped in the space between. Gravity pulled her toward the rushing waters below. She reached for security but only one hand was able to grab onto the rope. She felt herself slipping deeper. Bonnie saw her situation and quickly but cautiously stepped to the board where Willow was sinking. The bridge tottered and Willow struggled to keep herself from falling through.

"Help me, Bonnie. Help me."

"I got you, Willow. Grab my hand."

Bonnie gripped her hands tightly and pulled her to safety. Willow grabbed the ropes on both sides of the bridge and was able to steady her balance. Both feet were now firmly planted on the board.

"Are you ok? Do you want to go back?" Bonnie asked.

"I'm fine, Bonnie. You saved me," she pondered her choices. "Let's go on. I want to see what is on the other side."

The girls moved along and made it across without harm to where a narrow trail led up a hill. A thicket of trees encompassed both sides of the path, and the climb to the crown was a simple feat compared to the ordeal they just conquered. When they reached the end, they saw a wondrous meadow before them. Tall grasses filled the pasture. They walked further and came to the edge of the hill where they could see the farmhouse and the sunflower field. The view was magnificent and vast. Willow felt as if they made it to heaven.

"Bonnie," she called to her friend. "Look at the sunflowers."

This was the moment Willow had been waiting for. The sunflowers had reached their peak in the growth cycle and the petals were completely open. Standing tall against a luminous blue sky, the plant showcased a complete beauty and emanated a spirit unlike anything else Willow had ever seen. It was cheerful, like Bonnie. Willow put her arm around her friend and pulled her close. They were connected side by side. Their faces beamed with joy as they stood together below the bright and warm sunshine in marvel of the sight before them. The plant's brown center, bold and strong, held the richly, yellow-painted petals that spread outward like fingers, as if grasping the earth. Willow and Bonnie held their arms out with fanned open hands, to mimic the scene. They stood there, together, like sunflowers.

20

Chapter 20

Behind Us

Sure, Willow had friendships over the years, some friends she occasionally met with and confided in, but none like Bonnie. Reconnecting with her had perked Willow's life up like it did when she was nine. She received the bad news from her friend several weeks after their trip, and Bonnie confirmed that it was breast cancer. She was unable to give her more details other than her doctors were working on a treatment plan and she would keep Willow updated.

Bonnie also let her know she had lost the film case from their evening of being amateur detectives. Therefore, Clyde Weiss wouldn't be caught, yet, she added. It was the least of her worries right now but the recollection of sneaking around his house gave them another fond memory and a good laugh. She tried to sound like her normal, cheery self but Willow sensed the worry when she forced, *I'm going to be all right Willow* at the end of their conversations.

Willow did everything possible to support Bonnie from afar including sending her packages and calling her often, but she couldn't pull herself from the responsibilities at work to visit and Bonnie insisted there was no need; she was doing fine with the support of Scott, her family and co-workers. The hours Willow had to put in at her practice, compounded when one of the counselors left for another job. It made each day doubly taxing on her schedule and emotions. In the evenings, she came home to an empty condo and slumped in her high-backed armchair only having the energy to fix herself a bowl of cereal for dinner. Willow dropped weight and her clothes began to sag at the creases and excess material gathered at her ankles as if she was a burning candle, the wax dripping down the column and stacking at the base. Then, as if her life's trajectory wasn't already skewed enough, her mother received another letter from Floyd wanting to talk to Barbara, but Barbara, again, refused any contact with him. Finally, when Barbara began to have dreams that woke her night after night, making her toss until the wee hours of the morning, Willow decided she had to distance herself from Barbara's plight or she was liable to succumb to a breakdown like many of her patients who came to see her only after they couldn't function. We must put a plan in place before this point, she would always inform her clients when they showed up in her office raveled tightly in stress. Willow set her mother up an appointment with one of her colleagues. Mr. Keller had been in touch with Barbara, but he had not been able to make it back from Florida to finish the renovations. Willow convinced her mother that it was for the better and she needed to concentrate on putting the bad memories away for good.

"But I have been to counseling. I'm tired of conjuring up these old feelings. I want to get this house finished and live contently in Pequot," Barbara heatedly expressed to Willow over coffee one Saturday morning.

"Mom, my concern is that if you are having dreams, then you haven't quite put it away. One last try, please," She pleaded. "The counselor I can send you to is experienced in working with abuse victims."

"I work with abused women every day, so how would it look if I was the one who needed counseling. I need to be strong for these women."

"Going to counseling another time doesn't mean you are not strong, and it doesn't matter how many times you've gone. You go until you are

OK. This is about you and you will help the women at the shelter by knowing how to face this."

"All right, let me have the counselor's name."

Willow anticipated this outcome and had the counselor's card for the counselor in her purse. She handed it to Barbara, who dropped it on the counter next to the phone.

"I'll call tomorrow," she assured her daughter.

#

Barbara followed Willow's suggestion and made an appointment. The change that came over her was noticeable after only two sessions. She was lighter in her demeanor and the dreams waned after four sessions, but there was one last step she took to lift the heavy burden she carried for years, which Willow found out about over a dinner. It was late in the fall on a Sunday afternoon. The weather had dipped below freezing at nights and the leaves had dropped from the trees leaving the branches barren of life until spring. Barbara had the heat set at a comfortable temperature and the house smelled of roasted chicken when Willow arrived. A vase of flowers sat upon the table, a sign that Barbara was uplifted and subsequently gave Willow a hint that something was different. The dessert Willow made was a pumpkin cake drizzled with chocolate ganache and she set it on the table. Her mother showed delight in Willow's choice of cake.

"Is that the tasty pumpkin cake you always make for Thanksgiving?"

"Yes, mom. I know how much you like it and it won't hurt to have a taste of it a little early. How far away is Thanksgiving?"

"Two weeks," Barbara answered.

"That soon?"

"Yes Willow, you've been working too much."

After they shared a meal which included Chardonnay, cloth napkins, a deliciously baked dinner, and music, they cleared the table, stacking the dishes beside the sink. Willow started washing the dishes by hand. The dishwasher, which never existed in the carriage house, would be coming with the renovation but until then, the dishes were done the old fashion way. Barbara sidled up alongside Willow and took the plate she was holding from her hand, laying it in the sink. Willow stopped the water and eyed her mother with a questioning eye. Her mother had an air of happiness around her and it satisfied Willow in a way she couldn't explain.

"This can wait. Let's talk," she told her daughter and put the dish back in the base of the porcelain sink.

Willow followed her to the couch trying to unpuzzle the meaning behind the carefully planned dinner. Barbara brought in another glass of Chardonnay for each of them, a felicitous gesture for a celebration.

"Cheers," she said as she handed Willow her glass and clinked the rim with her daughter's.

"What are we celebrating?"

"I did it. I called your father. I confronted him and unleashed every bit of anger I had stacked up inside me for years. Willow, I was so brave."

"What did you say to him?" Willow's eyes were wide with a concerned curiosity.

"I told him what he did to me was wrong, a man should never hit a woman. I let him know living with him was frightening and it is despicable how uncomfortable he made us feel, walking on eggshells all the time, afraid to speak my opinion, tiptoeing around the house like we were afraid to wake the monster. In fact, I told him he was a monster. He took away my sense of freedom. I couldn't talk to anyone or have visitors. He wouldn't even let you have a birthday party. I couldn't have family or friends; I was only allowed to have him and you and then he took that away from me too. I let him know that he knocked me down physically and emotionally and took me away from the one pride I had in my life. Willow, I was proud of how I took care of you and he snagged that away too without so much of even trying to care for you in the way he should have. He made you think I didn't love you."

Willow saw pain leaving her mother as the tears fell. Barbara reached around and held onto her daughter as if she was that little girl who had just found her mom again. Her mother's crying reminded Willow of the sobbing she heard on the stoop many years ago, but this time it was different. She was healing. "Mom I always knew you loved me. I never believed what he told me. Even when you were gone that summer, I felt your love. We have something that can never be broken by the darkness of the Hitchen's family."

"I'm sorry, Willow. I'm so sorry I left you. I'm sorry I didn't get you out sooner."

Willow pulled back and fixed her eyes on her mother. "Mom, you don't need to be sorry. It's not your fault."

"No, Willow, I should have found a way to leave sooner, before that night."

"Mom, that's part of the cycle of abuse. You didn't realize and you didn't have any means to make money."

"Willow, I found a way, didn't I? Knowing that I let you live through nine years with an abusive man is what has been haunting me, that, and not confronting Floyd. You were right. I needed closure."

"Glad to know. Four years of college and two years of graduate school wasn't for nothing," Willow joked.

"Willow, after I unleashed all of that on Floyd, he was quiet for a moment and then," she paused and took a deep breath in through her nose and let it out her mouth, finding the courage to finish her story. "He said he was sorry. I expected him to yell at me. I was positioned for a fight and ready to defend myself. The night I left; I was afraid to defend myself. But on the call, I wasn't afraid, and I wasn't wrong. Floyd was wrong."

"Oh, mother. I'm so proud of you. You are brave."

"You are brave too, Willow. You've always been brave."

"I didn't feel so brave when you were gone but Bonnie and Miss Kora were the ones who saved me from falling apart. And watching the sunflowers grow somehow gave me hope. I knew I would find you again," she added.

"You forgave your father and I'm going to let go now. I'll forgive him. I'll never forget but I'll forgive. I have to let go of the regret."

"This is a celebration," Willow said.

"Yes, it is. We can put this behind us." Barbara dried her eyes with a tissue. "I think that is enough about me. How is Bonnie doing?"

It was Willow's turn to cry. Tears welled in her eyes and she was now clinging to the box of tissues. "Mom, she's fighting hard. She is going through chemotherapy and her hair is starting to fall out, but her spirit is upbeat. I don't know what to do for her. I can't get off work after taking three weeks of vacation over the summer and being short-staffed, I'm really needed at the practice. I've sent packages and I call her. Her sister and mother help her get to appointments, but I wish I could make her dinner at the very least."

"Just be there for her Willow. Be there to laugh with her and enjoy life like you did with her as a child. She needs a refuge. You can be that refuge."

"That, I can do."

Willow and Barbara were engrossed in conversation and didn't realize the phone was ringing. Barbara, startled by the third ring, jumped up from the couch and hurried to answer it before the other person hung up.

"Hello. Yes, this is Barbara. Oh, hello Bill. How are you?" Pause. "Is your mother doing ok?" Pause. "You'll be back when?" Pause. "That soon?" Pause. "No that's perfect. You can start the Monday after Thanksgiving." Pause. "All right, it's a deal. See you then."

Willow straightened her posture and shifted her ear closer to the kitchen, listening to her mother on the phone. She acted as if she wasn't eavesdropping and sat demurely on the couch, flipping pages of a magazine when Barbara sauntered back into the living room.

"Guess who that was on the phone?" Her voice tittered.

"Who?" Willow asked as if she didn't know.

"Bill Keller. He's coming back after Thanksgiving to start the bottom floor renovation."

"That's good news, mom." Willow saw happiness in her mother, one that wasn't there before. But lately, she was feeling quite the opposite.

21

Chapter 21

Back to the Valley

Willow called Bonnie every day for over a week without hearing back from her, yet when she finally received a call late one evening, she understood why. They had found more cancer. It spread to her brain and the doctors changed her treatment, she sounded hopeful as she told me, 'There are new treatments, Willow, I'm so thankful.' Willow didn't know how, but Bonnie spoke with gratitude. Another evening she called to tell Willow that Scott bailed on her. He couldn't hack having a girlfriend with cancer, she had said, yet with these struggles, she remained strong and determined to beat cancer, so Willow remained strong with her. She sent her novels Bonnie could read when she was stuck in a chair for hours having chemo. Her hair grew back but fell out again. Willow sent her scarves and in return, Bonnie sent her back a picture of her with one wrapped around her head. She looked beautiful; Willow noted. Cancer didn't take her joy.

Summer came and one evening, Bonnie called crying. It was the first time she heard that kind of anguish from her friend, and Willow cried on the phone with her as she revealed the news. The cancer had spread to her lungs and still, she was determined to fight. Willow would continue to fight with her. Her family rallied around her. She was thankful for every day she had but she was tired. Her body wasn't cooperating, she expressed through an email message. She ended her email with dire words that stuck in Willow's head. 'I can't keep living like this.' Willow pulled out her keepsake box and fumbled with the stones as she thought about what to do. She needed a Miss Kora remedy. Willow had to get back to the valley, where Bonnie was living now with her sister and mother so they could care for her. She had taken her pets and left the house in the mountains. 'It did not look like it did when you came', she confessed to Willow. She made plans to go back to the valley, and her mother decided to join her.

22

Chapter 22

The Last Day Together

The sunflowers were in full bloom and the bees were now pollinating. Willow and Bonnie dressed and went into the field. They ran up and down the rows and stopped to watch the bees collecting nectar. Bursts of humming noises buzzed, and sometimes the sounds of the honeybees were a continuous sonorous chorus. They hid behind the stalks, now almost twice as tall as they were, while playing hide and seek. The stalks became giants they had to battle or magical friends that whispered secrets.

The day was hot and humid, and their foreheads became beaded with perspiration, their shirts damp from sweat. Still, they played among the prolific crop of sunflowers incognizant of passing time for the summer day seemed endless. Mrs. Murphy had called them in for lunch once, but they forgot, and she didn't remind them again this time. Dirt streaked their ankles and their hands were brown from digging in the soil with sticks and making dirt pies. The flowers beckoned their presence as they engrossed themselves in imaginative play with nature.

This day would be the last day Willow spent with Bonnie as two carefree spirits. Mrs. Murphy came outside on the porch and stood before the field, her hands in the pockets of her apron. Willow caught a glimpse of her stiff posture as she stood appearing to mull over her next action. She watched for a moment before she broke her silence.

"Bonnie and Willow, you must come here at once," she commanded loudly with force. Willow had never heard this tone from Mrs. Murphy. They both stopped immediately to give her their attention.

"Mom must be mad we didn't come in for lunch," Bonnie said. She shouted in her direction, "Mom, I'm sorry, we forgot about lunch."

But when they reached Mrs. Murphy, she seemed more worried than she did angry. Her forehead scrunched with confusion, and her eyes lingered on Willow and Bonnie. As she led them inside, her silence revealed the seriousness, and Willow sensed it was about her. Without question, they followed Mrs. Murphy. Willow's heartbeat fast, and she knew that her life was about to change. The day, which had seemed as if it would go on forever, had abruptly altered its course.

She led them to the living room. The television was silent. Mr. Murphy was sitting in a high-backed chair, dressed in overalls and his boots, off, indicating he wouldn't be working outside anytime soon. Standing near the front window, was Joseph. He had his arms crossed at chest level and stood soberly as he waited. Willow glanced out the door and noticed his Buick parked in the driveway, behind Mrs. Murphy's station wagon. This time, they let Bonnie stay in the room. Willow was directed to sit down, and Bonnie sat next to her on the couch. Mrs. Murphy stood beside the chair next to her husband, waiting for Joseph to speak.

"Willow, it seems the police have some information about your mother." He uncrossed his arms. "She may have been found, and she is asking for you."

"Where was she?" Willow asked.

"We're not sure but a woman came to the police station claiming she is your mother. I haven't been out there to see if it is really her."

"I want to go see her," Willow requested.

"That's why I am here. I'm going to take you to the police station. Since I know your mother, I can make sure it is really her."

"Please Mr. Joseph. I have missed her," tears of relief streamed from

Willow's eyes. The knots that had tangled her heart for months were unraveling. "Please take me to her." She bolted from the couch and ran over to Joseph hugging his waist. He patted her back then kneeled to be at eye level with her.

"Now Willow, I'm not positive it's your mother but," he paused, "just in case, go get your things."

That wouldn't be much Willow thought. She only came to the Murphys with one paper bag full of clothing. Jenny had given her some clothes that she outgrew or felt were too drab to wear anymore now that she was sophisticated.

Bonnie helped Willow gather her belongings while the adults waited in the living room. Jenny came to her sister's room when she heard Willow and Bonnie opening drawers and scuffling around the upstairs. My mother is back Willow had told her. Jenny helped gather the items and the three of them returned to the living room. Willow had enough clothes to fill a plastic garbage bag.

Now that she had her things, it was time to go. She glanced around the room at the family that had so graciously taken her in as one of their own, fed her, clothed her, and loved her. Then there was Bonnie. Her sunflower friend. This was the moment she had to say goodbye. The Murphys gathered in to hug her. First Mr. and Mrs. Murphy, then Jenny.

"Keep reading," Jenny said.

"Willow, we loved having you with us. We wish you the very best and I hope you can come back and visit. You are always welcome," Mrs. Murphy expressed then she wrapped her arms around the little, innocent girl.

Mr. Murphy cleared his throat. "Willow you take care now, you hear." Then he patted her back just behind her right shoulder.

All the sudden a frantic knock pounded the front door. There was Miss Kora peering inside the screen with curiosity as if she knew. Mrs. Murphy cocked her head so she could see who was at the door.

"Kora. Come in," Mrs. Murphy said welcoming her to the gathering.

"I was at my mailbox and I just had a feeling something was going on that I needed to be here for," she stated opening the door, letting herself inside. The door squeaked as it swung shut.

"Well, as a matter of fact, you are correct," Mrs. Murphy responded to her inquiry. "We think Willow's mother has been found and Joseph is going to take her to the police station in town."

Miss Kora ran to Willow, who was standing apprehensively beside the couch, clutching her suitcase. She set the suitcase down and hugged Miss Kora, holding on a little extra longer than the others. "Bye, Miss Kora. Thank you for the rocks."

"Oh honey, they are more than just rocks. They are relics, relics that hold power. Hold on to them my dear."

Willow pictured in her head the carnelian stone that brought her courage and the pink crystal that brought her good luck. She thought that maybe Miss Kora was right, maybe they held powers. After all, she was able to survive this ordeal and now Mamma may have been found. But something was missing. Bonnie wasn't in the room anymore and she couldn't leave without saying goodbye to the best friend she ever had, the friend that made her pitiful circumstances into a journey of joy and adventure, a time when she felt free from strife.

Suddenly the back door slammed, and Bonnie came bounding in leaving a breeze behind her. She held onto two sunflowers, cut about six inches below the massive blossom. They were weighty in her hand, and the flowers bobbled as Bonnie struggled to keep them steady. On the other hand, she held the knife used to cut the stems, a knife that Mrs. Murphy quickly and gently took from her placing it on the dining room table.

"Willow, here," Bonnie said out of breath. "These are for you."

Willow took the flowers admiring the magnificent blooms as she grasped the stems.

Miss Kora, the guru of plants, took note of the type of flower exchanged and as one would predict, expressed her thoughts. "Ah, such splendid sunflowers, the protectors, they soak up the sun and anything that grows below will be protected by their bold blossoms."

Kind of like Bonnie and her family protected me, Willow thought.

Then her mind thought of Joseph, but she couldn't quite understand why.

"I think we ought to be going," Joseph hesitated after observing these loving exchanges but bearing the news that it had to end.

"Bonnie. Thank you for the flowers. Here please keep one of them, one for me and one for you. I'm going to miss you."

"I'm going to miss you too, Willow." Bonnie's eyes swallowed with tears.

At the same time, they reached out, their arms embracing the other, each holding a sunflower in their hand. Willow gripped her tight not sure if she wanted to let go but she had to. If only she could take her with her to the police station. If only they had one more day together. But Willow knew. It was time to let go. She unhinged her arms, still holding onto the sunflower, and picked up her belongings.

"Bye, Bonnie," she whispered.

"Bye, Willow."

Joseph took up the suitcase and led Willow out the door. The Murphys' family and Miss Kora came to the front porch and watched as they left Bartholomew's farmhouse. The air held that earthy smell and she could almost taste the dirt from the field where the sunflowers stood. Soon Bonnie would be able to harvest the seeds with her family Willow thought as she looked around before plopping in the Buick. Mr. Mann was coming down his driveway and paused for a moment before he pulled out on Marshland Road. She glanced down and saw Miss Kora's mailbox. It was leaning again, but it stood with an indomitable spunk clothed in its rustic exterior. Joseph settled into the front seat. His maroon-colored Buick had the same colored interior. The seats were soft and cushiony. He started up the motor and it purred. Oliver. She thought. I didn't get to say goodbye to him.

"Joseph. Can you hold on for one more thing?"

"What is it, Willow?"

"I have to say goodbye to Oliver."

"Who is Oliver?"

"The cat. He loves me. I can't leave without saying goodbye to him."

"But he's nowhere to be seen and cats don't come when you call them."

"Just let me try."

"Go ahead, Willow."

Willow pulled the handle and pushed the heavy door. Right at her feet, Oliver was sitting there waiting as if he knew, too. She bent down and stroked his head and down his back several times. He purred and stared at her then reached his paw to her arm.

"Bye, Oliver." Willow pecked his head with a kiss. She gave a wave to the Murphys' family and Miss Kora. She then gave one last wave to Bonnie.

Joseph backed out of the driveway and pulled onto Marshland Road. She saw the Sunflower field behind the house, the sassafras tree where she met Bonnie, and the old decrepit shanty. She noticed the yard where they drenched themselves with the hose, looked at the stars, and caught lightning bugs. She stared out the back window as Joseph drove toward the town. She watched until the last sight of the bright yellow sunflowers was out of her view and she could no longer see the outlines of the people standing on the porch. She watched until the farmhouse was a tiny speck sitting on a piece of green. Then she turned around and pictured Mamma.

#

Joseph talked all the way to Nelson. Willow supposed he was trying to make the best of an awkward situation. He told Willow how he had missed seeing us at church and then asked about her stay at the Murphys' house. She answered only to be polite; her mind focused on Mamma. They passed by a long stretch of trees and fields before the gas station sign came into view. Then Joseph asked Willow if she was all right because she sniffled a few times. Willow was sad to leave Bonnie, but seeing Mamma, well that is what she'd been hoping for. She wondered if Mamma knew Daddy wasn't coming home. She pictured Mamma's hair and wondered it was still long with soft waves. She remembered how her bangs curled around the edges of her forehead at the temples. She missed the flowery scent of her neck and wrists where she sprayed her perfume. She missed her loving smile.

Joseph passed the gas station and Lucille's and Powel's Market. The police station was a little further up the road, beyond the cluster of stores. Willow saw the almond-colored brick building and the flagpole that stood in front of the double glass doors. The American flag was raised to the top of the pole.

Joseph held the door and let Willow pass through the entrance as he followed behind. The place smelled of oil soap; the same kind Mamma used to clean the wooden furniture. Beyond the front entrance, Willow saw glass windows. Behind them was an office that reminded her of the office at school. Joseph led her there. A woman recognized him. She said hello and gestured for them to follow her to a narrow hallway. There was a row of rooms with desks. They stopped at the third door on the right and Willow was directed to a chair with brown cloth seats and metal arms, which were cold when she rested her arms on them.

A man sat at his desk chair. He was smoking. Willow noticed a pack of Marlboro cigarettes next to an ashtray. He announced his name as Officer Ronald Dean and to just call him Ron. He asked Willow her name and told her the same thing Joseph did; they think they found her mother. He asked Joseph to come to a room beside his office. It was surrounded by windows, but all Willow could see was a blinding glare. Joseph went with him and about five minutes later, he came back to ask Willow to follow them. It was cold with fluorescent lights that buzzed continuously. Willow walked into the room and saw Mamma sitting in a chair.

She was found

23

Chapter 23

Start Living

Willow and Barbara planned to leave in the early hours of the morning, the time when the cool air would create goose bumps on your arm. New windows lined the back of the house and let in a breath of light as the morning sun rose. The salvaged garage windows from the carriage house doors remained in the front of the house leaving an impression of the time period when the structure was built. The living area and dining room were completed but tarps hung to prevent dust from penetrating the freshly painted walls created by the nearly finished kitchen makeover. The first floor was still draped in work. During the second part of the renovation, Barbara spent much of her time upstairs or stayed at Willow's condo. Unlike the upstairs, the first floor took longer than planned. There were more snags this time. Material didn't come in as scheduled and asbestos was found in some of the original walls of the house. Willow was surprised at the strict procedures for encountering such a thing in an old house, but it only reinforced her approval of Mr. Keller. He upheld high standards. Barbara accepted several dinner invitations from Mr. Keller and she finally admitted to Willow, her fond feelings for him.

Willow drove from the coast, following the same route as the last time she went to Sol Valley. When they arrived in the town, Barbara gaped at its growth. 'The old shell gas station is still the same,' she remarked as they passed the sign. But there was a larger gas station with a mini-mart and several islands of gas pumps, Willow had said letting her mother know they didn't have to use the gas station that held the old memories. Willow thought of this trip as a milestone for Barbara. Being able to return to a place she once was forced to escape, was progress.

#

Willow and Barbara went out for a meal then returned to the hotel to settle into comfortable clothes and planned to watch a movie. Barbara was looking forward to seclusion and little activity. Not two minutes after they changed and found a movie on HBO did the phone ring. Willow guessed it was Bonnie returning her call from earlier, when she phoned to say she had arrived.

"Hello," Willow said eagerly, looking forward to hearing from her friend.

"Willow, this is your father."

"Floyd, how did you know I was here?" Willow noticed her mother's face wash over with a pallid hue. She shot her mother a consoling glance as she listened to what he had to say on the other end of the line.

"Yes, I can do that. Ok, see you tomorrow." She hung up and right away, turned to Barbara.

"I'm not going to see him," Barbara adamantly stated.

"Mom, I didn't even tell him you were here. He asked me to come see him, and I told him I would stop by."

"How did he know you were visiting?"

"He talks to Joseph once a week. I guess Joseph has been making calls to the farmhouse to check in on Bonnie and Bonnie mentioned it. I'm sorry mom."

"I understand Willow. He will never stop being your father."

Willow and Barbara went back to watching the movie when Willow's mobile phone rang. To her relief, it was Bonnie, who, contrarily to what Willow imagined, sounded energetic. She told Bonnie she would be by the farmhouse on the way back from her father's cabin in the morning.

#

Willow ate breakfast in the hotel lobby and returned to her room where her mother was just waking up. She was embedded in the mattress and snuggled comfortably under the covers.

"Mom, I'm heading over to Floyd's place, and then I'm going to stop at the farmhouse on the way home. I hate to leave you here by yourself all day."

"Willow, I'm in heaven right now. There are no hammering noises or screeching sounds of drills. There's no dust flying. I'm fine right here. I'll watch television and read my novel. Don't worry about me."

"I'm not sure how long I'll be gone. It might be late this afternoon before I get back."

"It's all right. I'd like to meet Bonnie, but you let me know the best time and I'll be ready."

"You look so comfortable and rested."

"I am, Willow. I haven't had a day to sleep in for so long."

Willow left her mother at the hotel to relax. She stopped at the market to pick up groceries for her father sticking mostly to the basics of bread, fruits and vegetables, and meat. She spotted a chocolate cake and figured her father would appreciate something sweet and delicious. She picked up a second cake to take to Bonnie's. As she was shopping for groceries, it occurred to her that her father's life since leaving jail, was somewhat of a charity case, and she would never know the feeling of having an intact family. A rueful feeling tugged at her for wanting that.

The drive was easy this time for she remembered the directions from her last visit. She knew exactly when to turn into Crumpler Road and soon she was making a left on 1008. The road had the same bumps as the last time, and she felt her sedan jump as she drove to the cabin. Her father was waiting on the porch. Willow fetched the groceries from the back seat and Floyd came over to take the bags out of her hands. Willow sat on the porch while Floyd put away the food. He came outside with a glass of tea and handed it to his daughter.

"Thank you, Willow, for bringing me food," he said and sat next to his daughter.

"Willow, I know you're here to see your friend. I'm sorry about the cancer."

"Me too."

Floyd continued to speak in a somber tone, "I realized what she and her family did for you when I was in jail. I know I wouldn't let you go to her house but I'm glad you did Willow."

"That was what saved me from misery. I had to stay at Bonnie's house when you went to jail. One day I was upset and ran back to the house. I saw grandpa in the garage. He put gas cans in the back of his truck and left. Mr. Murphy was missing a gas can and I only ever remember seeing one in the garage. Was Grandpa involved?"

"He put me up to the evil deed and then blamed the entire incident on me. I served ten years, he served nothing."

"What was his problem with the Ferebee's besides the fact he was prejudiced?"

"Mr. Ferebee worked for the state police. My dad was afraid of him."

"Well that's all wrong and what you did was wrong, Dad! The Ferebee's didn't deserve that."

Floyd shifted his gaze for a moment when he noticed Willow called him *dad*. "It's all wrong, Willow. My actions were hateful, but it eventually turned out the way it's supposed to be. I'm out here and your mom is doing good in the world, isn't she? Can you tell me what happened after she left that night? I always wondered."

"She hid. That's all I know. She hid until Joseph took me to the police station. I don't know what has haunted her more, your abuse or leaving me with you. She told me I kept you alive, I never quite understood that, but I think it's because..." Willow's voice trailed off into silence, hesitant to delve deeper into the darkness.

"I know what you were going to say, Willow. Yes, I threatened to kill myself with my gun to scare your mother. I did it for her attention, I realize now. I knew I didn't treat her right, yet I wanted her to stay. And I was jealous of Joseph. I suppose that's why he never told me anything about Barbara. He was the one who came to me in jail. He helped me, Willow. Before that, I was so against him and his religion. Irony," Floyd smirked after he said the word.

"What did you do at Bonnie's house that summer?"

"We had some adventures; we played in the sunflower fields and climbed trees."

"All the things kids should be doing," he said as if he realized his notions back then were wrong.

Willow agreed. Floyd asked her more questions about that summer and she told him the stories. She was surprised at how vividly she was able to remember from over twenty years ago and found herself smiling as she spoke about the memories. She even caught her dad smiling a few times. He retreated in the house to bring out the pitcher of tea, refilling her glass.

The sound of a vehicle traveling over the rocky road could be heard just beyond the cabin. Willow turned toward the sound, surprised that someone would be driving this deep in the woods.

"That's Joseph. He knew you would be here this morning and he wanted to see you."

Willow hadn't seen him since the day he reunited her with Barbara at the police station. Her heart flipped with a feeling of ardor. Joseph looked out for the people in the community unconditionally and Willow had never been able to thank him. Instead of a Buick, as Willow remembered, Joseph drove an SUV. He immediately recognized her as if he had seen her grow up and she recognized him too. His hairline had receded, and the rest was peppered with gray, but he held the same warm smile and his congenial manner remained unchanged. He carried a box of canned goods into the cabin then joined Willow and Floyd on the porch. She told him the story of her life since she left Marshland County without mentioning that her mother was in town with her.

They talked about Bonnie and Willow stated she was stopping by the farmhouse after she left. When Floyd excused himself to use the bathroom, Willow thanked Joseph for helping her father.

"Your father has been found. Anytime the power of God can change a bitter heart, it changes the world, even if it's minuscule," he told Willow.

Floyd came back out with more tea and the three of them conversed a bit longer before Bonnie said her goodbyes. She left the cabin watching her father talking to Joseph as she experienced the uncomfortable jolting from driving over the uneven surfaces.

When she arrived at the farmhouse, both trucks were parked in the driveway along with Bonnie's Subaru, so she parked on the side of the road. She carried chocolate cake and knocked on the front door and Mrs. Murphy was right there welcoming her inside with a hug. Bonnie was relaxed on the couch watching television. Willow thought back to the day they got their new television, and she and Jenny stayed in all morning watching game shows. This television, a more modern set with a bigger screen, was not encased in a fancy wooden box.

"Willow!" Bonnie sounded chipper which surprised Willow especially after seeing how much weight she lost. Her body was thin, and her cheeks were sunken. Still, her smile was lively revealing the same exuberant Bonnie she always knew. A blue paisley scarf wrapped her head. The color of the blue matched her eyes. Willow hugged her tightly after she handed the cake to Mrs. Murphy. "It's so good to see you."

"Well, I wish the circumstances were different..." her voice trailed off for a second. "We should be at the beach or in the mountains but whatever, you are here."

Mrs. Murphy offered Willow tea.

"No, thank you. I just drank about three glasses at Floyd's."

"You went to see your father. How did that go?" Bonnie asked.

"It's coming along."

Willow and Bonnie talked for several hours. Mrs. Murphy brought in sandwiches and pieces of cake which she had sliced and placed on dessert plates. Bonnie ate slowly and took in tiny bits at a time until she finished the food as she came up with the idea of having a picnic tomorrow evening and Willow decided it was a brilliant idea. The weather was predicted to be pleasant. Mrs. Murphy agreed and suggested that everyone bring a dish to share. Willow would stop by Miss Kora's on her way back and invite her to the celebration. After some time, Willow could tell Bonnie was losing her strength and needed to rest. Willow gave her a tender hug before she left the farmhouse.

#

The next day, Willow and her mother left the hotel and stopped at the market to purchase food. The store was quiet for a Saturday afternoon. Back in Pequot, the markets were always busy at this time of day on a weekend. The music flowed over the store speaker playing soft rock hits of the 70s and Willow hummed to the familiar tunes. After she picked up several buckets of fried chicken and a container of potato salad, she spotted large sunflower bouquets in the floral department.

When they arrived at the farm, Barbara placed the food on the table while Willow carried her flowers to where Bonnie was enjoying watching the sunshine shower over the field.

"Willow, thank you," Bonnie's voice lifted in excitement when she received the arrangement. "These are beautiful. Remember I gave you a sunflower on your last day with us. I can see that moment clearly, like it was yesterday."

It pulled at Bonnie's elbow when she gripped the stems, so Willow reached out to help Bonnie hold it steady and was concerned by the weakness her body exuded.

"I still have that flower. I dried it and keep it in a special box. Let me put these in a vase for you."

"Thank you. There are some under the kitchen sink."

Barbara walked out of the door with Mrs. Murphy, who must have saw the flowers through the kitchen window because she brought out a vase filled halfway with water. Willow introduced her mother to Bonnie for the first time. She hugged her, embracing her with affection as if she was meeting family. "Bonnie, it's so good to meet you. I've heard so much about you and your family. I can't be more grateful how you took care of my Willow."

"It was such a fun summer we had. I had just moved into this house and the only playmate that I had was my sister Jenny. I was grateful that Willow came along."

The other guest arrived with their hands full of food offerings. Joseph was with his wife and Willow was meeting her for the first time. Miss Kora brought a bowl full of greens complete with herbs from her garden. Jenny came downstairs with her husband Cliff and the twins, Michael and Marcy, came running from the barn each holding a cat. They were a few years older than the last time Willow saw them and starting to lose their young child faces. Michael was slightly taller than Marcy and both were a bit gawky being at that awkward stage before puberty. They dropped the cats when they saw the crowd that had gathered on the back porch; the cats stuck around as if they were invited, creeping along the railings before jumping to the porch floor and hiding under the couch. A noisy hum filled up the back of the house. Bonnie perked up with energy. Barbara and Joseph united with a hug and her mother became engrossed in a conversation with him and his wife. The children were playing in the yard; Bonnie was taking everything in on the couch and Mrs. Murphy, Jenny, and her husband, cliff, were fixing food in the kitchen. Miss Kora rearranged her herbal salad on the table. Willow took a moment to look around. The people surrounding her were all part of her life when she lived here but never gathered in one place. It was the culmination event of that summer but 22 years later. It was the way she wanted to live, surrounded by people she loved.

Joseph pulled Willow aside. "Willow," he started. "All those years ago when your mother was gone, I want you to know I looked out for you. I often stopped by the house to make sure you were all right. I was the one who put the clothespins on the line and left the strawberries on the stoop. I fixed the door so it wouldn't keep you up at night."

"That was you?

"Yes, Willow. I kept your mother safe, too. When I took you to the police station, I knew your mother was there. I kept it a secret so it wouldn't get back to your father or his father. Your mother was not well enough to take you back right after your father went to jail so the Murphys kept you for a little while. I prayed for you Willow and your parents."

"Well, Joseph. I felt like someone was at the house. I felt someone looking out for me." Willow paused. "Thank you, Joseph. You've helped me and both of my parents. You have a heart as big as this valley, Joseph."

"You have a special gift, Willow. You survived a challenging childhood. You're an overcomer, Willow, and this valley could use someone like you to work at the new clinic which is opening in the next few months. They are looking for a psychologist to work with young children. You would be perfect for the job."

"Oh, Joseph. I'm employed. I like my job, most of the time. Working with children?" Willow lifted her voice and wrinkled her brow as if giving the notion a second thought. "Now that would be a challenge but perhaps a good one. I don't know, Joseph. I don't know if I could leave my mother."

"Well, Willow, you don't have to say yes now. Maybe give it some thought," he suggested.

Mrs. Murphy organized the dishes on the serving table so that the supper foods were at one end and the desserts took up a smaller portion of the table at the other end. The vase of sunflowers stood in the middle residing over the bounty. "This is quite a gathering for being planned at the last minute. I think we are ready to eat, everyone."

A hush fell upon the picnic when Joseph announced for everyone to bow their heads in prayer. The afternoon cooled as they ate at tables in front of the cornfield. The gathering lasted the rest of the daylight hours. The sun remained vibrant as it started dropping from the sky and soon it exchanged with a silvery moon. Michael and Marcy started catching lightning bugs. Willow noticed Bonnie's energy waning and Joseph and Miss Kora must have noticed too because they announced they ought to leave. Willow hugged them goodbye, promising to keep in touch, and Barbara made another round of thanks for taking care of Willow years ago. Jenny and Cliff helped Mrs. Murphy gather up the dishes that were left and brought them into the kitchen for cleaning with Barbara following behind. Willow and Bonnie were left outside sitting on the back porch, feeling the soft silence that had trickled among them, except for the crickets that performed the evening song. Sassy, Bonnie's cat, sauntered to the porch and cuddled next to her. Her dogs, tired from the excitement of the picnic, laid motionless in random spots on the porch.

"I had a great day. I had more energy today and I was able to eat the food," Bonnie remarked. "Maybe it was the peppermint tea that Miss Kora has been bringing me. It's good for the digestive system."

"You're doing better," Willow said with a sense of hope.

"I'm going to be all right, Willow. My treatments are working." Bonnie said as she closed her eyes and took in a long breath. "This air brings back memories. I can almost smell the sunflowers."

"I can feel the dirt and sweat on my legs," Willow said, reaching to scratch her ankles. "What I would do to go back to that summer."

"Willow, we were as thick as thieves. I looked forward to your visits. On days you didn't show up in the morning, I climbed the sassafras tree and stared at the edge of the sunflower field wishing for you to appear from the woods. Mom would say, 'Bonnie what on earth are you doing, isn't it time you come down from that tree?' and I would insist that you were coming. Then when you came to live with us, I was thrilled."

"Bonnie you saved me that summer. Visiting with you was the only time I felt normal with my mother being gone and my dad, the way he is. I felt so free with you. I could be a child unbuckled by the afflictions that gripped my life. If only for the moment, I was able to forget my strife. When we spent time together over the past two years, I felt that same sense of freedom, like I had a chance to live, to breathe easy."

"Willow, maybe it's time you start living. You can breathe easily without me, you know. Take time to do something fun, something you've never done before like traveling."

"That's hard with the hours I work and looking out for my mother," Willow remarked.

"Your mother seems to be doing quite all right on her own. Willow, if you don't start living for yourself, you will eventually come up empty."

Willow thought she had it all figured out but now Bonnie was causing her to feel differently. Her job was secure, her mother was happy and safe, her dad was able to live without harming himself or others but there was something missing as Bonnie just made her realize.

Bonnie nodded her head a few times drifting off to sleep. Willow slipped a pillow under Bonnie's head, so she wouldn't wake up with a kinked neck and sat beside her in silence. She pictured every memory she could conjure of her and Bonnie here and played it in her head like a movie until Barbara and Mrs. Murphy stepped outside, finished with the dishes. Mrs. Murphy stated that she would help Bonnie to bed and lifted her from the couch. Bonnie woke up and hugged her friend. Willow hugged her back gripping on tightly.

"When are you heading back to Pequot?" she asked.

"Some time tomorrow, my mom and I are going to do some sightseeing before we head back."

"Call me so we can start planning next summer's trip when I'm healthier."

"I will do that. I love you, Bonnie."

"I love you, Willow."

#

Willow pulled into the carriage house driveway; she left the motor on while she helped her mother carry her luggage to the house. When Barbara opened the door, she remarked that the place felt different, 'airier', she had said. Willow wondered if her mother's feeling had something to do with the progress of the renovation. It was too dark to see and too late to ask her mother to turn on the hallway light. Besides, Willow was anxious to get home and into bed. The radio was playing Suite: Judy Blue Eyes and the song pepped her up enough to stay awake for the drive to her condo. "Do do do do do do do dah do do do," she warbled along to the music as she veered into the parking lot of building D. After she turned off the car, the motor purred one last time, and she heard the river ramble in the background. She schlepped her luggage to the door of her place. "How can you catch the sparrow," she sang in a low voice as she found her key and unlocked the door, letting herself in. She noticed the answering machine blinking. She must have a thousand messages she thought. It would have to wait until morning, but something propelled her to go over and push the play button. Work messages, a call from a friend, more work messages, and a message from Jenny.

"Hello, Willow. Bonnie is not doing well. We had to rush her to the hospital this evening. She is in ICU. My mobile phone doesn't work in the hospital so call Sol Valley Regional, ICU unit. Ask for me or my mother."

Another message played right after.

"Willow, Bonnie passed away. We are heading back to the farmhouse. Call us in the morning. There's nothing else we could have done. I'm sorry, Willow."

24

Chapter 24

God is Good

Willow called Jenny the next morning. She was groggy and seemed to be in a fog, reporting that she hadn't slept all night. Jenny told her they were working on arrangements, and Willow expressed her sorrows before they hung up. Likewise, Willow slept very little. She tossed and turned until five AM when she finally drifted off into a slumber dreaming about next summer's trip to the beach. She was sitting in a beach chair next to Bonnie, listening to her radio blare classic rock tunes. The sun was bright and pleasantly warm, and the waves rolled to shore dropping bits of rocks and seashells before it ebbed out to sea. Bonnie was sitting in the beach chair she had since she was a teenager. The ends of the material were frayed, and the wooden arms were streaked where the finish had worn off. They wore bug-eyed sunglasses with white rims. With their toes in the sand, they sang along to the music, untrammeled by who would hear their off-key singing. People smiled as they passed by. When she woke, Willow felt the heaviness in her heart. Willow told her mother the news and Barbara asked her to come over, but Willow couldn't get out of bed that day.

Willow wept through most of the day and ignored all phone calls from both her mobile and condo phone. She turned down the answering machine volume so her mother's voice wouldn't come through asking again and again if she was doing all right. Barbara couldn't grasp the bond she had with Bonnie, not that Willow blamed her. How could she? She was gone that summer and Bonnie replaced the missing part. When Willow was able to gather herself to get out of bed, the first thing she did was reach for the keepsake box and pulled out the dried sunflower, staring at it with questions and thinking about its cycle. Human life has a cycle too and Bonnie's had come to the end, too soon.

We were just beginning again.

She wondered why God takes the good ones. "The Good Die Young," she said out loud that day as Billy Joel's song came to mind. She thought of her father. Why hadn't God taken him? His life was full of strife, a strife he caused others to suffer and now, he was a continuous charity case. Willow felt guilty for those thoughts.

Bonnie was grateful for her life. Willow couldn't count how many times she had said "God is good" even after all the pain she suffered. Today Willow couldn't bring herself to think the same. She wanted God to bring Bonnie back. She was the bright spot that summer her mother was gone, and when she and her mother fled the valley, she held onto that. Their friendship erased the shame because Bonnie never saw that part of Willow. Bonnie never expressed pity or stared at her with sorrow because she couldn't read or didn't have birthday parties like the other kids did or because she couldn't pass fourth grade. She never saw her father get angry or her mother cry in despair. There were no judgments dropped or subtle hints of what she had were more than Willow had. If Bonnie didn't see her shame, then maybe other people wouldn't either. It stuck with Willow through every run-down place she lived, every bill her mother couldn't pay and every second-hand store she shopped in for clothes. And now, Bonnie was gone.

25

Chapter 25

The Spirit of the Sunflower

Willow went to the carriage house the next day. "Please come over, Willow," her mother had urged. Willow parked in her usual spot. The door was surprisingly unlocked, and Willow was able to walk right inside without the pause of her mother peeping through the hole or unfastening the locks. She was somber as she walked the short hallway to the kitchen, her legs moving slowly as if they were weighted with metal. The tarps were no longer hanging, the sounds of hammering were nonexistent, and the house was clean, free of dust particles floating aimlessly. It sparkled with a freshness Willow couldn't help to notice even with the dreariness that held her inside a bubble. Bill was standing next to Barbara and they were both gazing upon Willow with sympathetic faces. Barbara wrapped her arms around Willow and held her while she cried.

"It's going to be all right. Bonnie's in a better place," she said softly.

The typical things people say when someone dies, which didn't offer her any comfort, but her mother's embrace did. It brought her a feeling of safety, a feeling that it was going to be all right, eventually. When she pulled away, she soaked up the changes in the house. It took on a different aura. A sense of renewal washed over her as she found a glimmer of new life somewhere inside her melancholy. The renovation was completely done, and she breathed in the smell of fresh paint and new carpet. She looked around, admiring the transformation of the house. Her eyes stopped at the windows. Outside she saw the brightest sunshine she ever saw in her life. The kind of shine she remembered presiding over the sunflower field. It flooded the living room of the house and she felt its energy. Like the renovations renewed the carriage house, the sunlight renewed her spirit, and, in that moment, she felt Bonnie's presence. It reminded her of Bonnie's advice, 'It's time you start living' she heard her say. And Willow was ready to follow it. She was no longer that pariah from Sol Valley on Old Rock Road.

#

Willow packed the last box in the back of her sedan. The trunk took two extra tugs before it would lower and still, she had to use her palms to force the trunk to latch. The rear end bounced as if it was answering back to the brutality Willow imposed on it. She had sworn she was getting a new car even if it took most of her savings for the down payment but then she accepted the job. The bottom of her neck was warm with perspiration but good luck finding a hair tie. Everything she owned was packed, with most of her belongings in storage and the rest in her car. She used her hands to gather her thick long caramel hair, the ringlet curls roping around her fingers as she pulled it off her neck. Another glance at the condo, her first place where she lived independently. Now she was ready. Willow cranked the air conditioner on high then tuned rock music on the radio. This would keep her lively as she made her journey into Sol valley.

Willow stopped at the first light in town. She pulled out the contract and glanced at the address to the new clinic. The light turned green and she made a right, heading down the main street of Sol Valley. The police station was nearing, and Willow slowed her speed as she drifted by. The building and the flagpole remained the same as the day she reunited with her mother. Some things in the valley hadn't changed. But the clinic was new. Two blocks past the police station, and there it was, her new place of employment. She checked the address to make sure, but the sign confirmed it. Willow parked on the curb in front and lifted her eyes to the sign, Sol Valley Clinical. She would be here by eight AM tomorrow and now that she knew where it was located, the morning transition would be smooth, she hoped.

Willow drove west and made the left on Marshland Road. A few miles later, the farmhouse came into view. The sun hung over the field; this summer was soybeans. Willow parked in the driveway next to the trucks. She took one bag and her purse with her and knocked gently on the screen door, then didn't hesitate to walk in when it was not answered right away.

"Willow is that you?" She heard a scratchy but joyful voice from the kitchen.

"Yes, it's me, Mrs. Murphy."

She was standing in the entry to the hallway peering back at Willow. "Well of course it's you. No one has big brown eyes like you, Willow. Come in. I'm just finishing up dinner."

"Where should I put my bag?"

"Would you like to stay in Bonnie's room?"

"I'd love to, Mrs. Murphy."

"Willow, you're grown up now, you can call me Jean."

"Mrs. Murphy, I can't do that." Willow chuckled.

Willow took her bag upstairs and then retrieved the rest of her belongings from the car. She would be staying at the Murphys' house until she found a place to settle in Sol Valley, where she was starting a new position as a child psychologist. She was one of ten that interviewed for the position in the new clinic and was favored unanimously. Willow looked forward to the new challenge and the chance to work with children, whom she hoped to be easier at change than adults.

Mrs. Murphy set the table. She explained that Jenny and Cliff took the kids on vacation to the mountains so it would be just the two of them, this evening. The plates topped with shepherd's pie were steaming and smothered in brown gravy. After a quick prayer, Mrs. Murphy dug her fork into the mashed potatoes and blew to cool it.

Before she ate, she said, "You know Willow, there's this trail behind Miss Kora's cottage. If you go past her house, you'll find a suspension bridge. It leads to a path that will take you up a hill."

Willow knew exactly where to find that trail.

"And," she continued. "At the top of the hill, you can see the whole valley."

"Well, Mrs. Murphy, I'll have to find it. It seems like a wonderful trail to walk, especially on a sunny afternoon."

"It is, Willow. I took a walk up there with Miss Kora the other day and I found the darndest thing."

"What was that, Mrs. Murphy?"

"All the way up the trail and to the crown of the hill is filled with wild sunflowers."

26

Epilogue

Since Bonnie died, I continue to live in the valley. I take regular walks across the suspension bridge and follow the trail to the crown of the hill. My mother still mentions she has extra room in the house if I ever want to move back to Pequot but I'm hoping that Bill will move in instead. Maybe one day, but for now, I'm watching my mother be happy and fall in love with the man she deserves. I'm holding out for a man like Bill. I miss Bonnie and think about the good times we spent together. I wonder about the adventures we could have had if she was still living. I pictured us as two old kooky women with wrinkled faces, crepe papered skin, wearing floppy hats at the beach, or hiking trails in the mountains or maybe we would have found another sunflower field to run through. When a person dies and it leaves a deep impression in your life, a spot of permanent loss remains. Bonnie can never be replaced but she lives on through the place I hold in my heart. Every time I see a sunflower, I feel the spirit of Bonnie and remember the summer we watched the sunflowers grow.

27

Reading Group Guide

1. Which character had the most impact on the outcome of Willow's success? Explain. How did each character impact you? Who was your favorite? Least favorite? Why?
2. Willow encourages her mother to forgive Floyd but when she asked her daughter if she forgave her father, Willow left the question unanswered. Do you think Willow forgave her father? Does Floyd deserve forgiveness? Why was Willow not able to completely cut her father off from her life?
3. The novel dives into Willow's thoughts when she was separated from her mother, but we do not know where her mother was hiding or what she was thinking. What do you think the mother's state of mind was during the separation from her daughter? Where do you think she was hiding?
4. What do you think was Willow's most challenging obstacle to overcome?
5. How was Bonnie's innocence and approach to life healing to Willow? What was your favorite character trait of Bonnie? How was Miss Kora's approach to life healing to Willow? What was your favorite character trait of Miss Kora?

6. How is Joseph important to Sol Valley? Is there someone in your community that has had an impact as Joseph did on the people of Sol Valley?
7. Willow and her mother seemed to make it over many hurdles, but both of their lives came together at the same time. At which part of the story was this most evident?
8. What was your favorite scene of the novel? Why?

28

Acknowledgments

I read somewhere along this journey that an author is not to thank their reader, but how could I not include you in the acknowledgments. Without the reader, the words would be just words upon a page but once those words are ingested, the story comes to life. Thank you for choosing *The Spirit of Sunflowers* to add to your repertoire of fiction.

Behind every manuscript is the persistence of a writer but, if not for the constructive suggestions of Ella Marie Shupe, I would have not been able to fine-tune *The Spirit of Sunflowers* into its final revision. Your suggestions were key to the composition of this story. Thank you for your committed attention to help me get it right. You recognized how much this project meant to me and that was encouraging!

Craig Keller, thank you for the use of your name for the character of Bill. Not only was your last name a perfect fit for the contractor but the character's work ethic was inspired by you. Thank you for being my friend. Donna would have been ecstatic that you were included. She is smiling on us.

Thank you, Sassy cat, the pet I adopted from Donna. We are an inseparable, loyal pair. The purring and snuggles are much appreciated as well as being woken with your kisses at five in the morning (before my alarm sounds). You were right there by my side watching me type on my laptop. I love you, Sassy!

Hafsa Idrees. Thank you for the art that covers *The Spirit of Sunflowers*. Every piece you create is enriched with beauty and displays your passion. I saw the main character in Rahat. In fact, that piece drew me to admire your work. I am a fan! Readers check out her website, hafsaidreesart.com. You can find her prints on Fine Art America. You will be intrigued!

To the star of this story, Donna, my forever best friend. I thank you, posthumously, for your 43 years of friendship. I was six and you were five, I believe, when we first met. You brightened my life as Bonnie brightened Willow's life. The summer after you passed, I bought a sunflower at the grocery store because sunflowers were your favorite. As I walked by a woman who admired the plant which I held in my hand, her remark was, "That's cheerful!" That was who you were. And so, this story I began on the first anniversary of your passing, eventually became *The Spirit of Sunflowers*. I can only hope that I was able to capture the essence of who you were in the character of Bonnie. Donna, thank you for our bond that cannot be broken by death, your unconditional friendship, and your example of the strength that you portrayed to the world with your relentless fight against cancer. You have and always will hold a place in my heart. I love you, Donna Lynn Connolly!

29

About the Author

Kristine K McCraw
Photo by Megan D McCraw

Kristine K. McCraw is a special education teacher who has been teaching for almost 30 years. She attended Clarion University of Pennsylvania and after graduating, she left her hometown of Pittsburgh to live in Virginia where she began her career in the field of Education. She is married with two children who are now adults, which leaves her time to engage in one of her favorite hobbies, writing. Kristine plans to continue developing her talents as an Indie Author. She has already self-published *The River's Bend* and is currently nearing the end of her third novel. She would love to hear your thoughts about *The Spirit of Sunflowers*. Send her a message at KristineKMcCraw@outlook.com.